COMMITTED

BETROTHED #4

PENELOPE SKY

Hartwick Publishing

Committed

Copyright © 2020 by Penelope Sky

All rights reserved.

No part of this book may be reproduced in any form or by any electronic or mechanical means, including information storage and retrieval systems, without written permission from the author, except for the use of brief quotations in a book review.

For Dr. Joel Saal

The Man Who Saved My Life

CONTENTS

1. Hades — 1
2. Sofia — 9
3. Hades — 17
4. Sofia — 25
5. Hades — 31
6. Sofia — 39
7. Hades — 57
8. Sofia — 71
9. Hades — 75
10. Sofia — 97
11. Hades — 107
12. Sofia — 117
13. Hades — 123
14. Sofia — 133
15. Hades — 141
16. Sofia — 149
17. Hades — 159
18. Sofia — 167
19. Hades — 175
20. Sofia — 181
21. Hades — 187
22. Sofia — 197
23. Hades — 205
24. Sofia — 219
25. Hades — 233
26. Sofia — 245
27. Hades — 253
28. Sofia — 265
29. Hades — 271
   Epilogue — 277

Also by Penelope Sky — 281

1

HADES

Two Months Later

WE STOOD IN THE MIDDLE OF THE STREET, STREETLIGHTS SLIGHTLY illuminating us in the center of the city. Most of the buildings around us were dark because tenants kept their curtains shut and kept to themselves. Florence was a beautiful city, but everyone knew it was plagued by monsters like me. As long as they minded their own business, they knew they were safe.

Maddox stood beside me, in a long-sleeved shirt and dark jeans. He never wore a watch or any other kind of jewelry. He was slender and ripped, possessing a strong physique that wasn't burdened by a mass of muscle. The time I'd spent with him had yielded even less information about his character. He didn't have a concrete personality. Some days he was talkative, and other days he didn't say a single word. We'd combined our men together, like a sick blended family. As we waited for our accomplice to arrive, he turned his gaze on me. With his crystal-blue eyes, he stared at me with a burning gaze that was as cold as frostbite. There was no emotion in his eyes, just light intrigue.

I refused to show intimidation or fear. This man had taken away everything that mattered to me. I won't allow him to take control of my emotions too. I turned my head in his direction and met his look with stoicism.

He took a step closer to me. "We've made a lot of progress, huh? I knew the two of us would clean up this country."

The only rule he'd given me was not to assassinate him. That meant I could be as standoffish as I wanted. I didn't have to like him; I didn't have to respect him.

He never seemed to care about how much I hated him. He was either immune to it or oblivious. "Shouldn't be much longer now…unless he has a death wish." He turned back to the road and waited for the car to arrive.

A minute later, a black SUV parked in the middle of the street, and our distributor got out of the back seat and walked toward us. He had five men with him, but the protection was obsolete considering all the men we had positioned around the area.

Maddox glanced at me again. "About time, right? I thought I was gonna miss high tea."

I hated this motherfucker.

Richard walked toward us, with skin deeply tanned by the unforgiving sun. His thick, curly black hair was pulled back in a ponytail, and he had extra weight around his waist. He walked up to us with a stony expression on his face. "I'm only here tonight as a courtesy. But I won't change my mind." He was a distributor who had the only way into the Middle Eastern countries. He had all the soldiers and the government on payroll, so it didn't matter how war-torn the country was, he could make it happen.

"And why won't you change your mind?" Maddox asked. There was always a slightly cheerful tone to his voice, a contradiction to the seriousness on his face. It was impossible to figure out his feelings at any point in time.

Richard paused as he stared at Maddox, clearly swallowing his frustration. "There are new regulations. There are airstrikes happening as we speak. It's dangerous, reckless. Now is not the best time."

Maddox started to pace slowly, one hand in his pocket and the other rubbing his jawline. "The entire population is under siege. They are stuck in a country they can't escape, and all the asylum countries are rejecting refugees. It sounds like they are prisoners to their own terrible demise." He stopped and turned back to Richard. "It sounds like high-quality meth is exactly what they need."

I could detect the threat in Maddox's tone even though he didn't do anything visibly threatening. My eyes glanced back and forth between Maddox and Richard. Maddox did business differently than I did. It was more extreme, but also more effective.

Richard spoke again. "If I'm caught, I'll be decapitated."

Maddox shrugged. "Hasn't that always been a possibility?"

"Yes." Richard glanced at me before he kept talking. "But the laws have changed. They are searching everything that comes into the country. Tensions are high. I can't just pay off everyone."

"You can if you pay them enough." Maddox returned to my side. "Let's make this happen, Richard. I've got two thousand kilos just for you. Be a rich man and make me a rich man."

Richard shook his head. "The answer is no…at least for now. I came in person tonight in the hope we can continue this business relationship at a later time."

Out of nowhere, Maddox began to laugh. It was genuine, like he'd just remembered something hilarious. It was almost a shrieking sound, the noise of an animal dying. Then he stopped abruptly. "It's now or never." He suddenly turned ice-cold, making the air around us vibrate with hostility. "You're going to do this, or I'll decapitate you right here in the street." He snapped his fingers and motioned to one of his men, who brought him a large samurai sword. He'd prepared for this before even meeting Richard, which made it even creepier. Maddox stood with the blade slung over his shoulder, looking almost like a lumberjack. It was comical but terrifying.

Richard held his composure well, but it was obvious he was unnerved by the threat.

Maddox turned to me. "Would you like to do the honors?"

No, I wasn't going to chop off this guy's head. "I have a different approach."

Maddox made an elaborate bow. "The floor is yours."

I moved closer to Richard and spoke to him as a comrade. "What Maddox said was right. The people are more hopeless than they were before, which means they're willing to pay top dollar to forget their troubles. You could charge even more money for this product, and while there's more risk, there's also more reward. You could make double or triple what you made in the past. This is a perfect business opportunity for all three of us."

Richard considered what was said as he stood in silence. His arms crossed over his chest, and he glanced at Maddox. "Alright. I'll have to use more money to pay off the officials in the army."

"That's fine." The best way to encourage a man's ambition was through riches. "We'll transport the batch to the border for you. You're on your own from there. But we expect a drop at the usual time. Fail to deliver, and we'll drop our own airstrike."

Richard nodded in agreement before he looked at Maddox one last time. Then he turned around and walked away, heading back to his car and driving off with his men.

Maddox and I were left alone in the brightness of the streetlight. I had accomplished what we wanted through negotiation and a sprinkle of threat. It was an easy approach, whereas Maddox went from zero to sixty in a millisecond. It wasn't always clear if he was an evil mastermind or he was an unpredictable emotional train wreck.

Maddox continued to hold the blade like it was his favorite toy. "So, you're good cop. I'm bad cop."

"No. There are just more effective techniques than torture. The only thing stronger than fear is ambition."

He placed the tip of the blade on the concrete and rested both of his hands on the handle. "That's why we make such a good team. We get shit done. If your way doesn't work, then mine will." He stared down the long road into the night, an awed gaze in his eyes. "Look at everything we've done in just a few months. Imagine everything else we'll do in the years to come."

Years? Fuck me.

"I'll arrange for the transport of the product. If he doesn't make good on his word, it'll be your job to take care of it. I know you can do the dirty work. You've done it before."

Who could talk about the death of their brother so casually?

"So, how are things with the missus?"

I turned to him as I felt the blood boil in my veins. My wife left me two months ago. She left behind her name and her ring. I was just as devastated now as I had been then. Nausea constantly gripped my body, and I'd never felt so weak in my life. But I let her go because I had to. "You know she left me." I'd stopped wearing my ring because it was too painful, but I never took off the watch she gave me.

"Oh yeah, that's right." He snapped his fingers like he'd just realized it. "I think you're better off. She wasn't that great of a lay."

The cityscape in front of me suddenly had a red tint. I had a gun in my pocket, but that wasn't how I wanted to kill him. I wanted to take that blade and saw at his neck until his head came loose. My hands tightened into fists, and my rage could barely be contained. I suspected he was testing me, wondering if I'd snap under the pressure. The only reason I didn't lunge at him was because of the consequences.

The consequences Sofia and Andrew would have to suffer.

Maddox continued to watch me, clearly amused by the battle raging behind my eyes. Then a gentle smile came through like he was remembering an old joke someone once told him. "We should cut Damien loose. He's dead weight."

The sudden change in subject was jarring. Damien and I had our differences, but he definitely wasn't dead weight. When he wasn't fucking everything up, he was doing all the work. He was smart, reliable, and hardworking. "He's a vital part of this business."

"Three is a crowd. You and I are the vital parts of this business now."

Damien wouldn't blame me if he got pushed out, but I didn't want to be the only one stuck with Maddox. Even if we weren't friends anymore, Damien was still an ally against this psychopath. "He knows the ropes. He's integral to our success."

Maddox smiled slightly. "Loyalty." That was all he said.

I assumed the matter was settled.

"That's why I like you. Once your loyalty is earned, it's never broken. Personally, I don't think Damien deserves it, but I understand it. Maybe one day we'll have that kind of loyalty to each other."

Over my dead body.

"He can stay on. But he's not getting an equal cut."

I didn't give a damn about money anymore. I'd lost the only thing that actually mattered…my family. Money would never make me happy. "That's fine. I'll split my cut with him."

He placed the blade over his shoulder once again. "Generous."

No, I just didn't give a damn.

Before he walked away, he gave me an awkward clap on the shoulder. It was like he didn't know how to embrace a friend or an ally. He was always a bit out of place, as if human interaction were impossible for him to understand. "I know things are shitty right now, but when we take over the world, you're going to forget that things ever were less than perfect."

2

SOFIA

I was almost seven months along, and I was definitely showing. It didn't matter how loose my dress was or if I wore all black, my baby bump was impossible to miss. I wasn't ashamed of it, not in the least, but I was definitely getting uncomfortable.

I stepped inside the Tuscan Rose located in central Rome and greeted the staff at the front desk. After chitchat and a rundown of the latest at the hotel, I walked to my office, passing the flowers and paintings on the way. I lowered myself into my chair and looked at all the paperwork waiting for me.

This hotel was very different from the previous one. There were no shady characters having clandestine meetings in the bar and conference rooms. There were nothing but good people, honest people. It was much less stressful, and I never worried about seeing someone I didn't want to see.

I felt like I could move on with my life.

Of course, I missed my husband…ex-husband.

But I got everything else I wanted. My mother and I bought a nice place in the city, and I had the baby's room ready to go. I was close to a good school and walking distance from work. There was never any talk of drug dealers or crime.

It was normal.

Antonio, the hotel manager, came into my office. He was a young man to have been promoted to such a high level, but the more I got to know him, the more I understood why he deserved the position. He was meticulous about everything, just the way I was. He cared about the minor misalignment of the flowers in the lobby, if a painting on the wall was slightly crooked, if a tie wasn't perfectly straight. All the little details were just as important as the big ones.

He walked up to my desk and set a folder in front of me. "Schools are starting to get out for Easter vacation. Our hotel is at full occupancy."

"That's great." I hadn't seen full occupancy in Florence, not once. But Rome was a bigger tourist destination.

"We have a couple big clients staying with us, and another wedding has just been booked. I collected payment. You should see it reflected in your records by the afternoon." He wore a collared shirt tucked into his slacks with a tie, looking professional but not stuffy. He had classically olive skin and dark hair, and his nicest feature was his smile. He was always smiling.

"Thanks so much. I'll take care of it when I see it."

He glanced down to my stomach. "How are things with him?"

My hand immediately brushed over my stomach. "He's doing well. He's a bit feisty with his kicking, but he's good."

He nodded. "Maybe he'll be a football player."

I chuckled. As long as he wasn't a drug dealer, I would be happy.

"I'll see you later." He left the office.

Once he was gone, the sorrow settled into my bones. I was happy in Rome, and more importantly, I was safe in Rome. I had a life I'd always wanted, to run my own hotel and have a family.

But losing Hades was like losing a piece of myself. I loved that man and always would. I doubted I could ever love anyone else in the same way.

We hadn't spoken much since I left. He didn't try to get me to stay, and he didn't try to halt the divorce filing. He let me go with resignation, and that told me he knew this was the best thing for me, that it was the only way I would be safe.

Even if it was the right thing to do, it didn't make it easier for the two of us. But we knew we needed to give each other space because if we talked all the time, it would make the separation more difficult.

I knew Hades would always be in Andrew's life…but he wouldn't necessarily be in mine.

Maddox had ruined my life. Even if decades passed and I remarried, I would still hate him with every fiber of my being.

He took my husband away…and I would never be whole.

At five o'clock, I left my office and walked out of the hotel. While I was constantly aware of my surroundings, I wasn't paranoid the way I used to be. No one was out to get me. No one wanted me. There was nothing to worry about—and that was a good feeling.

"Hey, pretty lady." A man came to my side and kept up with my stride as I headed down the sidewalk.

I wasn't alarmed by the sudden company because I recognized the sound of his voice. It was similar to Hades's. I stopped and turned to Ash, my brother-in-law—my former brother-in-law. "What are you doing here?"

He used to be so dark and formidable, but now he was much more cheerful. The old hostility he used to show to Hades had disappeared. He usually had jokes up his sleeve. "I was in the neighborhood. Thought I'd stop by."

I hadn't spoken to him since the divorce started. I hadn't really spoken to anyone since we'd signed the papers. My world came crashing down, and I removed myself from society. I was so depressed, I didn't think I could go on. If I weren't having Andrew, I probably would've caved and gone back by now, but I had to do the right thing for my son. He couldn't live in a world where he was always in danger. I was happy to see Ash, but I really didn't know what to say. He looked similar to his brother, and that hurt my heart a little bit.

His eyes slowly softened with sorrow. "How are you?"

My hand glided over my stomach. "Andrew is healthy, and I've kept busy."

"So, my brother told you his real name."

I nodded. He shared everything with me.

"That's a good name. Ash would've been better…but it's good enough."

He successfully got me to smile a little bit.

"Can I walk you home?"

"I only live a few blocks away."

"Good. Because I hate to walk."

Together, the two of us walked down the street and headed to the three-story home I'd bought for my mother and me to live in. My mom had a few friends in the city, so she stayed busy socializing. She even came to the hotel and worked with the decorators to keep the ambiance fresh.

There was a lot of silence because I didn't know what to say. I liked Ash, but being around him only reminded me of what I'd lost. I had to move on with my life, move on from Hades, but that was impossible if I had to spend time with his brother. But since I was having Ash's nephew, I would always be connected to both of the Lombardi brothers.

I took control of the conversation. "How are you?"

He shrugged. "You know, all sex and money."

"So, things are good?"

"Very good. What about you?"

"You already asked that."

He gave me a serious look. "And you never really answered the question."

I shrugged. "What do you want me to say? It's been hard…"

"It's been hard for him too."

I never called Hades to shoot the breeze. I never asked how he was doing. I imagined he'd moved on with his life, replaced me in his bed, and I didn't want to know any of those things. I knew he was sad about our breakup, but he was probably bedding other women to get through it. And that made me sick to my stomach…even when it shouldn't. "Is he doing okay?"

Ash took his time before he answered. "As well as he possibly could be, I guess."

"It's been two months, but it feels like two days. It's been rough, but there was no other solution."

"Unfortunately."

I kept walking until we reached my front door. "This is me."

Ash looked up at the three stories then turned back to me. "It's nice."

"Thanks."

"I'd invite myself inside, but I don't trust myself around you now that you're single." He winked, telling me he was teasing me.

I smiled at his comment.

"You can call me if you need anything."

"Did Hades ask you to say that?"

He shook his head. "No."

My eyes softened.

"We'll always be family."

I lay in bed in the middle of the night. My hand rested over my stomach, and I focused on the feeling of Andrew's kicks. They were gentle but distracting enough that I couldn't sleep. Hades had never felt his son kick. I'd left too soon, and he never had the honor other fathers did. It was moments like these that made me miss Hades the most. I felt alone; I felt scared. We should be doing this together, not apart.

I grabbed my phone off the nightstand and looked at the screen. There was no message from Hades. There was never a message from him. He'd let me go with an aloof stare, like he knew it was the best thing for me, but he resented me all the same. I wanted to call him, but I knew I shouldn't. It was too soon to have a close relationship, to be friends who had a kid.

Could we ever be friends?

I stared at my phone for a while, considering what I should do. The silence was suffocating. I didn't just lose my husband, but my best friend, my everything. My life felt so much emptier without him. Maybe that would change when Andrew was here, but I knew there would always be a hole in my heart.

Maybe it was because I was lonely, maybe it was because I missed him too much, but I called him. The blue light lit up my dark room, and I pressed the phone to my ear and listened to it ring.

It didn't ring for long. His deep voice announced itself over the phone, quiet but strong. "Sofia." He didn't say it with the same affection he used to possess. There was a tone of melancholy in his voice, slight betrayal. But he was there, answering my call like he promised he would.

"I hope it's not a bad time." It was one thirty in the morning, so it was a stupid thing to say. If he wasn't asleep, he was working. Or worse, he had company over. I wouldn't be surprised if someone had replaced my spot in the bed. My ex-husband was the sexiest man in the world. With beautiful brown eyes and the body of a Roman soldier, he was the sort of man any woman would give up anything to be with. The thought of someone else made me weak, so I tried not to think about it.

"No." He never talked much, even during our happier times, but he was speaking even less than normal. The old camaraderie was absent. He almost felt like a stranger now. That was probably because he was. We hadn't spoken in weeks. His feelings, his opinions were totally foreign to me. "Are you okay?"

I missed hearing that question. When I was his wife, I was the center of his whole world. My well-being was the only thing that mattered. But now I wasn't his responsibility anymore, and that made me feel so distant from him. "I'm fine. Andrew is kicking a lot, and I can't sleep." My hand moved over my stomach as I lay under the warm blankets. I was on the top floor, and my mother was on the second floor. "He's been really ornery for the last couple of days. I've been eating a lot of spicy food, but I think that's just a coincidence."

He didn't release a chuckle or give any indication he'd heard what I said.

"I have a doctor's appointment in a couple days…if you want to come."

He sighed loudly over the phone. "Of course I do. I'll be there."

I wanted to stay on the phone with him forever, but there was nothing to say. I couldn't even ask him about work because that would mean I would be asking him about Maddox. I couldn't ask about Damien because they weren't friends anymore. I couldn't ask about anything…

But I continued to sit there because it was better than nothing.

"Are you doing okay?"

"Yeah. Just busy with work and my mother."

"That's one thing I don't miss…"

A small smile came over my face. But then I wondered if he missed me. He never told me he loved me anymore or stopped by for a random visit. When we'd decided to end things, he seemed like he wanted it more than I did. It was crazy to think we'd been so in love just months ago, and now we were so far apart. The only thing keeping us together was the baby we made.

It made me hate Maddox even more.

Hades's deep voice made the phone vibrate. "I'll let you get some sleep."

Disappointment deflated my lungs like popped balloons. I wasn't sure what I expected him to say. We had nothing to talk about other than how miserable we were. I didn't want to hear about his personal life, and I didn't have a personal life at all. We could talk about our son, but since he hadn't been born yet, there wasn't much to say. "Goodnight…"

"Goodnight."

3

HADES

I approached the table in the strip club. Music played overhead, and there were girls everywhere.

When Maddox saw me coming toward him, he dismissed one of his men. "Get the fuck up. My boy is here." Once his guy was gone, he kicked out the chair so I could sit. He had girls on either side of him, but neither one of them actually touched him. What was more perplexing was the fact that he wasn't facing the stage. Sometimes it seemed like he forced his sexuality when he really didn't possess one. He wasn't that interested in women, but he wasn't interested in men either. He was just interested in power, making people do things that he wanted…preferably against their will.

I sank into the chair and felt the usual wave of nausea drown me. Maybe he only wanted me because I seemed unobtainable for so long. I was a prize he got to put on display, a captive that showed his strength. Maybe that was all I was to him…a trophy. He was already filthy rich, he was already powerful, so what made him tick? What did he want? I honestly had no idea.

The waitress brought me a scotch.

I took a long drink, but nothing could get this taste out of my mouth.

There were cards on the table like they'd been playing blackjack before I got there. Maddox had a glass of water in front of him. I'd never spent extensive time with him so I didn't know him that well, but this was the third time I'd seen him in a bar setting and he hadn't ordered a drink.

Odd.

Maddox gently nudged the brunette beside him. "My good friend is down tonight. Why don't you cheer him up, sweetheart?"

Just as she rose to her feet, I shut down the offer. "No."

The girl returned to her seat, a little offended.

"No pussy tonight?" Maddox took a sip of his water, holding it like a glass of vodka.

"No booze tonight?" He said I couldn't kill him, but he never said I couldn't insult him.

Maddox set down his glass again, his expression slightly provoked. With a gentle wave of his hand, he dismissed all the girls at the table. Now, it was just the two of us, sitting in the center of an empty strip club, girls climbing on the bars like monkeys.

I knew I'd pissed him off because the air was different. It was tense, cold. I held his gaze and refused to be intimidated.

"You can have any girl you want tonight. I paid for them all."

"I don't have to pay for sex." I'd done it many times in the past, but now that I'd had the real thing, real passion, it was hard to imagine going back to anything else. I could pay a fortune for a woman to be what I wanted, but she still would never come close to what I'd had.

"They say the best things in life are free, but only poor people say that shit." He took another drink of his water. "Not sure why you're so hung up on that woman. There was nothing special about her. Sometimes she had a sharp mouth, but the rest of the time, she was boring."

My teeth started to grind together. "Sometimes I wonder if you want me to kill you."

He shrugged. "Sometimes I wonder the same thing. Life is so dull without murder, blood lust, violence… It just gets stale. Are you afraid to die?"

No one had ever asked me that before.

"I'm not." He went on. "In fact, I'd be impressed if someone could ever pull it off. I've got tricks on top of tricks up my sleeve, and I get off on preparing for any eventuality. I guess I'm hoping you will try, because I've gotten bored lately. I wouldn't mind torturing someone…"

What a sick fuck. There was no rhyme or reason to his madness. He was a lunatic who did terrible things once the entertainment stopped. He'd dropped thousands of euro renting out the strip club, but he clearly wasn't interested in the girls or the booze. He was just there because he didn't know what else to do. It was kind of sad. "You're so lonely that the only connection you ever feel is through death."

He stared at me for a long time. His blue eyes were so chilly that frost seemed to rise from his gaze. He was extremely still, like a mountain on a windy day. All the trees and bushes bowed in the wind, but he stayed exactly the same. He conveyed the most emotion when he conveyed no emotion at all.

I waited for him to say something, but nothing was forthcoming. I seemed to have punctured his skin, hit an invisible button. He liked to study and observe everyone around him, but he didn't want anyone to do the same to him.

He didn't like it one bit.

Damien sat across from me on the terrace. He used to come over all the time when we were friends. But now, he came over because it was the only place where we could have a private conversation. Our relationship seemed irrelevant at this point. We just needed each other to survive.

Damien looked out at the view and stayed quiet for a long time. "How is she?"

"Fine." I hated to admit it, but she was much safer there than she was with me. I used to be at the top of the food chain. I used to be the man who gave other men nightmares. But now I was dangerous…and not because I wanted to be. Everything I touched was destroyed. I was a slave to a man who got off on destruction. I had nothing to offer my wife…nothing to offer to my son. They were both better off without me.

Damien watched me for a long time. "So, that's it? After all that?"

"Yeah."

His eyes filled with disappointment. "It's not right."

"Doesn't matter. She wanted to leave, and I let her. She made the right decision for herself and our son. I wouldn't want her to have to see the man who'd raped her on a daily basis. I wouldn't want her to watch me be a fuck boy to the man that tortured her. I don't deserve her, and I know it."

"Then kill him. I don't understand."

"He wants me to. He's waiting for me to do it. He even told me that."

He sighed deeply. "Fuck. That's annoying."

"I've met some scary men. Some crazy men. But I've never met anyone like him. He doesn't want anything, he doesn't need anything, so he just does things. He likes torturing me because he has a twisted obsession with me. He likes to cause drama. He likes to cause problems so he has something to solve. He wants me to make an attempt so he could take my wife and torture me by raping her."

Damien shook his head.

"If I take a shot and I miss…it's my son on the line. He's not even born yet, and I love him more than anything, more than Sofia. Even if there's only a tiny chance I could miss, I can't take the risk."

Damien considered what I said and remained quiet. "What if I do it?"

"No."

"Why not?"

"Because it's the same thing in his eyes. Damien, do not go behind my back and do it anyway. You are not smarter than him, you are not stronger than him. Promise me you will not do anything."

He shook his head slightly. "I would never be so arrogant as to risk your family's safety. But I do think we need to come up with a plan. Letting him win is not the answer. We need to take our time and come up with a solution. There's got to be an answer. We just have to find it."

"I don't know…it's like he can see the future."

"Then we need to look further ahead. And if we don't kill him, someone else will…eventually. This isn't the kind of career that lasts a long time. It has a short shelf life. Someone will get Maddox eventually."

But it should be me.

"You should be with the woman you love. You should kill the man who hurt your family. We should not be his busboys. We can lie low for a while…but not forever. And if you wait too long, Sofia might find somebody else."

I knew Sofia loved me, but she broke my heart when she asked to leave. Marriage was about forever, for better or worse. She abandoned me and took our son with her. She did the right thing, but that didn't make it less painful. It was a betrayal…and it stung like lemon on a fresh wound. After our son was born, men would swoop in. She would have a million offers all over again. No one would care about the fact that she was a single mom. She would move on and forget about me. "I don't think Sofia and I are supposed to be together. The curse has never been broken—it just changes. She loves me and we get together…but then she leaves. Even if I kill Maddox and get her back, something else is going to get in the way. She's the only woman I'll ever love, and that's my punishment. It'll never change."

"I don't believe that. If you get rid of Maddox, all your problems will be solved."

I shrugged. "I'm tired of fighting for her. I'll always love her, always want her. But I can't keep doing this. She left me…and a piece of me died."

"But you said she made the right decision."

"She did—for her and Andrew. But she still left me. She still abandoned me. That fucking hurts. She didn't put space between us while keeping us together. She divorced me. She signed the papers and left."

Damien was quiet.

That week when she packed up her things and left was the most difficult of my life. We didn't have sex; we didn't have a tearful goodbye. It was all business on her end. We both shut down our emotions and stopped feeling everything. I didn't beg her to stay because I had way too much pride. I let her walk out of my life… and take my heart with her.

I sat on the couch in my sweatpants and watched TV. In the

morning, I would fly to Rome to join Sofia at her doctor's appointment. It would be the first time I'd seen her since she left. We hadn't spoken much either, barely checking in with each other over the phone. I knew she was safe because she was nowhere near here.

How embarrassing. My wife was safer without me.

When she'd called me a couple nights ago, I'd loved hearing the sound of her voice, but I also felt dead inside. I knew she wasn't calling me because she missed me. I knew she would never want to get back together. So every phone call was torture.

Thank god they were so seldom.

Now I stared at the TV screen and didn't pay attention to what I was watching. I was always thinking about events in my life, whether they involved Sofia, Damien, or Maddox. Those quiet moments I used to enjoy were long gone.

My phone started to ring, and it was my brother. We hadn't talked much either, so whatever he had to say was probably important. I took the call. "Yeah?"

"What a warm welcome," he said sarcastically. "You make me feel so fuzzy inside."

My brother had always been a smartass since we were boys. Some things never changed. "Is there something I can do for you?"

"Just calling to check in. How are you doin'?"

Fucking terrible. Thanks for asking. "Same."

"I ran into Sofia the other day…"

My heart kicked into overdrive anytime she was mentioned. "Ran into her where?" Was Sofia going to bars? Was she going out with friends? She was so solemn when she left me. Maybe she remained just as stoic as she moved on.

"At the hotel."

"So, you didn't run into her. You stalked her."

"Potato…potahto."

"How was she?"

"Even with that belly, she's hot. I didn't know pregnant chicks could be so sexy."

If I hadn't known he was joking, I'd fly there and kill him. "Ash."

"Alright…fun's over. She seemed okay. Says she's working a lot. Lives with her mom. I told her she could call me if she needed anything."

"Thanks for saying that."

"No problem. She's still a little sister to me."

Even though she wasn't my wife. "I'll be down there tomorrow."

"Yeah?"

"Sofia has a doctor's appointment."

"I'm glad you guys are working this out."

We didn't break up over something stupid. We didn't fall out of love. There was no cheating. Something ripped us apart. "We're still having our son together. I'll always be in his life, even though I'm not sure that's the best thing for him."

"It is. You're going to be a great father."

A great father would protect his family. I'd failed to do that. "I should get going."

"Maybe we could get a beer or something after?"

I suspected I would just want to come home after seeing Sofia. It would be a hard day, and the last thing I'd want to do was talk about it. "We'll see…"

4

SOFIA

Spring had come early, so it was a bit warm in the city. I wore a pink dress with a black cardigan, but the layers couldn't hide my swollen belly. I did my hair and makeup and felt my heart race a million miles an hour.

Hades would be there any minute.

He was supposed to pick me up and drive me to the appointment. It was the first time he would see my new place, the first time we would do something as a divorced couple. Our divorce would take a few months to be finalized, but we both behaved as if it was a done deal.

My mom walked in behind me and looked at my reflection in the mirror. "You look very pretty. But maybe some pearls would be nice."

I rolled my eyes. "Mom, I'm having a baby. Not meeting the Queen of England."

"I would really love to see Hades when he stops by. He was a good man."

Yes, he was. I told my mother the reason we had to leave, and she understood. But she was so fond of him…as was I. He was the father of her grandchild, so he would always be around. But

I thought today wasn't the best time for chitchat. "Maybe next time. It's probably going to be a little tense since we haven't seen each other in so long."

"Alright…I understand."

When I heard the doorbell ring downstairs, I immediately felt the jolt in my chest. I was nervous, uneasy, totally erratic. I'd seen Hades so many times before, but now everything was different. I wasn't even sure what we were anymore. Were we friends?

I headed to the bottom floor and then opened the front door.

He stood there. Tall and proud. In a black t-shirt that fit over his broad shoulders nicely, he was the same powerhouse I remembered. He had a wide chest that stretched the fabric tightly, and his bulging arms did the same thing. His flat stomach led to narrow hips, and his jeans were slightly low on his hips. His wedding ring was absent, but the watch I gave him was still on his wrist.

I stared at him for several seconds…speechless. He was more handsome than I remembered. Striking brown eyes, masculine cheekbones, and a jawline so hard it could cut glass. He was the perfect man.

I missed him.

His eyes landed on mine, and they didn't blink. He stared for a long time, as if he was sizing me up the way I'd just done to him. I probably looked completely different. My stomach was much bigger, along with the rest of my body. My thighs were thicker, my arms had more mass, and my tits were definitely a size larger.

He didn't make a single comment.

The quiet stretched on for a long time, like neither one of us knew what to say.

I wanted to move into his chest and hold him, but that didn't seem appropriate anymore. Just looking at him didn't seem appropriate.

He stepped away from the door and slid his hands into his pockets. "Ready to go?"

I grabbed my purse and walked with him to the car.

We sat together in the doctor's office. I was on the table in a gown. My bare belly was visible, and the sonogram machine was next to me and ready to be used.

Hades sat against the opposite wall, his gaze directed out the window like he purposely didn't want to look at me. He didn't make small talk or ask how I was doing, probably because our conversation over the phone had already been dull enough.

This was the man I used to speak to every day. Now, we didn't talk at all.

The doctor came inside and smeared the gel across my belly. He pressed the apparatus over the surface of my tummy and projected a picture of our baby on the screen. Andrew's heartbeat was visible, along with some of his other features, like the shape of his skull and the outline of his body.

Seeing my son brought tears to my eyes.

Hades came to my side and stood next to me, his eyes on the screen as well. He stared with the same intensity, as if he couldn't believe this was really happening. He took a deep breath and continued to stare.

"Everything looks healthy," the doctor said. "He's coming along nicely. Keep taking your vitamins, drink lots of water, and try to walk for at least thirty minutes a day."

I was on my feet all day at work, so that wasn't a problem. "Thank you."

After the doctor cleaned me up, he walked out so I could get dressed.

As before, Hades turned around and faced the opposite wall so I'd have my privacy to get ready. He didn't have to do that, but I guess it would be weird if he didn't avert his gaze.

After I got dressed, I grabbed my purse and headed for the door. "I already knew he was doing well, but it's nice to hear. There's no way he could kick me all the time and not have strong bones and muscles."

"Or maybe he's just feisty like his mom."

"Very true."

We left the doctor's office and got back into his car. Hades drove me home, driving through the streets as the sun set in the sky. Summer was still a few months away, so it got dark a little earlier than I wanted.

"You want to get dinner?" I wasn't sure what provoked me to ask the question. I was just sad at the way our relationship had become so quiet and uncomfortable. I'd expected it to be awkward in the beginning, but that discomfort wasn't wearing off.

He kept his eyes on the road with one hand on the wheel. "I have to be heading back…"

"Oh." I couldn't hide my disappointment. He used to drop everything for me. Now I wasn't the most important thing in his life.

After another five minutes of painful silence, he arrived at my home and parked at the curb in front of my door.

I was suddenly filled with sadness. It may be a few months before I saw him again, maybe even longer before we spoke again. This break was so clean that it was emotionless. It was hard to believe we'd ever loved each other when he was so indifferent to me.

He got out of the car and walked me to the door.

I got my keys out of my purse and unlocked it.

He stayed a couple feet back, like he was hoping I wouldn't invite him inside for a drink. "Keep me updated on Andrew. If you need anything, I can get down here in a couple hours. When it gets closer to the birth, I'll stay in the city so I don't miss anything."

How did we become this impersonal? We used to be so passionate and affectionate. Now there was no heat between us. All the fire that used to dance around had been permanently extinguished. "Alright…"

Hades turned away without even saying goodbye.

I didn't know what possessed me to say it, but I grabbed his attention. "Hades?"

He turned back around, but he didn't come closer to me.

"Is everything okay?"

"Yes."

I walked toward him until we were face-to-face again. "It just seems like…I don't know."

His eyes shifted back and forth as he looked into mine, but he didn't respond to my comment.

"It seems like you hate me or something."

He shook his head slightly. "No. I could never hate you."

"Then why are you so cold?"

His face tilted toward the ground as he considered how to respond. He lifted his head once again and looked me in the eye. "Because we aren't together anymore. This is how I treat everybody else."

"Well, I don't like it."

His eyes narrowed. "Then you shouldn't have left me." He turned to walk away.

I grabbed him by the arm and forced him back. "You have no idea how hard this has been for me. You have no idea how much I've missed you. You have no idea how much I hurt every day that you're gone."

"Then you could've stayed."

"You know I couldn't…"

He pulled his arm away from my grasp. "That was your decision, and I respect it. You were doing the right thing for you and Andrew, and I get it. But let's not forget that you abandoned me to the hellhole where I live. You get to start over with a new life. I don't. You were a prisoner to Maddox…and now I've become his captive."

5

HADES

When I got the news Andrew was doing well, I should've been happy.

Ecstatic.

But I wasn't. All I could feel was overwhelming resentment toward my ex-wife. She'd never looked so beautiful, never glowed so bright. Relocating to Rome was the best thing for her, and while she didn't look happy, she didn't look stressed either. She'd gotten everything she wanted…and she did it without me.

It made me bitter. Angry.

I wanted Sofia and Andrew to be safe, but I was miserable living under Maddox's thumb. I was his little bitch, practically a slave. I was a rich man in a powerful position, but I had no rights, no freedoms. I couldn't have the one thing I wanted more than anything else. It was like she didn't care…at all.

When Maddox took her and all hope was lost, I sacrificed myself in exchange for her freedom. I threw myself on the grenade so she could get away.

But she abandoned me.

I would've judged her if she stayed. In fact, I respected her for choosing herself and our son over me. But the darker side of me couldn't stop hating her for it. I'd sacrificed so much for this relationship, and it made no difference in the end.

How could she go to the doctor with me and be so calm? How could she be so pragmatic about this whole thing? It'd been two months, so we'd both had time to decompress. There had been a lot of tears when she first left. But I'd never gotten over that phase.

It seemed like she had.

How could she love me as much as I loved her but be fine with all of this?

I wasn't close to being fine.

It'd been a few days since I'd stormed off and left her on her doorstep. But I hadn't stopped thinking about that moment from the time I'd gotten home. I went right back to work with numbness all over my body and a scotch in my hand. I was stuck in a never-ending vortex of pain. My life was so meaningless, sometimes I wondered what the point was. If I were dead, Maddox would have no interest in Sofia. I wouldn't have to live without her.

It was late in the evening as I sat on the couch with the TV on. Living alone was suffocating. I'd preferred isolation, but after I was happily married, I couldn't imagine being alone again. Now it was just depressing…especially when I thought I heard her voice coming from the closet or the bathroom.

My phone lit up with Sofia's name.

She was calling me. I watched it ring but didn't answer. I'd never loved someone and hated them at the same time. But if she ever needed me, I had to be there. I would never forgive myself if something happened to her because I was too pissed off to be reasonable.

I answered the phone. Bitterness was audible. "Yeah?"

"Don't fucking yeah me." She launched herself at a million miles an hour, expressing all the rage she'd kept bottled up inside the last few days. She was like the sun, solar flares jumping out everywhere. "I didn't want this. I didn't want to lose you. I hate this so fucking much. You think I like being alone? You think I like being hours away from you? You say that you're a prisoner, but you have no idea what being a prisoner is really like. You don't know what it's like to be chained up and raped, so don't sit there and act like you and I are the same. We are not the fucking same." She was harsh in her tone and destructive in her choice of words. She didn't hold anything back, and her rage was mixed with the distant sound of tears.

I kept the phone to my ear and closed my eyes when she mentioned the most terrible thing we'd had to endure.

"I told you to kill him, and you refused. If you aren't going to do anything about it, then I have to move on. Don't you dare judge me for what I did. If I'd never married you in the first place, I never would've been raped. You were supposed to protect me, but being with you has caused me more harm than if I were alone. I don't regret being with you because I loved you, but I can't be stupid and expect a future to be any different from the past. I have a son to think about now. And what kind of mother would I be if I didn't give him the life he deserves?"

I continued to listen to her emotional monologue.

"It wasn't easy for me to leave. It isn't easy to live here alone. When I imagine you with someone else, it makes me sick to my stomach. When I told you I loved you, I meant it. That is something that will never change. So, don't paint me out to be a heartless bitch that turned her back on you. I wish things could be different, but for as long as Maddox is around, it can't be. Be mad all you want, but the person you should be mad at is you… not me." The phone went silent when she hung up.

I kept the phone to my ear and listened to the dial tone. I opened my eyes once again now that the conversation was over. Well, it wasn't really a conversation…just a very heated monologue. I should call her back and apologize, but I couldn't. She was right, but that didn't take away my anger.

I was angry at her for being so beautiful.

Angry that I couldn't have her.

Petty and spiteful that someone else would get her someday.

And I would be here…miserable and alone.

"Is it that time of the month?" Maddox stared at me from across the table in the conference room, leaning back in his chair while his arms were perfectly straight on the armrests. His blue eyes were always expressive, whether he was playful or angry. A week had passed since my incident with him in the strip club, and things had been a little tense since that moment.

I turned my gaze on him, keeping up the same apathy.

"I've got an Advil in my purse. Do you want it?"

I turned my look away and ignored him.

"Come on, we're friends. Unburden all your earthly troubles." He raised his arms, making a welcoming gesture.

"If you think we're friends, then you've never had a friend."

His eyes slowly turned frosty, his playful demeanor disappearing. "Careful. I'm the only friend you've got."

I continued to stare at him, feeling the slight threat in the room. I didn't have much concern for my own safety because I had nothing left to live for. Andrew would be better off without me, and there was no hope for Sofia and me. There was nothing Maddox could do to me that actually frightened me. "You really think that's what we are?" I didn't understand his psyche, so maybe he truly believed that. He wasn't fueled by women, money, or possessions. He seemed to have nothing, but everything. His men were loyal to him, but I suspected that was out of fear, not affection.

He cocked his head slightly, like a dog that was trying to understand what was just said. "What else would we be?"

"Do you rape all your friends' wives?"

He shrugged. "I've never raped anyone before. Your wife was my first." He winked.

I wanted to reach across the table and grab him by the throat. But since that was what he wanted, I stayed in my seat. I felt like a bug under his shoe. One wrong move and I would get squished.

"You want my advice?"

I almost laughed because it was absurd.

"Don't live in the past. There's so much shit we have to do."

I rubbed my hand across my jaw because I didn't know how else to bottle my anger. I couldn't imagine living like this every day, subjected to this cruel torture. How could I look at the man who hurt my wife every day…and let him call me a friend?

"This partnership will be much more fruitful if you move on. Look at everything we've done together. We've been more successful than you and Damien ever were. We're a match made in heaven. And now that Sofia is no longer your wife, you can focus much better."

I averted my gaze because I couldn't stare at him any longer. The only thing I wanted to focus on was killing him. I couldn't help but live in regret because if I had killed him sometime in the past, none of this would have happened. Or if I had killed Damien a long time ago, none of this would have happened either. Sometimes it seemed like all these things were happening because they were meant to happen. The universe wanted to keep Sofia and me apart.

Maybe it was time I started to listen.

Maddox continued to stare at me as if he expected some kind of rebuttal.

I had no rebuttal.

I had nothing.

I'd just stepped out of the shower when Ash called me. With a towel around my waist, I took the call. "Yeah?"

"Why do you always sound so gloomy when you answer the phone?"

"Because I am gloomy."

"How are things goin' at Maddox and Sons?"

I didn't say a single word because it wasn't funny at all.

Ash picked up on my silent hostility. "How are you?"

I was tired of people asking me that all the time, always timid like they expected me to explode. "Stop asking me that. I'm shitty, and I'll always be shitty."

"Alright…duly noted." He was quiet on the line for a bit before he changed the subject. "I checked on Sofia at the hotel today."

It was the first time I didn't want to think about her. The conversation we'd had almost a week ago was still fresh in my mind.

"The manager there is kind of a young guy, maybe your age. I think he might be into Sofia…"

That didn't surprise me in the least. "Everyone is into her."

"Including me," he said with a chuckle.

I was immune to his sarcastic remarks at this point.

"You want me to take him out?"

A bitter laugh wanted to escape my throat because it was so stupid. It was even stupider because she wasn't my wife anymore. "No."

"Are you sure? I can make it look like an accident."

"She's free to do whatever she wants."

"But she's carrying your baby."

"I doubt the guy has much of a chance with her anyway."

"Well, actually, he's kinda hot."

Both of my eyebrows rose. "What did you just say?"

"I'm just giving you all the information. He's not some fat, ugly guy. He's young, and he's in shape. And they work together all the time, so he has good access to her."

Someday, another man would sweep her off her feet, and she would forget about me. There was nothing I could do to avoid it. I was tired of trying to fight fate to have the woman I loved. It was too much work, and it always blew up in my face. "It's gonna happen sometime…let it be."

Ash was quiet for a while, as if he had no idea what to say to that. But he continued to sit on the phone with me, as if that was the only comfort he could provide. "I'm sorry all of this is happening to you. You don't deserve it."

I closed my eyes and let the words repeat in my mind. I didn't want anyone's pity, but I appreciated his understanding. The person who used to understand me down to my core was long gone. I pushed her even further away. I had no one to blame but myself. "Thanks, man."

6

SOFIA

Two weeks had come and gone since I'd screamed at Hades. Anytime I thought of him, my heart still palpitated with rage. I didn't want things to be this way, but I had to stand up for myself. I had to set the record straight.

I used to love that man with all my heart, but now I was so angry with him.

I stayed busy at work, working longer hours at the hotel because I had nothing else to do. Andrew's room was ready to go, and I didn't have any friends in the city. I had my mom, but she wasn't my favorite person to hang out with.

I was sitting in the office doing paperwork when Antonio walked inside. "Hey, how's it goin'?" I guess he was a friend. He was a person I worked with on a daily basis, one of the few interactions I had.

"Good." He sat down in the chair across from my desk. "I'm the hotel manager, but you seem to work longer hours than I do."

I shrugged. "I'm a bit of a workaholic."

"Not a bad thing. But you are an expectant mother. You should take it easy. I can handle things around here."

I smiled. "That's very generous, but I like to stay busy. Keeps me sane. If I stay home all day thinking about giving birth to a fat baby, I'll lose my mind."

He chuckled. "Understandable."

I turned back to my paperwork and expected him to leave, but when he continued to linger, I lifted my gaze again. "Is there something you needed?"

He leaned forward slightly and rested his forearms on his knees. "This is kinda awkward, but I've been thinking about it a long time."

Was he about to ask me for a raise? He'd been a hard worker, and he was there early in the morning and late at night. If he asked for a raise, I would give it to him. I believed your business was only as strong as your employees. If your employees were happy, your business would be happy.

He paused for a long time before he continued. "Would you want to have dinner sometime?"

I stared at him incredulously because I couldn't believe what he just asked me. I was a woman who was more than seven months pregnant with another man's child. I was twenty pounds heavier than I usually was…and that had nothing to do with the baby. "Uh…"

"If you say no, I totally understand. No pressure, no hard feelings. But we seem to get along so well, and I feel like we have a connection. Can't blame a guy for trying, right?" Now he looked at me expectantly, waiting for my answer.

I continued to be shocked.

The longer I was quiet, the more uncomfortable he became. "Forget I asked. It's unprofessional."

"No, it's not that. I just can't believe someone asked me out." I assumed I would be undesirable to men everywhere. I was pregnant, and when I wasn't anymore, I would be a single mom.

What kind of guy would be interested in that unless he were a single father himself?

Antonio raised an eyebrow as he looked at me. "I don't think it's that surprising…" He straightened in his chair and relaxed now that he knew I wasn't offended by the proposition. "You're a beautiful woman, you are kind and funny, and you are dedicated to your hotel. I think you have the whole package."

It was such a compliment that I didn't know what to say. My ambition was a turn-off for most men. One person who didn't care was Hades. He actually seemed aroused by it. "Well, I'm very flattered."

Antonio waited for an answer.

I was free to do whatever I wanted. I was single, almost legally divorced, and it seemed like Hades hated me. I'd relocated here to move on with my life, so that was what I should be doing. But I was still madly in love with Hades, no matter how angry I was with him. I wasn't ready to move on. I suspected I wouldn't be ready for a long time. Even if he were back in the dating scene already, that wouldn't entice me to do the same. "You know, I just got divorced a couple months ago… I'm not ready to date."

Antonio took my rejection in stride. "I totally understand. If you ever are ready and are interested, let me know."

"I'll keep that in mind. But I should be honest and tell you I'm still in love with my ex-husband." Our marriage didn't end because we wanted it to; it ended because it had to. And that changed everything.

Antonio rose to his feet and continued to keep the situation lighthearted. "He's a lucky man."

After I'd screamed at Hades, I'd expected some kind of retaliation, whether he showed up on my doorstep or called me in the middle of the night. But that never happened. The silence continued for weeks. Those weeks turned into a month, but I refused to call him, refused to apologize. To behave like this was easy for me was a slap in the face. I had to move away, pregnant with his son, and start over.

And he thought that was easy?

I should drop my stubbornness and pride because we had more important things to worry about, but I still wanted him to make the first move. I deserved an apology, and I wouldn't play nice until I got one.

When he didn't call in a month, I realized I wasn't going to get what I wanted.

I was eight months pregnant, and it was time to move on.

The hardest part about making the call was the admission that everything was different. That our relationship wasn't even close to being the same. We were distant, practically strangers. I was in bed when I dialed.

The phone rang for a long time, so long, I didn't think he would answer.

He'd never ignored my call before. I hoped this wouldn't be the first time.

He picked up, clearly in a flustered mood. "What is it?"

"What is it?" I asked incredulously. "That's how you want to talk to me?"

The sound of him walking and breathing hard was audible. "I'm working."

Now I understood he was probably doing some illegal shit with Maddox. There were probably guns and dead bodies involved. I refused to apologize for my call. "I have a doctor's appointment tomorrow…if you want to come." We hadn't spoken at all, so I wasn't sure how much affection he had for me anymore. We used to be so in love, and now all of that was gone. I never thought it would happen to us.

"Text me the time. I'll be there." He hung up without another word.

I kept the phone to my ear in the darkness, the light from the screen brightening when the call ended. I didn't know what else to do, so I continued to lie there, to let the painful feelings fester like an infected wound. I eventually dropped the phone and turned on my side to stare into the darkness. My hand went over my tummy, and even though I had life underneath my palm, I felt so alone.

I'd never felt so alone.

I glanced at the clock every couple minutes because I knew Hades would be there any moment. He was picking me up at the hotel, so it was the first time he would see my office. I was dressed in a black dress with flats, trying to look as slender as possible. Sometimes I wondered if he was still attracted to me or if I was just a big cow in his eyes. Was he screwing prostitutes and strippers, so I looked like hell in comparison? I wanted to ask, but I had too much pride.

A moment later, heavy footsteps announced his presence. They thudded against the hard wood before he turned the corner and stepped into my office. Tall, muscular, and with a brooding stare, he was a magnetic force that practically shook all the paintings off the walls with just his presence. He was in a t-shirt and jeans, his physique stronger than it used to be. He was clearly working out more than he used to, lifting weights and increasing his size. He gave me a stony look as if he didn't want to be there. He stopped in front of my desk and stared at me with an arctic gaze. Heartbeats passed, and nothing was said. His brown eyes were hot but not warm. His jaw was clean like he'd just shaved before he left to join me.

His powerful arms rested by his sides as he waited for me to stand.

I watched him for a full minute before I rose to my feet and grabbed my purse. The silence wasn't full of comfortable camaraderie. It was tense, uncomfortable, raw. We were both bleeding from invisible wounds.

His eyes glanced down to my stomach because I was much bigger than I used to be. The stare only lasted a couple seconds before he met my gaze once again.

I came around the desk and prepared to leave. There would be no chitchat or stupid conversation about the weather. We were both fine suffering in mutual silence.

Before I could step out, Antonio entered my office with a couple folders under his arm. He halted when he realized I was about to leave with company. "Should I just drop these on your desk?" He glanced at Hades, but instead of being polite and introducing himself, he turned his gaze back to me.

"I got it." I grabbed the folders and tossed them on my desk.

Hades stared at Antonio with silent hatred.

It was noticeably awkward, so I tried to break the discomfort. "Antonio, this is my husband…I mean ex-husband." I should've chosen better words altogether, but now the damage was done. I looked at the floor because I didn't want to see Hades's face. But when I lifted up my gaze again, I kept talking. "We have a doctor's appointment today."

Antonio gave a subtle nod before he shook Hades's hand. "Pleasure to meet you, and congratulations on the baby. I'm the hotel manager, so I spend a lot of time with Sofia."

Hades reciprocated the gesture but didn't say a word.

Antonio picked up on the tension and excused himself. "I'll see you tomorrow, Sofia. I hope everything goes well today."

"Thanks, Antonio." I watched him walk out and wondered why Hades was being so cold to one of my employees. I understood he was in a bad mood, but that was unnecessary. I wanted to tell him off, but I didn't want to ruin the day before it even started. "Let's go…"

We sat in the doctor's office. I was in my gown, but I didn't want to sit on the examining table, so I sat in the chair directly across from Hades. With my legs crossed and my hand on my large stomach, I sat there and suffered the silence.

Hades sat with his knees wide apart and his hands on his thighs. His face was slightly tilted toward the window, and his eyes were focused on the closed blinds. He couldn't see outside, but he continued to stare like there was nothing else for him to look at. The watch I gave him was on his wrist, but his wedding ring was still gone.

I glared at him, my anger slowly building as he continued to ignore me. We hadn't said more than a few words to each other, and he was clearly fine with the animosity between us. We were about to have a baby, but it seemed like we were just doing business.

It made me hate him a little bit.

I didn't care how handsome he was. I didn't care how much I missed him. I hated him. "Is this how it's going to be? We're just never going to talk to each other?"

He kept his eyes on the window. "We're talking now, aren't we?"

I actually rolled my eyes at the smartass comment. "Is this really how you want to have our son?"

A sarcastic chuckle escaped his closed lips.

"What?"

He shook his head slightly. "I don't need to answer that."

"Well, you need to say something. I'm getting sick of this little act, and I'm getting tired of waiting for an apology."

His eyes shifted to mine, finally. His gaze was cold like freshly fallen snow. The look was actually a bit scary. "You'll be waiting a long time, then."

I felt the rage and sadness as I looked at him. "We used to be so different… I can't believe this happened to us. We were in love when we made our son. Now you hate me…"

His eyes stayed on mine for a long time, his gaze so still it was like a frozen lake. There was a gleam of rage in his eyes, but it slowly simmered to calmness. For just a moment, he looked like the man I once loved. "I don't hate you, Sofia."

"It seems like it."

"I can never hate you. Ever."

I heard his words, but they felt like a contradiction to his behavior. I would just have to settle for the confession and believe his honesty. My hand rubbed over my stomach, and I felt a little more at ease. "How are you?"

Just as before, his eyes flicked back to the window. "I don't want to have this conversation."

"Then what kind of conversation can we have?"

After a long stretch of silence, he shook his head. "How's Andrew?"

"He kicks me all night long, makes me use the bathroom every ten minutes, makes me so hungry I have to eat a million calories a day…so I'm pretty sure he's an asshole like you."

Finally, a slight smile formed on his lips. "Sorry about that."

"It's okay. I'm sure he'll inherit some of your better traits."

"I don't have better traits."

"You do…I just haven't seen them lately."

His eyes switched back to me, and he stared at me endlessly. It was still hard to tell how he felt toward me. It seemed like he hated me but cared for me at the same time. But it didn't feel like he loved me anymore. That was a thing of the past.

The doctor came in a moment later and performed a sonogram of my stomach. The heartbeat was loud and strong, and Andrew was nearly fully developed. His head was so distinct, along with his fingers and toes. The doctor said the words every mother wanted to hear. "You have a very healthy baby boy. Now, all we have to do is wait for him to arrive."

Hades stood at my side and stared at the monitor with a stoic expression. He didn't seem to feel anything—at least, it seemed that way on the surface. But his eyes were glued to the screen like he didn't want to look at anything else ever again. Slowly, his eyes softened as he looked at our son.

The doctor excused himself and gave us privacy.

Hades didn't stop his stare.

"He's beautiful…" Tears welled in my eyes because I could see the person I'd been feeling for nine months. I already knew him so well, with every bout of morning sickness and every bit of pressure I felt against my bladder. Andrew was already a part of my life, but now I got to see him be a part of Hades's life.

Hades breathed a deep sigh. "Yeah, he is." His hand moved to my stomach, and he placed his outstretched fingers across the bump. He rested his hand there a long time, feeling the life we made together. His eyes shifted from the screen to my stomach, and he placed his other hand there as well, like he was hugging our son with both hands. "Our son…"

Hades drove me home then walked me to the front door. We

didn't say a single word on the drive, and we returned to the awkward silence neither one of us liked to experience. Once Andrew was no longer the topic, the only things we had in common were mutual pain and resentment. We were a divorced couple that couldn't forgive each other for the wrongs we did to each other.

I unlocked the front door then turned back to him. I didn't know what to say, but I wanted to say something. I didn't want him just to leave and we'd return to our broken relationship. I wanted things to be better… I wanted us to be better. "Thank you for coming."

He slid his hands into the front pockets of his jeans and breathed a quiet sigh. He kept a foot between us, a significant distance filled with resentment and distrust. "I'll always be here for him."

That wasn't the reply I'd hoped for.

He glanced at the door before he pivoted his body to the steps. "Goodnight."

I didn't want him to walk away. I didn't want him to leave us like this, in this perpetual pain. "Hades."

Instead of walking away and ignoring me, he turned back to me. His eyes were filled with impatience, as if the only thing he wanted to do was to get away from me as quickly as possible.

I wasn't sure what I wanted from him, but I knew I wasn't really angry with him. I just missed him…wished he understood just how much I missed him. I was angry with the world because of what happened to us. I was lonely, heartbroken, and wanted the man I loved. Telling him all of that seemed pointless, so I didn't know what else to do.

He continued to watch me with guarded eyes, prepared for whatever I would throw his way. There was a hint of indifference in his gaze, but it seemed forced. He wasn't himself at all…as if he had to watch his front and his back when he was with me.

I stared at my ex-husband with longing, missing the intimacy we used to share, the trust that was once unbreakable. He used to come home from work and kiss me as if he'd been thinking about it all day. He used to stare at my naked body as if he'd never seen anything so beautiful. He used to open up to me and confide every secret he never shared with anyone else.

All that was gone.

Before I knew what I was doing, I moved into him and let my hands brush over his chest to his shoulders. My mouth came close to his, and I watched the way he went rigid at my proximity. I could feel his muscles tense under my touch, feel his breath brush over my chin as he sucked in a deep breath.

I leaned in and let my soft lips touch his full ones. My hands slid from his shoulders to his muscular arms, and I closed my eyes as I felt that old spark. I took a deep breath as I touched him, felt all that heat and love rush back. Kissing him was different from kissing any other man. He was special…one of a kind.

I was still so madly in love with him.

That high disappeared when he pulled away abruptly. His arms were removed from my reach, and he sighed in annoyance as he positioned himself a few feet away from me. His hand rubbed the back of his neck before he looked at me.

I felt like he'd slapped me in the face.

Shocked by the rejection, I stood there and didn't know what to do. I couldn't even cover up my reaction to spare my dignity. I was embarrassed…and hurt.

Hades responded to my expression. "We can't."

I understood we were divorced. I understood we wouldn't get back together. But I didn't understand his words. "Why?"

He turned his gaze to the street and watched a few cars go by. The sun had begun to set ten minutes ago, and it would be dark very soon. He let the minutes trickle by before he turned back to me. "Because we can't."

The logical part of me knew we needed to remain platonic, make this easier for both of us. We had a son to raise together, and we needed to be responsible adults. Blurring the lines with a confusing relationship would make that difficult. But I wasn't logical right now. I was pregnant, emotional, and sad. "Are you not attracted to me anymore?" I'd gained an extra twenty pounds throughout the pregnancy, and I had a stomach I couldn't hide anymore. I was self-conscious about my looks, but I never thought Hades would care.

All Hades did was shake his head as he turned away from me, as if that was the dumbest thing he ever heard.

I knew he was with beautiful women all the time, all slender and toned. I saw the women he was with after we broke up the first time, so I knew his type. Perfect was his type. "Because I'm not skinny and perfect like your strippers and whores, you don't want me anymore? Now, you're used to the best, and I'm just some fat pregnant woman?" I felt the tears start in my throat, but I refused to let them be visible in my eyes.

He slowly turned back to me, the tint of his face slowly turning from tanned to red. His brown eyes now looked black, and the vein in his forehead was noticeable. Like a volcano, it seemed like he was about to explode and burn everything around him. "That's what you think I've been doing?" Spit flew from his mouth because he spoke with so much hostility. "You think I've been fucking around? No. That's fucking stupid. I've never wanted you more."

Reassurance washed over me, and I finally felt connected to the man I still loved. My isolation had made me question everything, made me question what I ever meant to him. As my clothes stopped fitting, I felt ugly…hideous. His words made me feel like me again, made me feel confident once more. "Then take me." I grabbed the front of his shirt and tugged him into me, bringing his lips to mine in a violent collision. Our lips crashed into each other, even our teeth smashing a bit. My fingers tightened on his shirt because I wasn't going to let him go.

Instead of slipping away, Hades remained in place. His lips didn't move against mine, but he didn't end the embrace either. His arms remained at his sides as he breathed against me, as he tried to find the strength to do the right thing and walk away.

I wasn't going to let him walk away.

My fingers released his now wrinkled shirt, and my hands glided over his chest. My stomach pressed against his and kept us farther apart than usual because I was much bigger than I used to be. One hand cupped his cheek, and I kissed his immobile lips, seduced him the best way I could. I never had to try with Hades. He was always ready to go, always thrilled to take me, even if it was in the middle of the night and he was asleep.

His lips eventually caved and reciprocated my demanding affection. They moved slowly, treasuring every graze of my lips, every breath that we exchanged. He kept his hands at his sides like he was still trying to fight the longing, but with every passing second, he gave up more territory. He allowed me to conquer him, then eventually he raised his white flag.

His hands slid into my hair, and he kissed me harder, cradling the back of my head as he gave me his tongue and his breath. His arm moved around my waist, and he gripped my lower back as he pulled me into him. One hand went to my ass cheek, and he squeezed it hard as he backed me up to the door and continued to devour me.

We made it inside and shut the door, our hands all over each other as we yanked on each other's clothes to pull our souls closer together. He pressed me into the front door and kissed me just the way he did on the balcony years ago. His lips moved to my neck, and he kissed me before his lips moved to my jawline. His hands hiked up my dress, and he pulled my leg over his hip as he pinned me into the wood.

This was what I missed about being married to this man. It was so easy to get lost in the carnal desires our deep attraction created. It was easy to become prey to this predator, to forget all the terrible things happening in my life. He chased everything away, calmed the storm in my soul, and created a new one in my heart.

I was too pregnant to screw up against a door like we used to. My stomach was in the way, and on top of that, I lived with my mom, so she could walk by at the wrong time and see me going at it like a whore with my ex-husband.

We made our way upstairs to the third floor and entered my bedroom. He kicked the door shut behind him and then pulled his shirt over his head. His tanned skin was the same as I remembered but also different. Now, there was hard steel just below the surface, muscles so strong they seemed bionic. He must have been working out more than he ever did before, picking up buildings and cars to get that kind of definition. He was beautiful and strong, an eight-pack leading to a deep V in his hips.

Now, I felt fatter than I had before.

He undid his belt and loosened his jeans so they could slide down his muscular thighs and fall to the floor. His shoes and socks were gone a second later before the grand finale. As if I'd never seen him naked before, he took his time dropping his boxers, clearly proud of the main event. Soon, they were gone along with the rest of his clothes, and he stood in front of me with a big-ass dick that nearly made me do a double take.

Was it always that big?

He watched my reaction to him, probably wanting to see my desire for him. I wasn't sure what he saw, but he probably noticed the way I tensed, the way I licked my bottom lip without thinking twice about it.

Jesus.

I grabbed my loose dress and pulled it over my head. I wore a black bra underneath, a couple sizes bigger from what I used to wear because my tits had swollen with my pregnancy. I unclasped it and let it fall before I pulled off my black thong.

All the insecurities I'd felt washed away when he looked at me like that. His eyes devoured my body like a teenager looking at a naked woman for the first time. His gaze was so concentrated he couldn't blink. He stepped closer to me as he continued to stare, appreciating the new curves I had as a woman. My tits were bigger and he clearly noticed, but he noticed other things as well, like the thickness of my thighs, the wideness of my hips, the way my stomach stuck out so far. But the arousal in his gaze told me he liked all those changes.

He looked at me just the way he used to.

He moved into me and grabbed me by the hips as he guided me backward and onto the bed. He moved on top of me as I lay back and got comfortable on my unmade bed. It was a place I slept alone every night, dreaming about the man I'd had to leave. No one else had ever been there, and it was hard to imagine a time when there would be someone new.

I only wanted this man.

He held up his powerful body by his arms as he lowered himself on top of me. He moved between my parted legs and slid one hand into the back of my hair. All the anger and rage he'd exhibited toward me in the doctor's office seemed to be gone. Now the man I used to know was with me, the man who loved me. He lowered his face to mine and kissed me, a slow kiss that was gentle compared to our embrace on my doorstep. Every kiss was purposeful, meaningful. Exchanges of hot breath, gentle moans, and easy kisses…it was all enough to make me come by itself.

My hands moved up his stomach and across his chest, my fingertips recognizing every dip and groove because I used to do this every night. My fingertips dug into his muscles, feeling the resistance of his solid frame. Now I had a big stomach in the way, but that didn't stop us from getting close together.

I didn't just want sex because I was lonely. I wanted this man specifically, the man who still had my heart, body, and soul. Maybe this was a bad idea. Maybe it would hurt more in the morning. But I didn't care. I wanted him now…and I would deal with the consequences later.

I didn't want to ruin the moment by saying something that could jeopardize our passion, but I had to be smart. "Did you bring anything…?"

His eyes didn't change with offense. He was as hot and hard up as he was a second ago. He grabbed his base and slid himself inside me, sinking in easily because I was so wet and ready. He closed his eyes and moaned quietly as he inched forward all the way and put his dick in place. "I haven't been with anybody else."

My hands stopped at his chest, and I stared into his warm eyes as I processed what he said. We'd been divorced and separated for months. He had every right to move on and spend his nights with other people. It would kill me, but I had no right to be upset. Knowing he chose to be alone resonated in my heart. I couldn't imagine being with anyone else either, and not just because I was pregnant. I knew he wasn't lying either because he wouldn't risk giving Andrew something. Not to mention, he wouldn't lie to me. "Neither have I."

"I know."

His hips slowly rocked into me as he kept his gaze locked on mine. Every inch he possessed was deep inside me, our bare bodies working together to be as connected as possible. When we kissed on the doorstep, it was hot and aggressive, but now, he slowed things down.

He made love to me, not fucked me.

His arms swelled from supporting his weight, but his expression didn't look strained. His chiseled stomach was the exact opposite of my belly, and he rubbed against it as he rocked into me. His breathing slowly escalated with his exertion, and he stared at me like I was the most arousing thing in the world. He bent his neck down and kissed me as he continued to move deep inside me, getting every inch in deep so his balls tapped against my body.

This was exactly what I wanted…to feel this.

Maybe it was the hormones, maybe it was the love, but I exploded right in the beginning. My thighs squeezed his narrow hips, and I dragged my nails down his muscular back and claimed him as mine as he gave me the greatest high I'd ever felt. It made me feel connected once again, made me happy again.

He pressed his forehead to mine and continued to move, his expression focused as he fought his need to release. He was so hard inside me that it was obvious he wanted to blow. But he held on because I wanted to make this last forever.

I looked into his eyes and recognized the man I used to be married to. I saw the love in his eyes, saw the beauty in his soul. It had seemed like things had changed because of his coldness, but he was still the same…deep down inside. We'd been separated for months, but that distance only showed me how much I loved him, how much I didn't want to spend my life with someone else. "I love you…"

He didn't say it back with his words, but he did with his gaze. His body worked at the same pace to make love to me, to keep the moment going as long as he could.

My hands slid into his hair, and I pulled his face close as I locked my ankles together around his waist. "Hades, I love you."

7

HADES

Was it possible to feel elated and feel like shit at the same time?

Yes.

I woke up the next morning with Sofia beside me. The bed was foreign, the room was unfamiliar, but it felt like home. She was cuddled into my side with her arm over my waist, her swollen belly nestled into my side. Her brown hair was all over the place from where I had touched it the night before.

She was perfect.

I stared at her for a long time because I knew it was the last chance I'd ever get. Last night was a mistake, but the temptation had been too strong to walk away. The second she grabbed me by the front of the shirt…I was a goner.

That'd always been my weak spot.

I'd had sex with the woman of my dreams, her belly big because I made it big. It was a fantasy of mine—except in reality, she wasn't my wife anymore. When I was home alone with just my hand, she was always my wife.

I was surprised she'd assumed I had been with other women.

How did she not understand how obsessed I was? How did she not understand how much I loved her? Sometimes I wondered if she was as smart as I gave her credit for. Hopefully, Andrew wouldn't inherit her ignorance.

I lay still because I wanted this to last as long as possible. Once I was gone, I would feel alone again. These months of separation were supposed to help me move on. Sleeping with her only reminded me of how amazing we were together. It only reminded me of what I'd lost.

Reminded me of what Maddox took from me.

Thirty minutes later, Sofia woke up. Her body tensed slightly. Before she even opened her eyes, she reached out for me like she was afraid I'd slipped out in the middle of the night without saying goodbye. When she realized I was right there, she relaxed.

Listening to her tell me she loved me was a dream…and a nightmare. Watching her love me like this was worse. I was still angry with her for leaving me, even if it clearly wasn't easy for her. My hand moved over her large stomach, and I put her at ease. "I'm right here." I didn't have the opportunity to spend much time with Andrew because we were living in different cities. If she were still my wife, I would be able to sleep with my hand on her stomach every night, feel my son kick when he was being ornery.

Maddox took all that away from me.

She placed her hand on mine and returned her cheek to my shoulder. She took a deep breath and relaxed again.

I rested my head against the headboard and enjoyed the comfortable silence for as long as I could. Last night was perfect. As soon as I'd finished, I was inside her again, making love to her throughout the night and fighting against a rising sun. She was just as sexy pregnant, actually more so. There was something about her curves and the changes to her body that excited me. It was probably an evolutionary thing since I knew her baby was mine.

It was sexier than the hottest piece of lingerie.

But I couldn't get attached…because I had to leave. It would've been smart to slip out in the middle of the night, but I didn't want to hurt her in that way. I didn't want her to feel abandoned, or like it was so easy for me to leave.

It was the hardest thing in the damn world.

When I'd waited long enough, I took a deep breath and spoke the words out loud. "I have to go."

She didn't move, as if she didn't hear what I said.

I was patient and gave her a few minutes to comply.

She eventually moved off me and left the bed. She grabbed her dress from the floor and pulled it on, hiding all her voluptuous curves and that gorgeous ass. Her tits were nearly twice the size, and while I liked them, I actually like the way her hips widened more, the way her thighs thickened. I liked all the changes.

I forced myself to stop staring and got to my feet. Piece by piece, every article of clothing returned to my body. My shirt was wrinkled from the way she'd yanked on it, but I would never throw it away. The silence filled the room as we both got ready, the occasional dressing noise filling the quiet. It was awkward for a million reasons, which was why I shouldn't have let this happen in the first place.

But I was weak.

After she fixed her hair, she turned to me, barely making eye contact with me. "I'll walk you out…"

We left her bedroom and took the stairs to the bottom floor. Because the universe hated us, Maria walked by, holding a cup of morning coffee, fully dressed. She opened her mouth to address her daughter, but when she realized I was with her, she shut it again. Our wrinkled clothes and messy hair made it obvious we'd spent the night together. And the stupid smirk on her face told us she figured that out. "Nice to see you, Hades." She excused herself down the hallway and ignored her daughter.

I wasn't ashamed of being caught. It was Sofia's problem.

We stepped outside onto the front porch to say our goodbye.

I didn't know what to say because nothing had changed. I could tell her last night was a mistake and it shouldn't happen again, but I didn't have the audacity to say something so cold. This was hard for both of us. Maybe it was better to say nothing at all. "I'll come down a few days before the birth."

Sofia crossed her arms over her chest and stared at the ground. Her makeup was a mess because she hadn't washed her face like she normally did. Her hair looked like she had just stepped out into a storm.

"And I'll stay for a week or two."

She gave a slight nod in acknowledgment.

I didn't see what benefit Andrew would get, having me in his life. I was a dangerous man who did dangerous things for money. My partner was a psychopath who was completely unpredictable. I would only be around once in a while, and when Sofia eventually remarried, her new husband would be more of a father than I ever could. I would have to sit there and watch some new guy replace me in every way imaginable.

Could I do that to myself?

Ash warned me about Antonio, and now that I'd seen the guy in person, I realized how much of a threat he was. He was young, good-looking, and judging by the way he treated Sofia, he thought the world of her. He was clean, simple, and they both had the priority of the hotel in common. It wouldn't take her long to realize he was the perfect partner.

And all the bad things that had ever happened to her…happened because of me.

"Do you need to leave right now, or can you stay a bit?" She lifted her gaze to meet mine, unease in her expression.

I wanted to stay, but I couldn't. "No."

"So, I won't see you until Andrew is born?" Her voice broke off in pain.

Last night was such a mistake. Shouldn't have happened. "Yes."

She tightened her arms over her chest and nodded.

I turned away and left…because I couldn't do this anymore.

I sat on the balcony late at night and drank my scotch alone. I leaned forward over the table with my temple resting against my hand. There was no amount of booze that could wash away my regret, my overwhelming depression.

What the fuck was I thinking?

I should've left.

I closed my eyes and tried to block the memory from my brain. Everything was so good, from the sex to the whispers she would utter in the dark, but it made my life so much worse. That was a tease, torture. It only reminded me of what I didn't have anymore. Now I had to sleep in a bedroom I used to share with her and pretend her ghost didn't haunt me every night.

How was this supposed to work? Really?

I was supposed to casually sleep with her every time the loneliness became too much? I would wait around for her even though there was nothing to wait for? And then when she started dating somebody, she would break it off with me? And I would just be fine with that?

I would never be fine watching my soul mate end up with another guy.

And watching my son go with her.

That was an outcome I refused to accept. I was a good man and didn't deserve that punishment. It didn't matter how much I loved her, how much I loved Andrew, I couldn't put myself through that. The years would pass, and I would see Andrew on Christmas with his new family. I would always be a stranger… always be second best.

I couldn't live like that.

The best thing for me to do was to disappear.

We stepped inside the factory and surveyed the damage we'd done. Some idiot thought he could flood the market with his own product since Maddox's original power had been disrupted and mine was questionable. Clearly, they didn't get the memo that we were in a partnership now.

Three men were in the center of the room, their guns on the floor and their hands by their sides. They were outnumbered, and no amount of negotiation would spare their lives. Their product would be dumped, and their unused chemicals would be seized for our own production.

Since this was what Maddox lived for, he took the lead and teased the men. "You want me to let you go?"

The leader did his best to be brave by keeping a blank expression, but the slight tremor in his left hand was his tell. The tattoos on his face made him seem more like a clown than a monster. "I have money."

"What a coincidence, I have money too." Maddox crossed his arms over his chest and paced in front of the men. Instead of his body moving with quiet rigidness, his shoulders slightly bumped up and down, like he was about to start skipping across the concrete floor. "So, if I have money, why would I want yours?"

The leader remained silent.

I got tired of watching him play with his food, so I moved to the back of the room to see what we could salvage. There were a lot of barrels of unmarked chemicals, but I was certain it was stuff we could use in the lab. I bent down and examined everything before I continued to move around the space.

"Call me old-fashioned, but I don't like to take shit from people." Maddox stopped in front of the leader. "I want to feel like I earned it, ya know? If I just take everything from my enemies, that's too easy. Where's the accomplishment in that?" He stared at the guy while he rubbed his fingers along his chin.

Maybe I was used to these stunts, but I could tune him out pretty well. I started to organize everything we would have our crew take away. When I was running my own regime, I rarely spoke to my enemies. I just killed them and moved on. But Maddox seemed to thrive on these tense conversations. He seemed to care more about them than all the money he made. I'd been working with Maddox for a while now, and I still didn't understand him.

Maddox kept talking. "How about we set up a poker table right here, and we play for it?"

The leader glanced at the other two men like he couldn't believe what was happening. "So, I can gamble my way out of here?"

Maddox laughed. "Not quite. I'll let one of you go. The other two, I'll gut your stomachs and your wallets. High stakes, first one out is gone." He clapped his hands loudly. "That'll be fun, right?"

I had just turned around to grab a case of their product when I heard the commotion.

The room was suddenly silent, and Maddox's energy

disappeared like air being sucked into a vacuum. I heard the distinct sound of a gun being drawn. Then Maddox spoke in a tone of voice I had never heard him use before. "Hades, duck."

Instinct kicked in, and I didn't think twice about it. I fell to the floor.

The sound of the gunshot was amplified in the factory, the boom echoing off the concrete floors and unadorned walls. That sound was quickly followed by a heavy body hitting the ground.

I looked behind me and saw the guy dead on the floor, a knife in his lifeless hand. He must've snuck up on me because he was hiding behind the barrels. He probably hoped to take me hostage so he could negotiate his way out of there.

Or he could've stabbed me in the back and killed me on the spot.

I rose to my feet and continued to stare at the corpse in front of me. There was adrenaline in my body even though there was no fight. I turned to Maddox, unable to accept the fact that he'd just saved my life.

Maddox looked at the three men in front of him, his nostrils flared in rage. He sheathed his gun and pulled out a knife instead. "Change of plans, boys. You come after my brother, and I come after you." He slit the throat of the first guy then gutted the next.

I stayed put and watched the slaughter… unable to believe what had just happened.

I sat at the bar across from Damien, still in a daze from what I'd witnessed a few hours ago. It was three in the morning and I should go home and get some sleep, but I was so disturbed by what I'd seen that I couldn't close my eyes.

If I did, I would relive it…over and over.

Damien was still a part of the business, but since Maddox didn't care for him, he sent him on mediocre errands. I was the one he wanted, but he put up with Damien to keep me happy. I took a big pay cut because of it. I never told Damien why.

Damien rested his fingers on his glass as he leaned back against the booth. It was late on a Tuesday, so we were the only two people in there. The bar closed an hour ago, but they stayed open for us. There was a distinct animosity between us, but we stayed diplomatic to get the job done. "So, you took those guys out?"

"They're gone."

"Well, that was easy. I admit Maddox has resources we never did."

There was a reason I couldn't kill him. "Some guy came up behind me with a knife…"

Damien leaned forward. "You kill him?"

"No." I swirled my glass before I took a drink. "Maddox did."

Damien continued to watch me.

"He saved my life." Instead of feeling invigorated with life, I felt dirty. I felt like I'd unfairly cheated death. A part of me was disgusted to be alive because I'd rather be dead than be saved by a man like him. And I'd like to be dead…just to be dead.

"Seriously?"

With my eyes focused on my glass, I nodded. "Yeah. The guy was about to stab me, but Maddox shot him."

Damien rested both of his elbows on the table and ignored his drink. "I'm surprised he would do that."

"That makes two of us."

"He must like you."

I shrugged. "I don't understand him. He's the sickest

motherfucker I've ever met. I don't understand what makes him tick. I don't understand what he wants. He goes to strip clubs but seems uninterested in women. He makes a fortune but then burns it. Now he has saved my life…when he doesn't even need me."

"I haven't dealt with him much, but you're right. He's weird."

"Not just weird…inexplicable."

Damien looked into his glass for a while. "I've seen him around women…but never with women. You know what I mean?"

I lifted my gaze to look into his.

"He's oddly obsessed with you…"

"Damien, what are you saying?"

He finished his drink before he pushed the glass away. "I don't know…maybe he doesn't like women. Maybe he likes men… Maybe he likes you."

The theory didn't faze me at all. "If he were gay, he wouldn't have raped my wife. I mean, ex-wife…whatever the fuck she is." There was so much pain in that sentence, I had to close my eyes for a second. We had both been through so much just to be together, and in the end, we weren't together at all. She was raped for no reason. It was all my fault.

Damien looked slightly uncomfortable by the statement. "I don't think that means anything."

He was right. It might not.

"The guy knocks off any guy who gets in his way. Why would he care enough to spare you? I understand not killing you himself, but stopping someone else from killing you? That's odd to me. Why does he care whether you live or die? He threatened to hurt Sofia if you rise up against him. It's genius. He got rid of your wife, and now you're alone."

"Doesn't matter if I'm alone or not. I'm not gay."

Damien shrugged. "Just an idea…"

I sat at my desk in my bedroom with a bottle of scotch, the watch Sofia gave me, and a black revolver lying on the wood in front of me. Maybe I had too much to drink. Maybe the alcohol didn't water down my sorrow. Maybe it only made it more potent.

But I didn't want to live anymore.

I was a prisoner of a psychopath who might be in love with me. I was also a prisoner of a woman, a woman hundreds of kilometers away, sleeping soundly in her bed. The sun would rise in an hour, and she would leave for work, while I sat there and considered the unthinkable. Terrible things had happened to her because of me, and that made me hate myself so much. But the fact that I loved her so much made me hate myself even more.

The curse was still in effect…because I was so miserable.

I didn't want to live because Maddox saved me. It seemed like I'd cheated death, like he'd taken away a merciful gift. If I were gone right now, everything would be better. I'd rather be dead than without the woman I loved.

How could I spend the next few years, torturing myself every day? Every time I visited her and our son, I would die a little more inside. I would have to watch her remarry, have more children with some other guy. I'd have to be mature and understanding about the whole thing. I couldn't just marry someone else…because I would never love someone else.

I had no other option.

This was the easy way out.

Without my existence, Maddox had no reason to care about Sofia or my son. He would forget about them like they never existed in the first place. Very few people would miss me. Sofia would be upset, but some other guy would take my place, and after a few years, she would forget what it was like to love me.

It was a coward's way out.

Well, what else was I supposed to do? If I tried to kill Maddox and failed…the consequences were unthinkable. But continuing to be Maddox's prisoner was just as inconceivable.

I grabbed the gun and checked the barrel. A single bullet lay inside. I closed it again, took off the safety, and cocked the gun. After one more drink, I would opt out.

But then my phone started to ring.

Sofia.

I watched her name flash across the screen as it continued to ring. I was tempted not to answer and to finish what I started, but the possibility of her needing me quickly changed my mind. What if she needed help? What if, in a few years, Andrew needed help? What if one day her new husband couldn't fix her problems? If I weren't here, what would she do?

I grabbed the phone and answered before the voice mail picked up. "Sofia?"

Her voice was quiet, like she'd been sleeping and recently woke up. "Are you busy?"

I looked at the gun sitting in front of me and clicked the safety. "No."

"Andrew is kicking so hard that I can't sleep…"

I didn't know what she expected me to do about that, but I did like knowing she thought of me. I'd never felt my son kick, and that felt like such a waste.

"And I hated the way we left things last week…"

We would never part on good terms. Our relationship was too

emotional, intimate. There would never be a time when we could say we were good friends and nothing more. At least on my part, she would always be the woman I loved…no matter how many years had passed. I could be fifty and still feel the exact same way. And that had nothing to do with the curse—that was all me. "We'll never leave on good terms, Sofia."

"I know…it's just so hard."

I closed my eyes as I listened to the sound of her voice, the pain in her tone.

"I don't regret what I did. But I just miss you so much…"

Tears escaped my closed lids. I let the two drops drip down my face like streams. This was my punishment for all the terrible things I'd done, the innocent people I'd killed, the prostitutes I'd paid, the crimes I'd committed. But it seemed too harsh…far too harsh. I didn't say a word because that was impossible to do without my emotions coming through. Last thing I wanted her to know was how broken I was, that I wanted to leave this world forever just to escape the pain, that the only reason I was still alive was because she chose to call at that exact moment.

It was almost as if it was meant to be.

8

SOFIA

Now I was so big, I was just miserable.

It was hard to sleep, hard to walk, and every time I looked at my naked reflection, I couldn't believe Hades actually wanted to have sex with me. My stomach had stretch marks, my petite frame was distorted by the life growing inside me. The time I had spent with Andrew had been magical, but now that I was at the end, I was ready for it to be over.

I finished up my final project at the office and prepared to leave. I'd be on maternity leave for a couple months, so Antonio would have to take care of everything. I made sure all my work was done before I walked out.

Antonio ran into me in the hallway. "You look a little uncomfortable…"

I rubbed my stomach and arched my back to decrease the pain in my spine. "A bit."

He smiled. "Go home and get some rest. I got everything handled here. And make sure you bring Andrew by whenever you're ready."

I headed home and waddled up the steps until I got inside. Summer was approaching, and the heat only added to my discomfort. I set my bag on the coatrack and heard my mom in the kitchen. "Please tell me you're making a grilled cheese sandwich." I walked inside and saw her cooking on the stove.

"No. I haven't made you one of those since you were eleven."

I leaned against the counter and rubbed my stomach.

"But I'll make you one now since it's a special occasion."

"Thanks, Mom. Or I should say…Grandma."

"I'm so excited to hear that in this house." She pulled out all the ingredients to make me a sandwich, a floral apron tied around her waist. "So…will Hades be returning soon?"

"I was going to call him in a little bit. I can tell Andrew will be here any day."

"Good. It's been a while since I've seen him." She waggled her eyebrows.

I ignored her double meaning.

"You think he'll stay here?"

"Mom, come on."

"What?" she asked innocently. "I'm just curious…"

Ever since she'd spotted Hades and me in the morning, she'd been hoping for a reconciliation. She loved Hades and would never give up on him. I explained to her why it would never work, but she didn't understand. "Well, don't be."

"This man is the father of my grandchild. Of course I care."

"Wherever he stays doesn't change his role in Andrew's life, so I wouldn't worry about it so much."

She rolled her eyes.

"I saw that, Mom."

She shrugged and kept cooking. "I didn't hide it, dear."

I was sitting in bed when I called Hades.

Hades picked up on the first ring. "Everything okay?"

"Yeah, I'm doing okay. But I'm getting really uncomfortable…"

His deep voice was slightly raspy, like he'd spent all day working. "I can imagine."

"I really think he could be here any day…so maybe you should come to Rome." I wasn't afraid to give birth even though it was incredibly painful, but I was afraid to do it without him. I wanted Hades with me every step of the way. Not to mention, I just wanted him here. Sleeping with him had made me forget all the fights we had. Now I just missed him.

"You have a week to go."

"I know, but I could use the help."

Hades was quiet. He didn't give me what I wanted or explain his trepidation.

I tried not to take offense to it, but that was difficult. "Unless you don't want to…"

"It's not that. I just have a lot of shit with work right now."

"Oh…" Sometimes I forgot that he worked with Maddox every day. I lived in a different city, so I didn't have to think about it on a daily basis. Sometimes it was easy to forget Maddox existed at all.

"But I'll make it work. I'll stay at the hotel down the street."

I didn't want him down the street. It was probably a bad idea for him to stay with me. I didn't want him in a different room on a different street. I wanted him right beside me, especially through times like this. "I assumed you would stay with me…"

A long, awkward silence extended over the line. "I don't think that's a good idea, Sofia."

His words cut me like a knife. "Why?"

"You know why."

The lull in our conversation stretched because there was nothing else to say. I wanted to get my way, but arguing over the phone wasn't the way to accomplish that. So I just let it be. "I'll see you tomorrow?"

His deep voice was reassuring. "Yeah…I'll be there."

9

HADES

I entered the hotel bar and saw Maddox sitting alone. It was a strange image, a very powerful man sitting alone by the window with a glass of water in front of him. The man never drank…at least not in public.

I walked through the sea of empty tables until I reached the small table up against the window. The Tuscan Rose was more overrun with shady characters than it had ever been, and if Sofia could see it, she would turn pale as milk.

I sat across from him and watched him look out the window. He seemed to be observing a group of girls walking by, holding bags of designer clothes as they ambled off together. His eyes studied them closely, like a cat stalking prey. His intentions didn't seem sexual…they didn't seem anything.

We hadn't spoken since the night he'd saved my life. After that happened, I worked on my own projects and took care of business from a distance. His kindness pushed me further away than his evilness ever did.

The waitress came over and brought me a glass of scotch before she disappeared.

Maddox slowly turned his gaze on me, his expression deflated.

His shoulders slumped with fatigue, and he seemed to be in a solemn mood. He wore his heart on his sleeve, and his emotions were very theatrical. When he was mad, he was really mad. When he was happy, he practically giggled. And right now, he seemed down.

I refused to ask him about his feelings. That implied I cared… and I didn't. "I need to leave for a few weeks."

After I spoke the words, Maddox gave me his full attention. He looked at me with crystal-blue eyes, eyes so bright they made the sky look black. Whenever he stared at me, he always seemed mesmerized, like he'd never really looked at me before. "Where?"

I hated answering to anyone. I wasn't going to start now. "Doesn't matter."

Maddox grabbed his water and took a drink. Instead of taking a sip like most people, he chugged half of it, like he'd just run a marathon. He set it down again with a heavy thud. "It matters to me."

"Personal reasons. Leave it at that."

"If it's personal, then you confide it to me. That's what friends do, right?"

If only I had the audacity to grab a butter knife and shank it up his rib cage. "I'll confide in you when you confide in me." He never shared anything with me, not that I ever asked. I'd made the statement just to prove a point and get him to leave it alone.

"Alright." He rested his elbows on the table and leaned forward, regarding me like a lover instead of a partner. "You killed your father, right?"

The blood slowly drained from my face.

"I killed my mother."

I didn't ask for the details because I assumed they were

disturbing. There was an innate creepiness in the air around us, like his mother's wounded spirit had entered the room to haunt him. But evil couldn't be haunted.

"I feel so much closer to you now." He said the words matter-of-factly, but there was a slight hint of threat to his tone. "Now, will you answer me?"

Out of principle, I refused to.

"I assume you intend to spend your vacation time with your new son in Rome. I suppose that's fine. If something comes up, I'll let you know."

I shouldn't be surprised he knew that information, but I still felt violated by it. This man knew everything about me. He probably kept tabs on me when I was off the clock. Every time I visited Sofia, he knew about it. He probably even knew I fucked her too.

He tapped his fingers against the table as if he were playing a song. But the music was chaotic and unpredictable. If anything, it just sounded like noise. Is that what he heard inside his brain every day? Noise?

"Aren't you going to thank me for saving your life?"

"I don't understand why you did."

His fingers stopped drumming. "I think it's obvious. And I would hope you would do the same for me."

I couldn't stop myself from shaking my head.

"When are you going to leave the past behind you? Hades, it's time to move on. We're partners now."

"No, I'm a hostage."

Maddox smiled like it was impossible to take me seriously. "You should look up the meaning of hostage because you clearly don't understand it. None of your rights have been revoked. You are paid handsomely. And you are protected."

He made it sound like I'd won the lottery. "Why did you save me?"

He cocked his head slightly.

"Why?"

His eyes narrowed.

"Answer me."

He leaned forward again and dropped his voice to a whisper. "Would you rather me not save you?"

"Yes."

He slowly leaned back, his body sagging with devastation. The pain entered his eyes, and it was the first time he actually seemed wounded. Up until that point, he'd seemed invincible. But something about my words hit him right in the heart.

He rose from his chair and didn't look at me again. He slowly moved through the tables and exited the restaurant. He didn't come back for me. And a moment later, I saw him walk past the windows, his hands in his front pockets…like he was just another person on the street.

I stood on her front doorstep and waited for her to come to the entryway. I was in jeans and a t-shirt, surprised summer had come so soon. Last summer, I married Sofia. That felt like a lifetime ago. I still remembered the way she looked in her wedding dress… I remembered taking it off when we came home.

My marriage didn't last long, but it was happy for its duration.

Sofia opened the door wearing a blue dress that fit her comfortably. Her hair was thick and curled, and even though she looked beautiful, she clearly looked distressed. Her stomach was considerably bigger than the last time I saw her. "Hey…"

Maybe when she looked in the mirror, she saw a large pregnant woman who wasn't the least bit arousing, but I saw something completely different. I saw a woman doing the sexiest thing in the world…giving birth to a son.

When she'd made a comment about me being with strippers and whores, it offended me because she didn't understand the depth of my feelings. Maybe they were thinner than she was, but they certainly weren't as pretty. Being with them would just make me lonely and depressed. This long venture into celibacy wasn't a good solution, but I didn't know what else to do.

I couldn't be with anyone else.

She opened the door wider, and she stepped aside. "Come in."

I moved inside, but I hoped I wouldn't run into her mother. The last time I saw her, it was awkward. I suspected an awkward conversation was about to follow, but when I stepped inside the house, it seemed quiet. Now that I was with Sofia, I didn't know what to do. It felt strange to go to her bedroom, but it felt odd to leave the house when she was so obviously uncomfortable. I stayed quiet and let her decide.

"Where are your bags?"

"I already checked in to the hotel."

Her eyes slowly fell with sadness. "Oh…"

I didn't want to repeat what happened last time. It had felt good in the moment, but afterward, I'd felt like shit. I was sure she felt the same way.

"You want to go to dinner?"

She stared at me blankly like she hadn't heard a word I said. "I don't want you staying at the hotel."

I'd hoped this argument wouldn't come up, but she seemed adamant about having it. "I think it's more appropriate."

"I don't want appropriate. I want you beside me every night so you can feel your son kick and move. And I want to make sure we're together when he comes. When my water breaks, I want you there for that. I don't want to be sleeping alone when the biggest event of my life happens."

I watched the emotion in her eyes and felt powerless to resist it. She didn't just want me for sex. She wanted us to be a family before the third member arrived. But there was no way I could sleep beside her without taking off my clothes and making love to her between the sheets.

It sounded like a nice picture…until I had to go home and be alone.

"So, you can stay here, or I can stay there. What's it gonna be?"

When she got like this, I knew there was no arguing. Besides, I didn't want to upset her when she was already so big, she was about to blow. I wanted her to be calm and relaxed, and if I was what made her calm, then so be it. "Alright."

She visibly relaxed.

"But what about your mom?"

"What about her?"

"You don't think that's awkward?"

"I don't care if it's awkward. She lives with me, I don't live with her. So, she can deal with it."

I'd prefer if we had more privacy, but Sofia probably would be more comfortable here than at the hotel, so I dropped my reservations. "Alright. I'll get my stuff, and I'll be back."

"Good." She walked to the front door and opened it again. "Hurry."

With my bag over my shoulder, I returned to the front door with hesitation in my veins. I knew I shouldn't do this, but I couldn't walk away either. When I got sucked into this beautiful connection again, it would just make it a million times harder to go back to my broken life. A few weeks of bliss would pass quickly, and then I would be back with Maddox, sitting across from him and trying to understand who he really was. That was my life now. This was just a glimpse…a dream of what I could have if things were different.

If I were a better man.

The door opened, and Sofia stood there, her eyes immediately going to my bag to make sure I'd followed directions. When it was clear I'd obeyed, she stepped aside and let me in.

I entered her large home and noticed all the old furniture that used to be in her house back in Florence before we got married. It was a nice place, just a little closer to the street than I would prefer. But it was near her work and a good school, so it was a nice spot for Andrew.

Sofia shut the door behind me then faced me. "Thank you."

She had no idea what I was about to put myself through. If she really understood the depth of this torture, she would never ask such a thing. I'd never considered telling her the truth about the gypsy and the curse. It seemed too ridiculous. But sometimes, I wanted to cave…and hope she would believe me.

Just when we were about to take the stairs, Maria appeared in the hallway. Her eyes moved quickly, spotting the bag in my hand and the tense expression on my face. A smile immediately emerged, and she moved toward me with genuine affection in her eyes. She was always kind to me, even a little clingy, so I knew her enthusiasm was real. "Hades, it's so nice to see you." She moved into my chest and hugged me, held me the way a mother held a child. There was a tight squeeze, and when she pulled away, that smile was still there. "I hope you'll be staying with us for a while."

She'd annoyed me in the past because she smothered me with her attention, but seeing her was actually nice…made me feel less lonely. "I'll be here until Andrew gets here. Don't want to miss anything."

Her eyes softened. "You're going to be a good father." She squeezed my arm before she excused herself.

Sofia watched her go before she turned back to me.

I knew we were having a son together, but it hit me hard that we were having a baby. I was about to be a father. I was about to be in charge of a whole other being. It wasn't just a son, but a boy who would be named after me.

Now, I felt so ashamed that I'd ever taken out the revolver.

What kind of man was I?

Sofia studied my gaze. "Are you okay?"

Not in the least. Just a few weeks ago, I'd considered suicide. But if I didn't take that way out, what choice did I have? I would be tortured every day until I was lucky enough to leave this earth. I wanted to be there for my son always…but could I?

"Hades?"

My eyes flicked back to hers. "Yeah…just excited for Andrew."

The last time I was in her bedroom, we were naked and doing what we did best. I hadn't had the opportunity to appreciate her bedroom, to notice her things in the space. There were paintings on the wall and a couple necklaces on the dresser. I carried my bag inside and put it on the armchair near the window.

Sofia came in behind me. She was in a loose dress with her hair done and her stomach stuck out so far that nothing she wore could hide it. "Are you hungry? I can make you something."

I'd skipped dinner, but I wasn't hungry. "You never have to make me anything." I looked out the window and admired the nighttime view before I turned around and faced her again. "I should be taking care of you."

Her hand moved over her stomach as her eyes softened. "This is the man that I miss…"

Things had been heated between us. Resentment bottled into rage. I never truly forgave her for leaving me, even though it was the right thing to do. I probably would've continued to be angry with her…until she put her lips on mine and forced me to buckle. "Don't expect me to be this way all the time."

"Why not?"

Because I was a bitter, angry, and sad man. "Because things change."

She held my gaze for a long time, the frustration slowly coming to the surface. Her hand slid from her belly and returned to her side. "Some things never change."

I didn't want to warn her of the things to come. This was the last time we would be together like this. Once Andrew was here, we would move on with our lives. We would drift apart. She'd fall in love with someone else…and I'd spend my nights with women I would quickly forget. This was the last time I would feel truly alive, the last time I'd want to be alive. I appreciated her faith in me, but it was misplaced. "I'm gonna get in the shower."

She seemed taken aback by the change in subject, but she didn't protest. "There are already fresh towels in there. Let me know if you need anything." She drifted away to give me privacy.

I got under the warm water and let the day's travel wash away. The smell of her shampoo and soaps was identical to her scent. I admired her loofa, the bar of soap she used on her perfect body, and even the razor she used to shave her sexy legs. To anyone else, they were just items that sat in the shower. But to me, they reminded me of what I lost. I used to see these things every day of my life. They were a part of marital bliss, sharing my space with hers.

Now all those things were gone.

My shower consisted of shampoo and body wash. That was it. Back to a simple bachelor life.

I took the longest shower of my life, letting the warm water drip down my body and wash away the stress and pain. When I returned to the bedroom, the most beautiful woman in the world would be waiting for me. But it was just a mirage, an oasis in a desert. It wasn't real. It was temporary. Everything that would happen at night would quickly turn to old memories.

Maybe I should tell her how hard this was for me…so she would let me leave.

But I didn't want to go either.

After my shower, I stepped out of the bathroom in a new pair of boxers. Sofia was in bed, reading a book on her large stomach. She was in a nightgown with her makeup gone. It was just the way it used to be…like we were married again.

There was a small table near her balcony doors, and on the surface was a plate of dinner along with a small vase of flowers. The food was covered with clear plastic, and the steam from the food was fogging the covering. It was chicken with rice and vegetables, probably her mother's cooking, but touching nonetheless.

Fuck, I missed being married.

Even though I wasn't that hungry, I sat at the table and ate the food she'd placed there for me. I should look out the window and admire the view, but my eyes kept shifting to the woman in bed. To any other man, she was just some pregnant woman reading a book. But to me, she was the most desirable woman on the planet. From her dark hair to her beautiful fair skin, she was perfect. She had a faint glow that radiated from the boy inside of her. Her full lips were softer than a cloud, and they fit in her perfect face like God put them there himself. I absentmindedly ate my food while I studied every single aspect of her face, committing it to memory as if I didn't already have a million pictures of her on my phone, pictures that I stared at in my darkest hours. I could be sitting in the back seat of a car waiting for our enemies to arrive, and my phone would be pulled out with my favorite picture on the screen. The sight of her face gave me a reason to keep going…even if she would never be mine again.

She must have finally noticed my stare, because she turned my way.

Ordinarily, I wouldn't have averted my gaze because I didn't give a shit if I was caught. But now, it seemed inappropriate, to stare at her like a man stupidly in love with his woman. She wasn't mine anymore…and she wouldn't be again.

She set her book on her lap. "How's your dinner?"

I finished chewing before I answered. "Good." I couldn't really taste the food because I wasn't paying attention. I never appreciated my meals anyway, because they were flooded with scotch.

"My mom's not a bad cook, huh?"

I shrugged. "She won't take Helena's job, but she's good."

Sofia chuckled. "I miss that woman. My mom tried to cook like her…doesn't work."

"You want her?"

Sofia's eyebrows rose off her face. "What?" she asked with a laugh.

"Well, you can have her if you want her." Sofia could have anything that she wanted.

"I'd love that, but she's yours. I'll find my own Helena."

We'd been divorced for months, but comments like that still killed me. Still ripped open old wounds. My hand ached like I'd just gripped a pen too tightly and signed our divorce papers. My heart bled the same as the night she told me she was going to leave. I was stuck in a time vortex. Months passed for everyone else, but for me, everything stayed the same. I couldn't bed another woman because it felt like I was cheating on my wife.

Even though I didn't have a wife.

So I was jerking off like a fucking teenager.

I'd killed my father and committed other horrendous crimes… but did I deserve this?

I finished my plate and left the dishes behind. I continued to sit in the chair because I knew what would happen the second I got into bed. I dreamed about that moment, but I also dreaded it. "I can take these dishes downstairs and wash them."

"Nonsense. I'll carry them downstairs next time I go down."

"No, I will." I stacked the dishes and covered them with my linen napkin so it wouldn't make the bedroom smell like room service in a hotel. I rose to my feet and walked to my side of the bed. My phone was placed on the nightstand, along with my watch. It was just the way I had it at home. My watch used to be tucked into my dresser because I chose a new one every day, but since Sofia gave that one to me, I didn't have the heart to ever change it. I still remembered the moment she gave it to me so vividly. In that instant, my life changed forever. I got everything I ever wanted, and I was happy. I wasn't happy anymore, but I continued to wear it…because the memory was strong enough to lift my sorrow sometimes. I wasn't sure I would be able to wear it once she remarried. Knowing she'd told another man she loved him would just make it too difficult.

"Are you alright?"

I didn't realize I'd been staring at the nightstand for over a minute now. I couldn't live in the moment with her because I was constantly dragged into the past and the future. I turned to her then finally got into bed without answering her question. I turned off the bedside lamp and let the room descend into darkness.

She closed her book and set it on her nightstand before she got comfortable beside me. She didn't reach out and touch me, keeping her hands to herself.

I lay on my back with my hands on my stomach, my blood running hot because I knew she was right beside me. In a nightdress with her long hair falling to my fingertips, she represented the strongest kind of temptation. She was practically a sack of a billion euro…and I forced myself not to take it.

"Come here," she whispered in the darkness. She beckoned to me with the beautiful sound of her voice. It was intoxicating in tone and affection.

I tried to resist as long as I could, but I knew how this would end. What was the point in fighting? I turned on my side and faced her, getting a jolt of pain when I saw how beautiful she was with her cheek to the pillow. With her hair flowing around her, she looked angelic.

Her dress was pulled up to her chest so her belly was visible. The swell of her stomach was so enticing, the way her natural arch deepened because her weight distribution had changed. There were stretch marks below her belly button, but even those were sexy. "Touch me."

I hadn't felt my son as much as I would've liked. Being apart for months had denied me the luxury. I couldn't resist the offer now, so I placed my hand over her large stomach and noticed the distinct hardness, the vibration of life underneath my palm. It was a riveting experience, but it also made hair stand up on the back of my neck, made me so hard that my boxers barely fit. I couldn't explain my powerful attraction. She'd been my wife when she was petite, curvy, and fitting into a size zero with no struggle. She was a million times sexier like this, with this belly sticking out from her frame. The words left my lips entirely on their own. "You are so sexy, baby…" I stared at my large palm as it rested on top of her. I was a big man, but even my large hand couldn't cover her entirely. My eyes drifted back to hers to see her reaction to my bold confession.

She used to be so confident, but now she was timid with self-doubt. She dropped her gaze for an instant because she didn't have the fire to hold my look. "I have stretch marks now. I'll probably always have them."

"What's wrong with that?"

"My skin isn't perfect anymore."

"I think it is perfect. Now you have scars, and scars are sexy. Men go to war, and they're proud of the permanent changes to their bodies. Women like men who've seen challenges, who've survived scary things." My fingers gently rubbed her stomach. "You're going to do the most difficult thing a human can do… give life. Of course, your body won't be the same, but it'll be better. You'll have battle scars…and that's so sexy." No guy would ever lose his arousal at the sight of her, at least, a real man wouldn't. Maybe I felt differently because she was giving birth to my son—and that was the sexiest thing she could do.

She lifted her gaze to meet mine again, this time less afraid. "You always know what to say…"

"I'm not saying anything. I'm telling you the truth. You are…" My words left my mouth and my brain when I felt a distinct movement under my palm. There was a definite vibration under the skin, a jolt of activity that was coming from inside her. My eyes returned to her belly and I became very still because I wasn't sure what I'd felt, but I was prepared to feel it again.

She placed her hand on top of mine and guided me to the exact location where Andrew was moving. She was used to the way he moved, the way he lived inside of her. "Hades, meet your son."

Sofia had an extra room across the hall, so I used it as an office during the day. I sat there with my laptop open so I could manage projects at the bank while I was away. Damien was in town, so he could handle things in my stead. I didn't have to ask permission to leave…like I did with Maddox.

I spoke to Damien on the phone about a couple things. I hadn't figured out what to do about our jointly owned business. We both had too much at stake, and neither one of us wanted to be bought out. At the end of the day, we both liked our jobs. That forced us to work together and play nice.

"How long are you going to be gone?" Damien asked.

"Probably two weeks."

"Well, alright. I'll handle all the meetings. How's Sofia?"

"Uncomfortable. She's pretty big."

"Well, tell her I said hi and congratulations."

"I will." I hung up.

A few minutes later, Sofia walked inside. She wore a short floral dress with her hair styled prettily. She waddled into the room and came to my side. "You've been working all day."

My eyes started at her ankles and drifted up her legs until I stared at her stomach for a couple seconds. I'd been sleeping beside her for a few nights, my hand on her stomach as I drifted off to sleep. It was the most comfortable I'd been in months, just feeling my son inside her. Sometimes, he woke me up when he kicked, but I didn't mind the interruption at all. I'd assumed we would be sleeping together, but that was all we did…sleep. It was what I preferred, but I was disappointed by it.

Maybe Sofia knew sex was a bad idea. Maybe it was too emotional for her last time, made her miss me so much it was painful. She'd whispered how much she loved me and wouldn't let me go until the next morning. Maybe she didn't want to put herself through that either.

I closed my laptop. "Taking care of stuff at the bank."

"Everything okay?"

"Yeah. Just bureaucratic stuff."

"If you're free, would you want to see Andrew's room?"

The room where he would grow, cry, and sleep? The room I would never get to see again? I wouldn't be there for the diaper changes and the nighttime feedings. I would never get to keep my son for a couple weeks in Florence. My relationship would always take place from a distance. "Yes."

She took me down the hall, and we stepped into the baby's room. It was painted blue like the sky, and there was a gray crib against the wall. There were already diapers piled on the dresser and so many toys he wouldn't know what to play with first. I stepped into the center of the room and looked around, feeling a million emotions at once.

Then I noticed a picture frame on the dresser.

It was a picture of me.

I stood in a suit and leaned against a balcony. It was a candid shot, and I must've been talking to somebody because I was smiling. It was clearly taken on our wedding day, but my bride was nowhere visible. I stared for a long time, feeling touched and scarred at the same time.

Sofia followed my gaze. "I know you won't be here as much as you'd like, so I want Andrew to be able to see you whenever he wants."

I felt a million emotions at once. I wanted to burst into tears, but I also wanted to demolish that whole room. I felt like a ghost observing someone else live my life. I felt like I was watching my life before my death. This wasn't a punishment; it was a crime. I didn't deserve this regardless of the things I'd done. This life should be mine, but after my son was born, I would be back to the shadows…back to the prison.

I no longer had control of my body. My feet moved on their own, and I was in the throes of an emotional breakdown. I gave her no explanation before I stormed out and left the house. If I stayed, I would say things I regretted. If I stayed, she would watch me collapse and combust.

I barely made it to the street corner before I burst into tears.

I ended up in a bar close by. Scotch was the only friend I'd had throughout the years, so now I leaned on it more than I ever had before. There were people everywhere, but I felt alone. The free drinks sent my way were disregarded, and I stared into my glass as I calmed myself down.

Sofia gave me space and didn't call me. It'd been hours since I stormed off and disappeared. I just needed a break from the suffocation, from the reminder of all the things I couldn't have.

Sometimes I wish I didn't love her.

My phone lit up with a text message. *Heard you were in the city. Wanna get a drink?*

It was my brother Ash, and I quickly deduced Sofia had reached out to him. *I'm already having a drink.*

Then have another.

I texted him the bar and waited for him to show up.

Fifteen minutes later, he sat on the stool beside me and ordered a gin and tonic. He stared straight ahead and didn't say anything for a while. The nice thing about my brother was that he didn't immediately interrogate me.

It was nice because I'd never been much of a talker.

"Sofia told me you could use a friend."

No, I could use a wife. I could use a son. I kept drinking and sat quietly.

"You want to talk about it?"

I shook my head.

"Alright." He sat there quietly with me…just being with me.

"What exactly did she say?"

"That you left the house abruptly and were upset. Didn't say much else."

Why didn't she come after me herself? Not that I wanted her to…

"I know this is hard for you, man. You're entitled to be upset."

I never said otherwise.

"You should tell her how you feel."

I slowly turned to him, my eyebrow raised. "What good would that do?"

He shrugged. "It won't change anything. But it might make you feel better…get all the shit off your chest. She used to be the person you confided everything to. Just 'cause she's no longer your wife doesn't mean you can't still do that."

I shook my head slightly. "I'm not her problem anymore."

"If she didn't love you, she wouldn't have called me. And as long as she still loves you, you'll always be her problem."

I walked into her bedroom late at night. It was almost eleven in the evening when I arrived back at the house. I was hoping she would be asleep, but I also knew she would be sitting up waiting for me, a book in her lap.

When I walked in the door, that was exactly what she was doing.

She shut the book and put it on her nightstand before she got out of bed. In the same nightdress she wore every night, she looked so damn pretty. Made me hate her even more. "Are you okay?"

Scotch was on my breath, and I was in a sour mood. I hated her because I loved her. And the more I loved her, the more I hated her. "I fucking hate this. We've been apart almost as long as we were married, but I somehow love you more now than I did then."

She turned still on the spot, listening to me with emotion in her eyes.

"I haven't fucked anyone else because I'm still in love with you. I dream of you, I miss you. And walking into Andrew's room only reminds me of what I'm missing, what I can never have."

A thin film of moisture developed in her eyes. "I know…"

"I'm happy we're having this baby. If I'm going to have kids with anyone, I want it to be with you. But I also want to be a family. I want to come home to you every day. I want Andrew to piss all over me when I'm changing his diaper. I want all that stupid bullshit that most men hate. I assumed this time apart would weaken my heart, but it's only made it stronger."

Two tears escaped her eyes and dripped down her face.

"I fucking hate this…"

She wiped away the tear tracks on her cheeks with her fingertips. "I hate it too. I can't picture myself being with anyone else but you. Antonio asked me out, and I just couldn't imagine myself going out with him…or anyone else. When I talk about you, I always call you my husband, even though you aren't anymore. I know this is hard for you. I just want you to know it's hard for me too."

It'd never be as hard for her as it was for me. I was stuck with Maddox…and I'd never escape.

"Hades, I love you so much."

I closed my eyes because I regretted my outburst. If I'd kept my emotions in check, this conversation wouldn't be happening. It wasn't helping either one of us. Only making it a million times worse. I liked knowing she was still in love with me…but I also hated it at the same time.

Now I didn't know what to do. I could leave and wait until Andrew was born, but all the emotions were already on the table. I was already hurting, and I couldn't hurt more. It didn't matter what I did next because the end result would be exactly the same.

Sofia crossed the distance between us and moved into me. When her hands went to the crooks of my elbows, I knew what would come next. But this time, I didn't want to fight it. This time, I needed it.

She cupped the back of my head, her fingers moving into my hair, and she pulled my face to hers and kissed me. She instantly took a breath when our mouths combined. The electricity burned her just the way it burned me.

My hand wrapped around her waist, and one hand dug into the back of her hair. I tugged her flush against me, feeling our son between us as I kissed her with all the feeling in my heart. I released all my longing, all the aches and pains in my chest, and I threw myself into her.

She clung to me just as hard, crushing our lips together as she kissed me with more passion than she ever had. Her tongue moved into my mouth, and she found mine before they danced together.

I pulled her nightdress over her head and continued to kiss her without skipping a beat. My hands moved to her thong and yanked it down so I could grab her cheek with one hand and squeeze. This woman could be mine for a little longer before I had to let her go forever. When she'd left me, I didn't really have the opportunity to treasure her. Everything happened so fast, and we were both too upset to appreciate our final moments together. But now we were ready to say goodbye, to have this final chance.

She pulled my shirt over my head and got me undressed, barely pulling her lips away from mine long enough to take a breath. She tugged my boxers over my hips and got me down to my skin before she guided me to the bed. She was the one who shoved me back.

I lay back on the bed and propped myself up on my elbows. The sight before me was so erotic, I forgot to breathe. Both of my hands formed fists, and my entire body turned just as hard as my dick as I watched Sofia move on top of me. She straddled my hips and widened her thighs so she could sit on my dick and slowly lower herself until only my balls were free.

I closed my eyes and moaned because it was almost too much to take. Her belly, her tits, everything was so perfect. I lay there as if restrained and watched her bounce up and down and ride my dick just the way she used to. I was too weak to do anything but enjoy it, to let my broken soul escape my chest and wrap around hers. "I love you, baby."

She moved up and down and rolled her hips, her eyes on mine. "I love you too…"

10

SOFIA

I sat across from Hades at the restaurant. It was the middle of the day, and we'd decided to get out for lunch. The last two days had been spent mostly in silence. He told me he loved me, and I said I felt the same way…but we never really spoke of it again. He'd slept beside me for the last few nights, and we weren't bothering to try to resist what we really wanted.

We went at it all night.

I appreciated every second we were together because it calmed the chaos around us. I missed being connected to someone like that, to feel the passion and so much love. I missed this man with all my heart, and I didn't know if I could ever let him go.

I was uncomfortable all the time because of my ridiculously big belly. The chair was hard on my back, and I couldn't sit close to the table because I was too big. But it was nice to get out instead of sitting at home and waiting for the baby to come.

Hades glanced at the menu before he lifted his gaze and looked at me. "What are you getting?"

"Everything."

The corner of his lip rose in a slight smile, a rare event for someone like him. He set down his menu and continued to look at me.

I missed seeing him wearing his wedding ring. When he used to wear it, he didn't attract so much female attention. But now most women looked at him, trying to figure out if he was available or not.

I had that pregnancy strength, so I would knock them out if they tried.

He continued to watch me with his brown eyes, the same eyes that looked into mine when he was on top of me in the darkness of my bedroom. There was always a slight hint of affection in his gaze, his heart on his sleeve.

The waitress came over and took our orders, then we were left alone again.

We spent so much time talking about us, I never asked him about him. "How are things in Florence?"

He took a long time before he answered. "The same."

"And things with Maddox…?" I never asked about that man because I despised him, but I wanted to know that Hades was okay.

His gaze darkened noticeably, and his mood soured like he'd been provoked. "I don't want to talk about that."

"Why?"

He shook his head slightly. "I just don't."

"You can always talk to me about anything." I knew he didn't have Damien at his side anymore, and Ash was here in the city. If Hades wasn't sleeping around, then he had no one to share his life with. Regardless of what happened between us, I would always be there for him.

"Maddox is crazier than I ever thought he was. He's smart, calculating…but his greatest asset is his unpredictability. I've never met anyone like him. Now I understand how he's survived so long."

"You talk about him almost like you admire him…"

Now, he looked consumed by rage. He was dead silent, so rigid it looked like his muscles would tear. It seemed like he wanted to say so much in response to my observation, but the only thing he managed to get out was a simple response. "No."

I knew I should let it go because he was so angry, he couldn't see straight. The thing keeping us apart would keep us apart forever. I wanted to go home to Florence and move back into my bedroom, but then I realized I'd made the right decision staying in Rome. I could never go back…not while that psycho was in charge.

"Don't ever ask me about him again."

I held my silence and didn't provoke him. Maybe he was right. Maybe we could never talk about this. I grabbed my glass of water and took a drink, my lipstick smearing on the glass. When I set it down, I rubbed my hand over my stomach. "I can't believe this is almost over. I've loved being pregnant, but I'm so ready for it to end. I can't wait to see if he looks like you, if he has your eyes or mine."

"I'm sure he'll be perfect."

"Are you nervous?"

"Why would I be? I'm not the one who has to push him out."

I smiled at the comment. "I'm not worried about that. But raising a son…that's a big deal."

He nodded slightly then fell into a quiet composure. His eyes drifted away, and he looked at nothing in particular as he remained deep in his thoughts. Minutes passed before he turned his gaze back to me. "You're going to be a great mother, Sofia. I have no doubt."

I lay beside Hades in bed, our naked bodies tangled up like cords in a drawer. Our faces were close together, and my fingers brushed through his hair as I listened to him breathe. I treasured the sight of this beautiful man because I knew I wouldn't be able to much longer. I loved everything about him, from his strong chest to his soft heart.

One of his hands rested on my stomach, and it remained there when he fell asleep. He'd been spending more time with Andrew in the last week than he had throughout my entire pregnancy. He slept with me every night, made love to me like I was his wife, and kissed my belly like he couldn't wait to be a father.

Knowing this was nearly over almost made me cry.

I didn't want to close my eyes because I didn't want this memory to pass. But my eyelids grew heavy, and I fell asleep with my hand against his chest. I could feel his heartbeat against my palm, strong as a horse.

But then my eyes snapped open when I felt something.

I was in momentary shock. My mind couldn't process what had just happened, couldn't determine if it was a dream or if it was real. But then I felt the sheets grow wet underneath me, and I knew the time had come.

"Oh my god…" My hand moved to my stomach so I could feel Andrew at my fingertips. The moment I'd been waiting for had arrived, and I was both excited and absolutely terrified. For a second, I didn't know what to do because I was paralyzed by the stress.

Hades must've noticed the dampness of the sheets or my frantic movements on the mattress because he opened his eyes and looked at me. After a couple of blinks, he was able to focus his gaze. He touched the wet sheets then moved his hand back to my stomach. He was the exact opposite of me, so calm it was annoying. "Let's get going." He got out of bed and grabbed my bag from the closet.

"Do you understand I'm having a baby?" I asked, somewhat hysterically.

"I took a health class in college. Give me more credit than that." He grabbed a dress from the closet and helped me to my feet so I could get ready. "Let's get you to the hospital."

"I'm having a baby…"

He pulled the dress over my head and got me ready when he realized I wasn't going to do it myself. "Everything's going to be fine, baby." He grabbed the bag off the bed and then wrapped his arm around my waist.

"How are you so calm right now?"

"Because I know you've got this." He pulled me in close and kissed my forehead. "We're about to meet our son."

I looked up at him, and the confidence in his gaze made me relax. I let the moment between us linger, let the joy last a little longer. I couldn't imagine loving anyone more than Hades, but I had a feeling that was about to change. "I'm so happy you're here with me."

His eyes softened, and he pulled me in for a kiss on the mouth. "Me too."

After twelve hours in the hospital room, it was finally time for me to start pushing. Every contraction I was subjected to was so painful, it brought tears to my eyes. My body was under such supreme stress, I wasn't sure how I was going to do this.

Hades sat in the chair at my bedside, dressed in scrubs with his hand in mine. He watched me with steady eyes, seeing the way I breathed into my nose and out my mouth. He gave my hand a gentle squeeze and continued to be a rock under my feet. "The doctor said it's time to push."

"It hurts…"

He placed his other hand on mine. "I know. You've been at this for twelve hours, and you deserve a medal. But you have to keep going. I know you can do this. You've always been a tough-ass woman. This is nothing to you."

"It's definitely not nothing…"

"Andrew has to get out of there, and the sooner it happens, the sooner he'll be in your arms."

I sighed because the comment went straight to my heart.

"It's time for both of us to meet our son. You can do it, baby."

After Hades gave me the pep talk I needed, I pushed through and made it happen.

Thirteen hours after my labor started, Andrew Lombardi was born.

He rested in both of my arms at the perfect size. He had ten fingers and ten toes, and it was clear he was a healthy baby. It took so much work to get him here, but he was more beautiful than I ever could've imagined.

He opened his eyes, and of course, he had Hades's coffee-colored eyes. "He looks just like you." That was exactly what I wanted, for my son to look like his father. Now I could see Hades every day, even if he was nowhere nearby. A piece of him would always be with me, no matter what the future brought. I brought Andrew close to me and placed a kiss on his forehead. All the instinctive feelings mothers described were true.

I would never love anyone the way I loved him.

Without even realizing it, I had tears on my cheeks. They were even in my heart. The pain of labor was quickly forgotten because I was so happy to have this little baby in my arms. He was a precious gift, an unexpected surprise.

Hades was quiet as he watched me hold our son. Wordless and still, he was like a spectator at an event, experiencing the moment from a short distance. He let me have all the time I wanted without asking for his chance to hold the baby.

Now that I had him, I never wanted to let him go.

"He's beautiful, isn't he?"

Hades was still quiet, absorbing the moment at his own pace. "Yeah…he is."

"I know I should hand him over, but I don't want to."

He chuckled quietly before he placed his hand on Andrew's stomach. Hades's fingers were so large compared to our son's small size. He could pick him up with a single hand so easily. "That's okay. You've earned this."

I kissed Andrew on the head one more time before I handed him over. "Andrew, this is your father."

Like a natural, Hades took him like he'd done this a million times. He cradled his head and the rest of his body, and then brought him into his chest with a single arm. He rested back against the chair and made sure the blanket was wrapped tightly. Then he was quiet as he regarded our son, studying his face like it was the most interesting thing he'd ever seen. His other hand rested on his stomach so his thumb could feel our boy's little heartbeat. Hades showed no emotion and kept everything beneath the surface, but a few thoughts escaped his eyes. There was so much love there, pure and whole love. He used to look at me that way from across the room when he was stuck in a conversation he didn't want to be a part of. But now he looked at Andrew that way because I wasn't the only person in his heart anymore.

I'd been replaced.

Hades continued to stare at Andrew with no signs of stopping. He took to his role so well, instantly looking like a father with no effort at all.

I wished every day could be like this…that Hades would come home from work and pick up our son out of the crib. I wished he were still my husband, the person I would grow old with.

The thought was so painful I couldn't bear it. I wiped the thoughts from my brain and just concentrated on the scene in front of me. My heart rate gradually slowed as peace descended. Before I knew what happened, I drifted off to sleep.

I was only in the hospital for a day before I got to go home. My life was completely different the second Andrew was born, and there was really no way to prepare for that. Now my world revolved around this little person, and I had to navigate everything with that in mind.

I sat in the back seat with Andrew on the way home instead of sitting beside Hades. It was difficult to leave my son in the car seat when I thought my arms would be a safer place. He cried like all babies, but most of the time, he was asleep. He looked so cute when his eyes were closed like that.

When we returned to the house, Hades carried everything inside so I could take care of Andrew. My mom was just as infatuated with the baby as I was, but since she understood what it was like to be a new mom, she knew I needed this time for myself. We went to the third floor, and I showed him his room before we returned to the bedroom.

I'd already fed him and changed his diaper, so all he wanted to do was sleep.

That was fine with me.

I got into bed and laid him beside me so I could watch him sleep as I lay there.

Hades joined me and lay on the other side. "Now what?" His voice came out as a whisper so he didn't wake Andrew.

"We take care of him."

Hades continued to stare at him. "Looks like he's doing okay on his own."

"Babies sleep a lot. They need their rest so they can keep developing."

"Like I said, I've taken a health class."

I shot him a glare across the bed.

He gave a faint smile in return. He hadn't slept much since we'd gone to the hospital because he took care of Andrew while I rested. But he didn't seem tired now. He wanted to lie there with me and enjoy the little boy we'd made together.

"Should you invite Ash over?"

"Why?"

"Because this is his nephew…"

Hades shook his head. "He'll turn him against me. I'm not gonna give him the opportunity so soon."

I knew he was kidding, but I still gave him a glare.

"I'll tell him. I just want us to enjoy him for a while, ya know?"

"Yeah…that's probably a good idea."

Hades turned on his side and placed his palms underneath Andrew's feet. He gently touched his toes and heels as he admired his son's peaceful expression. Hades spent his life dealing with criminals and living a fast life on the street. He was usually dressed in a tailored suit and shooting bullets full of power, but now he was just a father loving his son.

It was beautiful.

"I never want him to grow up. I want him to stay like this…forever."

He lifted his gaze and looked at me, a solemn expression in his eyes. "Yes…I wish it could stay this way forever."

11

HADES

My son shared most of my likeness. He was too young for his features to be concrete, but I could tell he would have my warm eyes, my olive skin, and a rugged jawline the ladies would like.

One thing we didn't have in common was sleep.

This guy could sleep all day and all night.

Most of the time, I was awake at three a.m.

When I thought of babies, I imagined these blobs of people shitting in diapers all day and crying nonstop. I never had an affinity for children and found them to be a nuisance. But I felt entirely differently toward my own son.

He was the coolest person in the world.

When he was awake, he stared at me with fascination. Sometimes, he would reach his hand out to grab me, to explore me. But a part of me believed he somehow knew exactly who I was. Sofia gave me a beautiful baby boy, and I felt so much gratitude the likes of which I'd never felt before. I'd only loved one person my whole life.

But I loved this guy even more.

I spent the next few days helping Sofia care for the baby so she could rest and recuperate. I also took advantage of the time to get to know my son. He was mostly just a doll wrapped in blankets, but our staring contests were intriguing nonetheless.

Sofia and I stopped having sex because the doctor said intercourse wasn't an option for many weeks. But I still held her tightly throughout the night. I still kissed her as if I never wanted to stop. Knowing she was the mother of my child made me fall in love with her in a whole new way.

Sofia was trying to get some sleep, and Andrew wouldn't stop crying. I attempted to feed him, but he wasn't hungry. I changed his diaper, but it was already new. I eventually took him into the nursery and rocked him in the chair in the hope he would calm down and drift off to sleep.

He never closed his eyes, but he did stop crying.

Now he stared at me in the dark while Sofia slept in the other room.

I knew I had to leave soon. I'd probably stayed far too long as it was. Maddox would grow frustrated with me, and the last thing I needed was for him to appear on the doorstep to fetch me himself.

So I had to go.

But when I looked down at this beautiful boy, I didn't want to leave. "I'm sorry, son. I have to leave…and I won't be seeing you as much as I'd like. I'm just trying to protect you, and I'm not sure how to do that by staying here."

He hung on to every word as if he could understand what I was saying.

"I love your mother very much, and I loved you the moment I felt you kick. But you and I live in different worlds. I don't expect you to understand that. Even as a grown man, you may never understand." The time I'd spent here for the last few weeks had brought me such joy. But once I was in Florence, that joy would turn into despair, the kind of despair that would swallow me whole.

I wanted to be a husband and a father, but I knew I never could be. Sofia would never be mine again, and I would just be a ghost that drifted in and out. I would have to stand by and watch Sofia love someone else. I would have to watch my son get more attached to his stepfather than he ever would to me. That didn't sound so bad a few weeks ago, but now that I'd met this little boy, I knew it was insufferable.

I would live a life full of regret…every single day.

I would never be the father who went to all the football games and watched him try on his suit for prom. I would never be a good role model for him, a father who would be there at times and not at others. I was a liability to both him and Sofia. I could do nothing beneficial for either one of them.

Their lives would be better without me.

And every time I would see him, it would just hurt more…and more.

Could I do that?

Could I come over for a visit and shake Sofia's husband's hand?

Could I listen to my son call him dad?

Could I watch some stranger have everything that should be mine?

I was lost in my son's eyes when my phone rang. I looked at the screen and saw the name I despised. I took the call and kept my voice low. If I ignored him, he would just appear at an even worse time. "I'll leave tomorrow." I wasn't ready to go, but I didn't want to argue for my freedom either. It was easier just to settle.

Maddox was quiet for a while before he responded. "Good. I need you here."

"Bye."

Before I could hang up, Maddox spoke. "Congratulations on your son. I hear he's beautiful."

I turned the speaker away from my mouth so he couldn't hear me breathe hard. Icicles formed in my blood because I turned so cold. I still held my son in my arms and rocked him gently, but all the muscles in my body tightened because I wanted to chop off his head. "Come near my son, and I'll kill you."

"Whoa…chill. It's all good."

I spoke through gritted teeth. "Don't threaten my son again."

"Threaten? I believe I gave you a compliment."

"Fuck you. You know what you did."

"Hades, let's both take a deep breath and calm down. You're probably just sleep deprived and a little on edge."

When I looked at Andrew, he was still calm. The same fascination was still written in his eyes.

"I probably wouldn't care so much about your son if you were here. Just something to think about." He hung up.

I set my phone on the table beside me and stared into the darkness. The lights were off, but I could feel the red tint creep into my vision. Both of my hands tightened into fists, and I felt the blood lust pump in my heart.

As if Andrew could feel everything I felt, he opened his mouth and began to wail.

I waited until the next morning before I told Sofia I had to go. It seemed like she'd been dreading this moment since I'd arrived because she hadn't mentioned it once. Over the course of the last two weeks, we'd fallen right into our old relationship, and it felt like we were husband and wife once again. I knew she didn't want that to end. God knew I didn't want it to end either.

But now it was time to close the curtain and walk away…for good.

Andrew had breakfast and then was put down for his early afternoon nap. He preferred to sleep with us at night, but during the day, he was fine with the crib, probably because the sun was still out.

I walked into the bedroom and grabbed my bag from the closet.

The instant Sofia noticed my movements, she visibly clenched, like a schoolboy about to be slugged in the stomach. And she refused to look at the bag. She even refused to look at me. Pretending the moment didn't exist was easier than allowing it to be real.

I didn't want it to be real either.

I put the strap over my shoulder and waited for her to turn toward me. I would give her the time she needed to tame her watery tears and rip off the bandage that would tear her skin. I pitied her heart, but I pitied mine so much more. She would get everything…and I would get nothing.

With her arms crossed over her chest and her gaze out the window, she let the minutes trickle by as she composed her response. She probably rehearsed every argument she wanted to make, but then realized there was no fight she could win. Our relationship couldn't work, and now that we had a son, it worked even less.

She finally turned to me once she had enough courage. Her green eyes were slightly glossy, and she pressed her lips together tightly as if she wanted to stop them from trembling. Her body was still recovering from the miraculous thing she did, giving birth to another person, so she wore baggy clothes to hide what she saw as her flaws.

They weren't flaws to me.

She walked toward me with her arms crossed over her chest, her eyes on the ground. She stopped in front of me, her long dark hair pulled over one shoulder and her plump lips begging for comfort.

How could I say goodbye to the love of my life?

I kept a stoic expression, and my emotions were hidden in a cage. I was about to do the hardest thing I'd ever have to do. She would hate me, and I hoped she would because it would make all of this a lot easier.

"I'm not ready for you to go yet…" She'd just had a baby, so she was exhausted. Her makeup was absent, and she didn't have time to do her hair. Her glow was gone because Andrew took it with him. But she was still the most stunning thing I'd ever seen. Listening to her ask me to stay was practically poetic.

"I don't want to leave either."

She moved closer into me and cupped my face. There was so much love in her eyes, love that had been absent for most of our relationship. Now it shone bright, like the North Star in a sea of clouds. She pressed her forehead to mine and took a deep breath. She closed her eyes for a moment before she kissed me.

I never wanted that kiss to end.

My arms wrapped around her, and I pulled her close. This should have been the beginning for us, not the end. This should have been a time for us to fall further in love as we bonded with the child we'd made together. But now it was going to be the hardest moment of my life.

She pulled away and let her hands trail down my chest. "When will you be back?"

I held her gaze and felt my pulse quicken in both wrists. It was impossible to look this woman in the eye and not say what she wanted to hear. It was nearly impossible for me not to get on my knees and give her whatever she wanted. "I'm not coming back…"

Her eyes slowly changed as she processed what I said, morphing from sadness to confusion. They shifted back and forth quickly so she could take in my expression as much as possible, to absorb any detail she may have missed. Her fingertips were suddenly light against my chest. "What's that supposed to mean?"

I saw the fire before the spark. I saw the inferno before the rage. "It means what it means. I'm not coming back."

Her hands slid the rest of the way until she no longer touched me. Like her fingertips had been burned, she stepped back. Her eyes smoldered in anger, and there was practically smoke rising from the surface of her eyes. "Hades." That was all she had to say to explain how she felt, to ask the questions she couldn't provide answers for on her own.

"I can't keep seeing you. It's too fucking hard." I took a deep breath before I continued. "Every time I go back, I'll have to start over. I can't keep torturing myself over and over again. I wish there were another way, but there's not."

She crossed her arms over her chest. "And our son? Your son?"

I shook my head slightly. "I can't see him either." That hurt more than losing Sofia. My boy would never know me. I would never know him.

Her eyes became so ferocious so fast. "So, you're just going to abandon your son?"

"Having me as a father will do him more harm than good. I'm a liability."

"That sounds like a shitty excuse to me."

If only she knew the whole story. "I can only come down once in a while, so he'll hardly see me anyway. And one day, you'll be married to some other guy, so I'll have to come and see your happy life and know I'm no longer a part of it. I'll have to watch my son look up to some other man as a father because I was never around. I can't do that to myself… I can't."

There was no sympathy coming from her. "It shouldn't matter what happens with me, if I do get remarried or not. Nothing should ever get in the way of being with your son. If you really never want to see me again, Ash can always pick him up. We have options."

It was still too much. "I can't do it, Sofia."

Her entire face began to flush. She'd never looked like that before, like a red-hot volcano about to destroy everything around her. "You can't be serious."

"I'm never going to move on if I have to watch you have your own family, if I have to watch my son love some other guy. It would be torture."

"Coward." She said the word slowly, like she was feeling it on her tongue for the first time. "Fucking coward. I don't like this either, but I would never turn my back on my boy."

"Because you get to keep him." My temper flared. "You get to start over with a new life. You can work at the hotel and raise a family without looking over your shoulder. You have no idea how shitty my life is, all the bullshit I have to put up with. Don't call me a fucking coward. You have no idea what I've sacrificed for you. I'm doing this for both of you. All I ever do is cause you harm. And I can't do that to my son."

Tears billowed over the edge of her lashes and dripped down her cheeks. "So, what? That's it?" She spoke through her tears, her voice cracking. "We're just never going to talk again? I'm never going to see you again?"

"You can always call me if you need anything…but that's it."

She turned her head slightly as if I'd slapped her. "I don't need anything from you, Hades. The only thing Andrew and I want is you."

My heart thudded in pain, but I kept up my expression.

She watched me as if she expected me to change my mind, to come to my senses and realize how harsh this decision was.

But there was no other choice. The best thing for both of them was to have nothing to do with me. And the best thing for my sanity was to never see them again. It was depressing as fuck, but there was no other way. Right now, I looked like a coward, an asshole. But that still wouldn't change my decision.

I wanted to kiss her one last time before I left, but that wasn't an option. I'd killed her affection the moment I'd abandoned her. Her opinion of me would always be low. When people asked about me, she would say I was a coward who deserted our son. I ruined the most beautiful thing in my life, but I was done trying; I was done fighting. This wasn't meant to be.

It was time to shut the door forever. "Bye, Sofia." I gave her a chance to say something back before I turned away and walked out of the house. If she wanted to scream and yell at me, now was her chance. But when I was out of the house…it was really over.

Her eyes shone with wetness, and her face was puffy from all the tears. The white parts of her eyes were now red. She trembled slightly with devastation. It was the moment of truth, but she didn't know what to say. She refused to say goodbye to me. She couldn't do it.

I couldn't keep my emotions in check much longer. I'd done a good job pretending to be heartless, but I wouldn't last more than a few seconds. When I was about to cave, I turned my back on her…and walked away.

12

SOFIA

The joy I felt at Andrew's arrival was quickly extinguished when Hades walked out on me. I'd already lost him once, so I shouldn't be so devastated. But knowing I may never see him again and he wanted it that way left permanent scars on my bones. He didn't just want nothing to do with me…but also Andrew.

The most amazing person in the world.

I'd had a much higher opinion of Hades. He was loyal and committed, but all those qualities I'd once adored were gone. Now I sat in Andrew's room, staring blankly out the window as he slept in the crib. I was heartbroken, and no bandage was strong enough to fix it. I understood it was hard to see each other when we used to be so happy, but I still couldn't justify his decision.

Andrew would never know his father.

I looked at the picture frame on the dresser, the image of the man I loved. I wanted Andrew to see his father's face whenever he wanted, to know his father was there even when he was hundreds of kilometers away. But now I couldn't look at it… even considered taking it down.

Was this my fault? If I had never slept with him again, would he still be here?

Did I push him when he wasn't ready?

I considered calling him many times, but I had too much pride. If he wanted nothing to do with me, then I wanted nothing to do with him. I knew I was just bitter and sad at the moment, but I meant it all the same.

He abandoned us.

My mom called to me up the stairs. "Honey, you have a guest."

I'd just given Andrew a bath and changed his diaper. He was in a blue onesie, and he looked so cute in his comfortable crib. There were many times when I had to stop and stare because he looked so much like Hades. I stepped into the hallway at the top of the stairs. "Who is it?"

"A very handsome young man."

I rolled my eyes. "That doesn't help at all, Mom. What's his name?"

"I don't know…Fire or something."

He was a hot guy named Fire… Took me a couple seconds to figure it out. "That's Ash. He's Hades's brother."

"Whatever. He's here."

I walked downstairs to meet him in the entryway. I was in a loose t-shirt and jeans. I'd put no effort into my appearance, but I was too sad to care if I didn't make a good impression. I opened the door and looked at my former brother-in-law. "Hey, what are you doing here?"

"Taking your mom on a date since she thinks I'm hot."

I rolled my eyes.

He smiled. "And Fire is a kinda cool name."

I opened the door wider and welcomed him inside. Just like my son, Ash looked like Hades. They had the same eyes and the same build. "How are you?"

He shrugged. "You know." He didn't elaborate on what that response meant. He was a man of few words, and he rarely shared his life with outside people. "I wanted to meet my nephew. According to Hades, he's gonna break some hearts when he gets older."

Like a typical mother, I was already so proud of my boy. "Yeah, he's absolutely beautiful." Ash mentioned his brother and I wanted to ask what else was said, but at the same time, I didn't want to know. "Follow me."

We went to the third floor and entered Andrew's room. Ash clearly didn't have much experience with kids because he stood at the rail with his hands in his pockets and just stared.

I came to his side and looked down at the baby boy wrapped in clean clothes with a warm blanket draped over the side. I watched Andrew look at our new guest, and I wondered what he was thinking, if he recognized him as his father since they looked so much alike.

Ash whispered quietly, "You guys did a good job."

"Thank you…"

"I guess some good came out of you having sex with my brother."

I smacked his arm playfully. I grew up as an only child, and Ash felt like the brother I'd never had. He teased me but made me feel loved at the same time. "You want to hold him?"

"Like, pick him up?"

"Yeah…that's what you do with babies."

He shrugged. "I don't know. You think I can handle that?"

"You're gonna have to. You're his uncle." I picked up Andrew and placed him in Ash's arms. "Support his head and keep both arms under his body. See? It's not so hard."

Ash stared at his nephew for a couple minutes, and naturally, his eyes softened a little bit as Andrew worked his magic. He moved to one of the rocking chairs against the wall and took a seat. Like a mother, he grabbed the blanket to make sure Andrew was comfortable.

I took the seat beside him and watched him fall in love with my son.

After Ash stared for at least ten minutes, he turned back to me. "He's pretty cool."

"I know."

"And he's super cute."

I raised an eyebrow.

"What? He is."

"I've just never heard you talk like that before."

He shrugged and returned his focus to Andrew. "There's a first time for everything." He gently rocked the chair back and forth as he supported Andrew with one large, powerful arm. Like his brother, he had a watch on his wrist.

Since he was here and he knew Hades wasn't, that must mean he knew Hades had left us. He hadn't mentioned it, and I suspected he wouldn't. "Since Hades is gone now, I guess you and I can get together…"

He slowly turned his head back to me, his eyes wide as if he couldn't believe what I'd just said. "Yeah, that'd be pretty hot. You and I make more sense than you guys ever did. But…I can't. I couldn't do that to my brother."

Maybe he didn't realize I was joking. "Why? He doesn't want me anymore."

He looked at my son for a little while before he glanced at me again. "We both know that isn't why. It's because of the exact opposite."

Tears welled up in my eyes because the sadness was too much. I would never forget the way Hades had walked out of here with no intention of coming back. It was so cold, so harsh. "Whatever the reason, he's a coward. He can treat me however he wants, but it's not right to abandon Andrew."

Ash continued to rock Andrew as he let the silence snuff out the conversation. He probably didn't want to get involved, but he also felt obligated to defend his brother. "You abandoned him, Sofia. Let's not forget that."

An invisible knife went into my gut, and I felt so betrayed. All I could do was stare because I couldn't believe he'd said that to me. "I didn't abandon him. I told him to kill Maddox."

"And you know he couldn't do that. He doesn't give a damn about his life, only yours."

"He still didn't leave me a choice." I felt my voice rise as the rage started to get to me. "I had to protect my child. I had to protect myself. If I continued to live there under that asshole's reign, I never would be able to sleep at night."

He held up his hand to calm me down. "I get that. But you still left him, and that wasn't easy on him. He got the short stick of this whole thing, and you know it. He still suffers every day, living as his fucking puppet. He's a goddamn prisoner. Seeing you and Andrew once in a while is just torture for him. You really don't get that?"

"I do, but…"

"No, you don't." His eyes suddenly turned harsh. "He's trying to do the right thing for everybody. He loved you so much and sacrificed everything to have you. When Maddox had you, he made the ultimate sacrifice by forfeiting his life. My brother and I have had our differences, but he is not a coward. That guy would slit his own throat just to make you happy. He's trying to do the right thing for everybody…and of course, he's the bad guy for doing it. I promise you he feels a million times worse right now than you ever could."

The tears swelled to an enormous size, and I couldn't keep them in place. Their weight was too much, and they cascaded down my cheeks to my chin. I sniffled loudly then wiped away the moisture with my fingertips.

"You know he's not a coward, so don't ever say that again."

13

HADES

I WAS SITTING AT MY DESK, STARING BLANKLY AT MY SCREEN SAVER when someone walked into my office. He helped himself inside without knocking, being both intrusive and annoying. He scanned my shelves as he strode to the armchair facing my desk. His fingers brushed up against the leather before he fell back and got comfortable in the chair.

My eyes followed his movements as my hand shut my laptop.

With both arms on the armrests and his legs crossed, he looked practically giddy to see me. "Have a good holiday?" His blue eyes were deep like the ocean. But instead of being full of life and intrigue, they were full of unpredictable mystery.

"Wasn't a holiday."

"You weren't working. So I'd say so." He cocked his head slightly, displaying the movements of a dog considering turning on its foe. "So, the wife and baby are healthy? What a blessing."

I didn't want him to mention my family ever again. "I went to see the birth of my son, but that is the extent of my relationship with both of them." If he knew I was no longer attached to them, he would lose interest.

"Oh no. Not getting along with the baby momma?"

My eyes narrowed. "Our relationship is over, so I never want to talk about her ever again. Or my son."

He raised both hands and surrendered. "Alright, alright. Just trying to be a friend."

"I don't have any friends. And I'm not looking either."

He lowered his hands. "Well, I suspect that's gonna change. You and I are the same man."

I'd never been more insulted. "We are not the same."

He started to count on his fingers. "We both killed a parent." He held up a second finger. "We're both drug dealers." He held up a third finger. "We both fucked the same girl…"

I was out of my desk so fast that some of my shit went flying to the floor. I jumped over the wood and rushed him like a player in the Super Bowl. I lunged at him and got both of my hands on his neck. I squeezed hard and slammed him down onto the coffee table. His back hit the surface before it collapsed underneath him.

I was out of control. I wanted this man dead more than anything else. I couldn't see straight…I couldn't think. I wanted to rip his eyes out of his head and shove them down his throat.

Maddox was so calm. He didn't fight me at all…like he enjoyed it. His hands rested at his sides, and he didn't fight the constriction around his throat. He looked deep into my eyes just the way a lover looked at their partner.

Fucking psychopath.

The door opened, and Damien walked inside. "What the hell is going on?"

He must've heard me launch into Maddox and destroy the furniture in my office. I continued to choke him and wait for him to pass on to hell. My knuckles ached because I was squeezing so hard. Regardless of the consequences, I needed this. I needed to unlock these shackles that bound my wrists and my ankles.

Damien kneeled on the floor at my side. "Hades, stop." He tried to grab my hands and pull them off Maddox.

I shoved him hard in the chest. "Fuck off." I watched Maddox's face turn red as the strangulation began to affect his entire body. Only one more minute and he would be gone forever.

Damien came back. "Hades, you don't want to do this. This is what he wants."

I started to think about Sofia and Andrew. What if this was all a setup?

Damien grabbed my wrists and yanked. "Sofia. Andrew."

I finally came to my senses and let him pull my hands away.

Maddox gasped for air and rolled over onto his side so he could cough and recuperate. He was red as a tomato and weak as a piece of straw.

I dragged my hands down my face and suffered my self-loathing. I'd lost my temper and could've lost a lot more.

Damien watched me with pity in his eyes.

Maddox eventually got to his feet. "I was just trying to bond with you."

I was still on the ground, so I spat on his shoe. "Fuck off."

He looked down at his shoe and watched the glob of spit reflect the light from the ceiling. He stared at it for a long time before he kneeled down and wiped it up with his fingertip. Then he stared at me like he was considering wiping it on my cheek or my clothes. But then he did the unexpected and placed the finger into his mouth and sucked.

Weeks had passed since Andrew's birth, and I seemed to be getting worse.

There were times when I became so weak, I almost called Sofia to apologize. I wanted to tell her it was all a mistake, that I couldn't live without her. I wanted to text her and ask for pictures of Andrew. I wanted to return to Rome so I could make love to her.

I couldn't do any of those things…and they were torture to think about.

Could I live like this forever?

Maddox and I continued to work together like nothing had happened. He was just as obnoxious as always, but he dialed down his intensity so he was somewhat tolerable. I wondered what would've happened if I'd killed him in my office.

Would I have gotten away with it?

Or would Sofia and Andrew be dead right now?

I sat on the balcony outside my bedroom and watched my brother sitting across from me. He'd stopped by for a visit because he was in the city. His large shoulders covered the back of the chair, and his tight t-shirt showed off all the muscles of his arms and chest. He eyed the bottle of scotch in the center of the table and grabbed it without looking for a glass first. "I knew you were gonna look like shit, but I had no idea you would look this bad."

I stared at the table. "What did you expect?"

He shrugged. "Not sure." He took a drink. "How are things here?"

I was living in the underworld…and I wasn't even the king. "I almost killed Maddox last week, but Damien stopped me."

"Good thing he was there."

I still wondered what would've happened if I'd gone through

with it. Did Maddox have spies in my own office? Did he always have an escape plan anytime he was near me? I wouldn't put it past him. "I spat on his shoe."

Ash cocked an eyebrow.

"He wiped it up with his finger…and then sucked it." I'd seen a lot of terrible shit, but I'd never seen anything so disgusting in my life. I'd dealt with a lot of bad men, but they were logical and respectable. This guy was just a lunatic.

"What the fuck?" Ash stared at me blankly before he cringed. "Who does that?"

I shrugged before I took a drink.

"Is this guy in love with you or what?"

I shrugged again. "I have no fucking idea. He is obsessed with me, that's for certain. He says we're the same."

"Same, how?"

"He killed his mother… I killed my father. We're both in the same business. Even when we weren't partners, he never wanted to kill me. If anything, he wanted me to succeed. He's practically indifferent to Damien, but he can't get enough of me."

"Is he gay?"

"No idea. I've never asked him anything personal."

"But do you ever see him with girls?"

I shook my head.

"Maybe he wants to be you."

"I don't understand him, and I don't want to." If he wanted to be me, that was just odd. And if he was in love with me, I never wanted him to think I felt the same way. It was best just to leave it alone.

After minutes of silence, Ash changed the subject. "I saw Sofia last week."

I knew he'd gone to see Andrew, but I never asked him about it.

"Your son is cute, man."

Thinking about him nearly brought tears to my eyes. "Thanks."

"She told me that you left. Was really upset about it."

No surprise there.

"Said you were a coward. But I set her straight."

"You don't have to defend me to her. It's better if she hates me anyway. It'll help me move on."

Ash looked at me for a long time, a mixture of pity and sadness on his face. He rubbed his forefinger against the scruff along his jaw as he considered what he would say next. "Can you ever really move on?"

I walked through the bazaar and watched the fire dancers delicately place knives into their throats before they blew fire out like dragons. Black cobras hissed on the ground before they listened to the hypnotizing music of the performer. There were bonfires everywhere, belly dancers in the square, and camels being led to their next destination.

With my hands in my jeans pockets, I walked forward and ignored the solicitations from the carts and the flirtatious gazes of the gypsies. Since I'd been to the tent many times, I knew my way there. I turned when I saw the large pottery station, and I spotted it exactly where it had been before. Still purple and still abandoned. There was no one there.

I walked to the flap and let myself inside. Timeless, it was exactly the same. Oils burned and filled the tent with a suffocating scent. The wooden chair looked like it was on its last stretch of life. The reading cards were on the table.

The gypsy flipped through them, wearing a dark scarf wrapped around her head and neck. She didn't look up even though she knew I was there. "I've never had so much business from one client."

"You've only taken my money once, so I don't think I'm good for business." I helped myself into the chair and watched her arrange the cards. I didn't believe in magic or superstition. But whatever the fuck this was, I believed.

She continued to play with the cards. She would flip them over, and if she found a complementary pair, she would take them off the table. "How can I help you, Hades?"

"I need you to read my fortune again."

She stopped what she was doing and finally lifted her gaze to meet mine. "One fortune per customer. That's the rule."

"Rules are meant to be broken."

She smiled like she found me charming. "The answer is still no."

I reached into my pocket and grabbed an envelope stuffed with money. I set it on the table in front of her. "Please help me."

She eyed the cash but didn't take it. "What do you hope to achieve?"

"I just need to know if there's any chance. If there's a chance that I can kill Maddox and get my family back." I couldn't take the risk when two people I loved were at stake. If I made the wrong move, I could lose the most important thing in the world. I had to be sure.

She pushed the cash back toward me. "Your money is no good here. I told you, one fortune per person. Period." She pulled the cards toward her and then stacked them into a pile. "That's the way this works. No exceptions for anyone."

"Why?"

"Would you really want to live that way? To always know the outcome of every decision before you even make it? That's a dangerous power, and it would destroy you." She rested her hands on the table and stared at me with a fearless expression. She didn't seem to pity me at all. "I'm sorry I couldn't be more help. I wish you well."

I remained in the seat because I had a backup plan I'd hoped to avoid. It was a terrible decision, but I'd been thinking about it for a long time. It felt cheap to take the easy way out, but I didn't see the point in suffering when there was no hope that things would change. "You said there was a way for me to stop loving her. Is that still on the table?"

She was still as a statue as she considered my question. "It's always on the table."

"Then that's what I want." I pushed the cash toward her as payment.

She didn't take it. "Hades, do you know what you're doing?"

It was a devastating decision to make, but I couldn't live like this anymore. I'd worked so hard for Sofia to love me, and in the end, I got what I wanted…but not the way I wanted. I wanted to live a life where I didn't think about her every second of the day, where I could just have a normal existence without being smothered by this devotion. I'd tried everything else first, and nothing worked. This was my last option. "Yes."

"It can't be reversed."

"Good."

"You can't walk into this tent and ask me to give it back. It doesn't work like that."

"I understand."

She was quiet for a long time as she considered the request. "But this woman loves you. You are cursing her to the same existence you've had to endure."

"It's not the same. She gave up on me. She chose this. I can't keep fighting for her when she won't fight for me. I can't do it anymore—I won't do it anymore."

She grabbed the envelope of money and took a few bills before she pushed it back to me. "Alright…as you wish."

14

SOFIA

It'd been a month since Hades left.

It didn't get easier. If anything, it got harder.

Ash's words echoed in my ears long after he said them. He defended Hades and said he was the wounded one. I was the coward who'd abandoned him. I was the one who'd caused him all the pain.

It was impossible to look at my son and not think of Hades. It was impossible to sleep at night without him beside me. I wanted my husband back. I wanted a marriage. I wanted us to be a family.

Could I really end up with another man someday? Have children with somebody else? Never see Hades again?

I wasn't sure if I could do it. Now that I had Andrew, I felt more connected to Hades than ever before. I thought of my ex-husband every time I looked into that little boy's face. Sometimes I considered packing my things and showing up on his doorstep. I considered forgetting about Maddox and just doing what I wanted.

But then I thought of Andrew…the tiny person I had to protect.

If it were just me, it would be different. My life was okay to gamble.

But with a baby, I didn't have that luxury.

When Andrew was asleep, I called Ash.

He picked up right away. "Sweetheart, I told you we can't be together. Have I thought about it? I'd be lying if I said no. But it would be wrong…no matter how good the sex was."

I wasn't in the mood for jokes, so I ignored what he said. "Can I see you?"

"Always. But is everything okay?"

"I'm fine. I just need to talk to you."

"I can meet you in fifteen minutes. Where?"

"My mom's not home, so I need to stay with Andrew. Could you come here?"

"Of course. But you aren't trying to seduce me, right?"

I hung up.

The first thing Ash wanted to do was visit with Andrew. He stood over his crib and watched his nephew sleep. He gripped the wooden rail and continued to stare. "Can we wake him up?"

"God, no. You never wake a sleeping baby."

"Why not?"

I rolled my eyes because he would never understand. I took a seat in one of the chairs so we could have the conversation I wasn't sure how to have. I patted the armrest beside me.

Ash took a seat and started to rock the chair even though he wasn't holding Andrew. "What's up, sweetheart?"

"I know this is a lot to ask, but I need you to do something for me."

When he realized how serious this was, he stopped rocking and his face turned as hard as a concrete wall. "You know I would do anything for you."

"Good…because I need you to kill Maddox."

He stilled further, his chest frozen because he stopped breathing. His eyes remained unmoving as he absorbed my expression and let my final words linger in the air.

"I have to get my husband back. The only way to do that is by getting rid of that guy. Hades needs to be free, and we need to be a family. I can't not see him for the rest of my life. I just can't."

He turned his gaze away and stared at the crib.

"Ash?"

He ran his fingers across the shadow on his jawline before he answered. "I can't do that."

My heart tanked.

"That would be a betrayal to my brother…and I can't do that."

"How could freeing him be a betrayal?"

"Because if I fail…" He turned his gaze back to me. "You and Andrew will suffer the consequences. I couldn't live with that guilt. And Hades would kill himself if he lost you both. It's way too risky."

That was the answer I had been dreading. "You just said you would do anything for me."

"Anything that won't hurt you. I just saw Hades a few weeks ago… Maddox is complicated. I might think it's the perfect time and be completely wrong. I'd be gambling with your life. I'm not confident enough to do that." When he saw my devastated expression, he continued, "I'm sorry…"

I'd been hoping to get what I wanted. It seemed like such an easy solution, but if that were the case, Hades would've orchestrated it already. No one would help me in this endeavor. I had to do it on my own…or it wouldn't happen at all. "Then I'll do it myself."

His eyes narrowed on my face. "You can't be serious."

"Dead serious. I couldn't do anything about it before because I was pregnant. But now I'm not anymore…"

"You're still a mother. If something happens to you, who will he have?"

"You."

His eyes softened even though he did his best to hide it.

"I gave up on Hades because I had no other option. But now I do have an option. And I'm going to use it."

He shook his head. "No. You have no chance against him."

"All I need is a gun and a target. I can do the rest."

"You don't understand…"

"I'm going to do this no matter what you say. So, you might as well just help me. You can tattle on me to Hades, but he's not gonna talk me out of it either. Maddox said he would hurt Andrew and me if Hades tried to kill him, but he never said anything about me trying."

"You're taking a big gamble on a technicality."

"It's not a gamble if I win."

I was torn.

Whenever I was with Andrew, I questioned what kind of mother I was, if I was able to risk my life to save someone else. If I failed,

Andrew wouldn't have a mother. On top of that, he may not have a father either.

But when I looked into those warm brown eyes, I knew I had to do it. We needed to be a family again, to be happy. When Andrew was older and asked why his father and I weren't together, I wouldn't know what to say. I wouldn't want my son to think his father was a coward who'd abandoned him.

Hades was so much more than that…but my son would never know.

Ash needed a week to think about what I said. Initially, he was too repulsed by the idea to consider it. There was too much at stake, too much of a risk. I had no special skills in fighting or gun handling, so my chances of success were low.

So, we had to come up with a plan.

Ash came over after dinner and sat in the nursery with me. Andrew had just had dinner so he was still awake, but he would drift off to sleep quickly. I gave Ash an opportunity to spend time with him, to hold him in the rocking chair until he went to sleep.

"So, you'll help me?"

He stared at Andrew for a while before he met my look. "I've thought a lot about it."

"I'd hoped you would. Otherwise, I'll have to figure it out on my own."

He rocked the chair for a long time before he stopped. "You'll never be able to hunt him down and take him out. Hades and Damien have tried that many times to no success. Your only chance is to get him to come to you."

"And how will I do that? Call him and tell him I'm in town?"

"No. He has to think he's catching you off guard. That's your only chance, your only leverage."

"And how am I gonna do that? I could visit Hades at his office…I guess."

"No. You can't involve Hades at all." He looked down at Andrew and noticed he was asleep. He lowered his voice as he kept talking. "I'm certain Maddox has people who keep tabs on you. He knows where you are and what you're doing. Since he's using you against Hades, that's the only way for him to keep his word."

"I've never noticed anyone following me."

"That's the point."

"So, when I go to Florence, he'll know?"

He nodded. "Exactly. Hades told him you aren't together anymore. So, Maddox will probably assume you're in town for personal reasons. Go straight to the hotel. Knowing him, he won't be able to resist stopping by."

That did seem like something he would do. He wouldn't touch me or threaten me, but he'd want to watch me squirm in his presence. I'd left my husband and moved all the way to Rome because I was afraid of Maddox. He would probably get off to the sight of my fear. "And then what?"

"Wait in your office. When he walks in…shoot him."

"I'm not quick with guns. He might shoot me before I could even draw."

"That's why you have your gun hidden. Wear a jacket and leave it in your pocket. That way, he'll have no idea."

"You don't think he'll figure that out?"

He shrugged. "He might figure it all out. Like I said, I don't condone this. But I think it's your best option. The fact that you're letting him come to you gives you the upper hand. He'll think he outsmarted you…when in reality, you outsmarted him."

My heart started to pound with adrenaline. I was exhilarated but also terrified. Squeezing that trigger would give me so much satisfaction. Watching his body go limp on the ground while his blood stained my floor would be the best retribution. But it could also go the other way…and I could be the one on the ground.

Ash watched the emotions dance across my face. "Are you sure you want to do this?"

I knew Hades wouldn't want me to. If he knew what we were plotting, he would scream in my face and tell me I was stupid. But I didn't want Hades to be a prisoner any longer, to live under the thumb of that horrible man. I wanted us to be together…like we should've been this entire time. "Yes…I'm sure."

15

HADES

Now that Maddox had taken over my facility, he'd also taken over my office. He was never in one place very long because he moved around constantly. Sometimes he used my office; sometimes he worked somewhere else. I still had no idea where he lived and where he kept all his other assets.

The guy was a nomad.

I collected the money from our distributors and carried one large bag into the office that used to be mine. Maddox was sitting behind his desk with his feet up when I walked inside and placed the black duffle bag on the corner of the surface. "It's all there. I counted."

He eyed the bag before his eyes turned to me. "Congratulations. You did your job."

Even when I was in charge, I never spoke to anyone that way. A good leader was someone who inspired people, not shit on people. "Congratulations. You're a fucking asshole." I turned around to walk out.

"Hades."

I turned back around and didn't look the least bit pleased about it.

He lowered his feet from the desk and righted himself in the chair. "Let's have dinner tonight."

The last time we'd had any serious interaction, I'd almost killed him. So this request was a bit off-putting. "You got something to say to me, say it now."

"I don't have anything to say to you. I just want to have dinner."

I hated this motherfucker. He was evil and weird…strange combination.

"Be at my place at seven."

Now, I was just confused. "I have no idea where you live."

"I know. I think it's time we got to know each other better." He smiled at me, a sick, twisted smile.

He had a place out in the Tuscan countryside. It was a modest house, but he had lots of land. It was so remote and private that it was easy for him to hide from all the major roads. He had at least three dozen men guarding the perimeter, so no one could cross him in his sleep.

The place left a bad taste in my mouth.

Was this where he took Sofia?

I sat across from him at the dining table and watched him pour me a glass of wine. There was no chef in the kitchen and no maid to help with the dishes.

"Cooking is a hobby of mine." He filled his own glass before he set it off to the side. He held the glass, brought it close to his face, and smelled it. Then he returned it to the table without taking a drink.

"Are you gonna drink that?"

He scooped the pasta onto his plate and grabbed a piece of chicken. "You know I don't drink, Hades. I just like the smell."

Fucking weird.

After he filled his plate, he pushed the utensils toward me. "I took a couple culinary classes on the French Riviera. I enjoyed it so much that I've been cooking ever since. It's a great way to wind down after a long day."

A long day of raping and murdering people?

"Do you like to cook?" He handled his utensils with perfect manners and even spun his pasta against his spoon. He practiced a refinement he didn't display on a daily basis.

"No." I served myself and took a bite. It was good, but I refused to say that.

"I could always teach you."

"No."

Maddox didn't acknowledge my rudeness. He continued to eat like this was a pleasant experience for us both. Our silverware tapped against the plates, and the sound was so loud because there was no conversation to muffle it.

"What did you want to talk about?"

"Who said I wanted to talk about anything?"

I had a million things to do, and I didn't want to waste precious time looking at someone I hated. "Then what's the point of this?"

"The point is for us to have dinner and enjoy each other's company. I don't understand why that's so difficult for you to comprehend." He chewed his food slowly as he stared at me across the table. Then he picked up his glass and smelled it again.

"I don't enjoy your company."

He chewed his last bite and didn't cut into his food again. He stared at me with lifeless eyes, like he didn't know how to respond to my cold statement. "I don't see why you feel that way. We work well together. We're good partners. We're good friends."

"Good friends don't lick each other's spit."

He turned his attention back to his food and cut another piece before he placed it in his mouth. After a long time chewing, he spoke again. "But good lovers do."

I heard his words and also the message underneath. It gave me a sense of dread I'd never felt before. I'd been faced with killers and thieves, but I'd never been faced with this kind of threat. He didn't want my money or my connections. The only thing he wanted was me.

I set my fork and knife on the plate and ignored the dinner I had been forcing myself to eat. Now I was too nauseated to choke the garbage down my throat. My eyes focused on his, feeling the urge to run but also to kill.

Maddox took another bite and chewed slowly, his eyes taking me in with a mesmerized gaze. His mouth moved slowly, and his eyes remained so intense, they were like two suns. He put his truth on the table and watched me react.

I didn't know what my next move would be. I wasn't entirely sure of what was happening. This man had been focused on me for years, and then he invited me over for dinner…like we were more than friends. "Is this a date?"

Maddox finished chewing then shrugged. "Do you want it to be?"

My eyes narrowed. "I like women."

"I like women enough…doesn't mean anything."

I'd never felt so targeted before. I'd had a gun pointed at my head and a knife to my throat, but being the source of infatuation for another man was creepy. In that moment, it made me understand the fear all women had every time they walked down a street at night. It was disturbing, disgusting. I'd had women corner me and make their best move, but that was totally different. I always had the right to say no…even though I never said no. Maddox had me under his thumb, and he clearly had no issue with raping someone.

For the first time in my life, I actually felt weak. "Why have you been obsessed with me all these years?"

He clearly had a lot to say because he pushed away his plate and utensils. His arms rested on the surface, and he leaned forward. "We are the same. I told you that." His eyes moved down to my plate before he looked at me again. "I noticed it a long time ago when you killed your father. Made me feel less alone…that someone else would do something so heinous. I watched you progress in your career. You're a self-made man. I admire that."

I listened to every word and hated myself for the attention I gave him. It was the first time I'd wanted to understand him fully because he was the kind of opponent I had never faced before.

"My respect and admiration only grew through the years. You were just a pawn in a game, but then you became the knight. I've watched you cut down everyone around you, and the pride grew inside me like a balloon…even though I didn't know you. Once you became my primary adversary, I'd never been so impressed by anyone in my life. You're a special man, Hades. I can never kill you because that would be a crime against humanity."

I'd never been fearful of someone's respect. I was afraid of people's murderous intent, but not their praise. "So, you've always wanted me as a partner. You've plotted all of this to keep me tethered to your side." Realization dawned on me that Maddox was far more intelligent than I'd ever given him credit for. He was patient and calculating, seeing the big picture when everyone else could only see the immediate event before them. He maliciously removed Sofia from my life so he could have me all to himself. It was so harsh, I almost stopped breathing.

"In so many words…" He grabbed his glass of wine and took another sniff, like the fumes from the alcohol could affect him through his lungs. "I've never felt this way about anyone…never wanted anyone so much."

I was actually scared of this man. He had me by the balls, could get me to do anything he wanted. All he had to do was threaten Sofia and Andrew, and I'd be bent over and ready to be fucked like a whore. It made me so sick, I nearly threw up everything I'd just eaten. I felt even worse for what happened to Sofia…that she'd had to endure this for weeks. "You've forced a partnership, so it's not based on loyalty or respect. It's empty because you know I despise you. If you forced any other kind of relationship, the results would be the same…empty." I refused to beg for my freedom, but I also refused to lie down and give in. Suicide returned to my thoughts because I'd rather be dead than have to live like this.

Maddox set down his wineglass and looked at me with disappointment. The silence continued for a long time, as if he was considering the perfect thing to say. Both of his arms rested across the table, and he leaned forward again to regard me. "If we solidified our partnership, we'd be unstoppable. Our reign wouldn't only be in Italy. It would stretch all over the world, and it would be so much sweeter if we were more."

I'd never been hit on by a dude, and it wouldn't bother me so much if the request were optional. But I knew it was only a matter of time before Maddox pressured me to give him what he wanted. He wouldn't have been this obsessed with me for so long if I'd really had a choice. I would be spared tonight, but not spared forever. "We'll never be more, Maddox. Let's not forget what you did to my wife. Maybe you've forgotten, but I never will."

"It wasn't personal. And she's your ex-wife."

My right hand tightened into a fist. "It doesn't matter if I hate her. She was still my wife, and you did something you can't take back. I will always despise you for what you did to my family. You've threatened my son many times, and I'm not going to pretend that didn't happen. I will never reciprocate your feelings, not just because I'm straight, but I absolutely loathe you. If you want me, you're going to have to force me."

His gaze was impassive, and his eyes were wide open like he didn't need to blink. His body tensed in the subtlest way, like he was channeling his rage to every part of his body. He could express so much with so little, and that's what made him innately creepy. Both of his hands formed fists on the table. "You know I have no problem doing that."

16

SOFIA

Handing over my son was the hardest thing I'd ever had to do.

I looked into his brown eyes and saw the man I loved. I saw Andrew's perfect skin, his little fingers and toes, and I felt like I was leaving behind a piece of myself. I hadn't had much time with my son, and this might be the last time I got to see him.

I kissed him on the forehead before I made the transfer into Ash's arms.

For a man with no experience with children, he handled Andrew like a pro. He held him in his arms like he was a father himself. He looked at him with affection, but then he looked at me with sadness. "I'll take care of him."

I would have left Andrew with my mother, but she didn't have the resources to protect anyone. The best thing she could do was run away and save herself. As far as I knew, Maddox had never threatened or mentioned my mother, so she was probably safe. Ash was the strongest man I knew besides Hades, and if something happened to me, he was the best protector I could find. "I know you will." I felt the tears start deep in my throat. It was so painful that I reconsidered leaving at all. Hades would want me to stay with our son and abandon him.

But I had to save them both.

Ash put him in the crib in his bedroom and turned back to me. "Are you sure you want to do this? It's not too late to change your mind."

"Yes…I'm sure."

Ash opened one of the drawers and pulled out a pistol. "You know how to use this, right?"

"Well enough to kill someone." I took the gun from his hand and put it in my pocket.

He continued to stand there as if he didn't want me to leave. When we'd first met, he was a cold jackass, innately distrustful. But now he was warm and thoughtful, becoming soft like his brother but retaining his masculinity. "If he doesn't meet you at the hotel, just come home and forget it."

I couldn't believe I wanted Maddox to hunt me down. I couldn't believe I wanted him to follow me and provoke me in my own office. I knew he wouldn't hurt me or touch me, but he'd want to terrify me. If that didn't happen, I would have no other way of killing him. I certainly couldn't hunt him down. "Alright."

Ash pulled me into his arms and hugged me. One hand rested between my shoulder blades while the other wrapped around my waist. His build was similar to his brother's, but his affection felt familial. He gave me a gentle squeeze before he let me go. "Be safe. And if you don't come back…at least Andrew can help me pick up more women."

I appreciated the joke to shatter the sorrow in the room, but I was too depressed to issue a chuckle. "Wouldn't he make it more difficult?"

"Have you seen how cute he is?" he asked incredulously. "That kid is gonna be a babe magnet."

A slight smile broke through on my lips. "I guess that's true…"

He gave me a last gentle pat on the back before he walked me out. "I know you can do this. Just stay calm and squeeze that trigger. And don't shoot him once. Shoot him until the barrel is empty."

I knew I would never stop shooting him. I'd shoot him in my dreams…shoot him in my nightmares. His death wouldn't erase my hatred. That would continue into his grave. "I will."

The driver pulled up to the hotel and let me out.

It'd been six months since I'd last seen the Tuscan Rose with my own eyes. It was the place I used to work every day. My passion for it got me up every morning. It was a place where Hades and I had our clandestine meetings in a luxurious suite, the place where I married the man I loved. It held so much significance for me, especially since both my father and stepfather had bled for this place.

It was home.

I walked inside wearing a blue dress with a black leather jacket. It was almost summer, so it was warm and a jacket was conspicuous, but it went with my outfit, so hopefully it wasn't that odd.

I entered the lobby and immediately noticed subtle changes I didn't like. The flowers on the table were wilted, and there was dust on the surface. The crystals on the chandelier hadn't been cleaned in months. The tile on the floor was scuffed because they'd stopped waxing. Those details weren't important to anyone else, but they gave a sense of pride to me.

A few people recognized me and said hello, so after I made small talk, I went down the hallway into my office. It was abandoned and cold. A stack of papers was on the surface of my desk, and my laptop hadn't been touched. There were no flowers to admire, no pictures on the desk to look at.

I sat in the leather chair and opened my laptop even though I had no work to do. I just played the part and did my time until Maddox appeared. I could only linger for a couple hours. Any longer than that would be suspicious.

If he didn't show up, I would be relieved. But I would also be devastated.

But if he did come…I would be terrified. I'd never killed anyone before, never took a shot at anyone. I didn't have any reservations about putting Maddox in a grave; I was just sick knowing I had to do it. It wasn't just revenge for Hades and me.

It was freedom.

Two hours passed, and I resisted the urge to call Ash to check on my baby. I also thought about calling Hades, but the second I got him on the phone, I wouldn't be able to lie about what I was doing. He would march down there and sabotage the whole thing. So I had to sit there…and wait.

This plan probably wasn't going to work. Maddox was an asshole, but he had bigger fish to fry. I didn't matter to him. He used me and tortured me… I was old news. The only person he really wanted was Hades, and now he had him.

He didn't care about me.

I was about to throw in the towel when heavy footsteps sounded outside my door. They reminded me of Hades because the distinct thud sounded like it could come from his substantial size. It was like an animal coming around the corner.

I slowly rose to my feet and slid my hand into my right pocket. My heart was beating so frantically, at the speed of a hummingbird's heartbeat. I perspired immediately, beads of sweat forming on my forehead and the back of my neck. My fingers found the handle of the gun and wrapped around the trigger. The metal felt hot in my hand, and I could hear the distant click as I let off the safety.

I was ready…but terrified.

I saw the shadow before the man. Then he stepped into the doorway, tall, muscular, and looking smitten with himself. His blue eyes locked on to mine, and he stepped into my office with a slight smile on his face. With his arms resting by his sides, he seemed pleased by the look of horror on my face.

I didn't have to act scared or surprised. I'd hoped this would happen, but I was still sick to my stomach. I would never forget the way he held me down and forced himself between my legs. I would never forget those painful nights when I wished I were dead. It was so easy to portray myself as a terrified victim… because that was exactly what I was.

He stopped in front of my desk and tilted his head slightly. "It's been a long time, hasn't it? How are you?"

I despised his ego, despised everything about him. He assumed he'd cornered me like a brilliant villain, and he didn't have the humility to wonder if he was wrong. Maybe he was playing me and he knew this was all a setup. But I suspected he had no idea…and he was about to pay for everything he'd done. "Things have been rough. But they're about to get better."

His eyebrows furrowed, and he barely had the chance to tense at my ominous threat before I squeezed that trigger as hard as I could.

The sound of the gunfire was piercing in the small room. It echoed off the walls and reverberated throughout the hotel. I could feel the gun lurch back as the bullet left the barrel. I couldn't see my gun, so I couldn't aim. I just had to hope I was pointing in the right direction.

And I was.

The bullet hit him right in the gut, making his body jolt when the momentum struck him in the center. He staggered back slightly, and as if he didn't know what had just transpired, he moved his hand over his stomach and let the blood drench his skin. He looked down at his palm and rubbed his thumb and forefinger together, feeling the blood against his fingertips. He slowly looked up again, his reaction sluggish because he couldn't process his own demise, the realization that death was slowly creeping in.

I didn't pull the trigger again because I wanted to relish this moment. I wanted revenge for what he had done to me, but what I wanted most of all was revenge for what he had done to Hades. He'd been controlling him for months now, making him miserable. That was the inspiration for my blood lust and violence. I cared more about Hades than I cared about myself.

I pulled the trigger again.

Like last time, he staggered with the hit, moving back slightly, growing weaker by the second. When he couldn't keep himself upright any longer, he moved to his knees on the floor and pressed his hand into his abdomen to stop the bleeding. He was in such shock, he didn't know what to say. His sick and witty comebacks were no more.

I walked around the desk as I pulled the gun from my pocket. With a strong arm, I raised the weapon and looked down the barrel as I pointed right between his eyes. I watched with satisfaction as the fear crept into his features, as he wrestled with the painful finality of death.

He dropped his hand from his stomach and bowed his head as he gave up. He'd already lost so much blood that he couldn't think straight any longer. His heart was beating fast, beating hard. The pulse was quickening in his ears, and the devil had begun to knock on his front door.

"This is for Hades." I squeezed the trigger and watched his brain splatter against the opposite wall. His body fell a millisecond later, lurching backward until he was a corpse on the floor. The blood made a puddle under his body, and his skin started to turn white as death settled in. My office had been demolished by the corpse bleeding out in front of me. It was almost poetic, the way he died where he'd first cornered me years ago.

I lowered the gun and stared at him for a long time, treasuring the sight of his dead body. I was supposed to unload every bullet into his body, but I just wanted to stare…to treasure this moment as long as I could. His regime was over, and now I could get my life back.

I could get my husband back.

Other employees of the hotel came by to see the commotion, and when they saw the body, they immediately turned away, some of them throwing up because it was such a disgusting sight. People offered to call the police, but I told them I already had it taken care of.

I called Hades.

He answered after several rings, and he was in a cold mood. "What?"

He said he never wanted to talk to me again, never see me again. Only if it was important was I allowed to reach out to him. Judging by his response, he assumed this call was not important at all. "Come to the Tuscan Rose in Florence. I killed Maddox, and now I need to get rid of the body."

There was such a pregnant pause over the line, like the calm before a storm. My words were so incredible that he probably didn't know how to respond. And rightfully so. "Repeat what you said."

"I killed Maddox. Meet me at the Tuscan Rose." I couldn't stop the smile from coming into my voice the second time I said those words. It was true… Maddox was dead. The thing keeping us apart was no longer a threat. We could finally have what we'd always wanted.

Instead of asking a million questions like he wanted to, he just obeyed my orders. "I'll be there in ten minutes. Make sure he's really dead."

"Trust me. He's gone."

Hades burst through my office door in a t-shirt and jeans. Instead of looking at me and rushing to my side, he tilted his head down and stared at the body. He clearly needed more definitive evidence that it was really Maddox, because he grabbed a piece of paper and placed it over his hand so he could reposition Maddox's body and get a look at what was left of his face.

He stared for a long time.

Seconds trickled by until a full minute had passed. Hades took in Maddox's expression; his bright blue eyes were unmistakable. When he had the evidence he needed, Hades released his body and let him fall back to the floor.

He slowly rose to his feet and ran his fingers through his short hair, like he couldn't believe that this moment was true. His greatest adversary was dead, and now he was a free man. He finally turned to me, his eyes open wide and his expression incredulous. "What the fuck happened?"

"I killed him."

"Obviously. But how did this happen?"

I understood he was in shock, but I'd expected a different reaction. Once he'd confirmed Maddox was no more, I'd expected him to move into my arms and hug me tightly. I'd expected a deep kiss that celebrated our reunion. "I came to the hotel because I assumed he would follow me. When he walked in the door, I shot him."

He placed his hands on his hips as he continued to stare at me in disbelief. "Just like that?"

"Yeah…just like that."

His eyes widened. "I don't understand…"

"I assumed if I came into the city, he would confront me…because he's an asshole like that. He enjoyed hurting me, enjoyed scaring me. I moved to another city because I couldn't stand being anywhere near him. I assumed he would take advantage of the fact that I was alone here. So, I had my gun in my pocket, and when he walked in, I shot him." I pulled the gun out of my jacket pocket and clicked on the safety. I set it on top of the desk and looked at him again.

"There's no way you thought of this on your own."

I didn't want to throw Ash under the bus. "Doesn't matter. He's dead. End of story."

He ran his fingers through his hair again. Even though the threat had been eliminated, he still seemed stressed. He looked down at the body again before he stared at the wall, thinking a million things at once.

I slowly moved toward him then made my way into his chest. One hand cupped his cheek while the other wrapped around his neck, and I pulled his face to mine as I kissed him. I felt our bodies and souls reunite, felt our connection explode with affection and joy. All the suffering was over. We could be us again. My lips slowly moved against his, feeling a kiss I hadn't felt in weeks.

He kissed me back hesitantly, his mouth automatically moving with mine, but that fire didn't burn from his core. He seemed confused, like he didn't know what was happening. He grabbed my hands and pulled them from his body as he ended our kiss.

I stilled at the rejection, hoping for a reasonable explanation for his coldness. Maybe he was disgusted by the blood and brains still on the wall. Maybe he was so relieved to be free that he didn't know what to do.

He stepped away from me and gave me no apology. Now there were several feet between us, and it felt like miles. "I've got to take care of this. The police won't do anything to you, but our relationship is a lot better if they don't have to pretend they don't notice anything."

I let him walk away and get to work as I nursed my wounds. He had never pushed away from me like that before, and something felt wrong. But I reminded myself that he had been subjected to this man's cruelty for a long time. He probably felt so many things, and he just needed time. "Is there anything I can do to help?"

"No." He pulled out his phone and made a call. "Just stay out of my way."

17

HADES

It was hard to believe.

Just a few days ago, I was having dinner in his home, worried I would end up in his bed.

Now, he was dead.

I pulled his body out of the truck, and with the help of my men, we carried it into the lab where the furnace was located. I never used it to burn bodies, only to dispose of evidence and chemicals. But it was the perfect place to get rid of someone I despised.

Together, we heaved his body inside and watched the flames lick his skin. It only took seconds before his body caught fire. I wanted to watch him burn until he was ash, but the smell was acid in my nose. I closed the stone door and locked it.

Then I stood there and listened to the body burn.

The furnace connected to the ceiling of the building, so pieces of him were escaping into the atmosphere. His organs were turning to dust, his brain was evaporating with every passing second. Death was already so final, but cremation truly made it irreversible.

I was glad this was really the end.

This monster couldn't torture me anymore.

He didn't own me anymore.

I stood there until the heat dissipated and there was nothing left to burn. The weight was off my shoulders and the shackles removed from my wrists. I could sleep easy at night and know I was the victor in this fight.

Even if Sofia did the dirty work.

Maddox was at the top of the food chain, and now that I'd defeated him, I took his place. Everyone would fear me more than they already did. It was a good feeling.

Damien walked up behind me. "Fucker's really dead?"

The high I felt was quickly extinguished when he drew near. I slowly turned around and faced him, feeling the adrenaline and rage in my blood. I could barely look at the guy without breaking his nose. "What the fuck were you thinking?"

His blank stare was so convincing. "I got here as quick as I could…"

"Don't play dumb with me. I know you're stupid, but not that stupid."

His eyes narrowed, and his shoulders squared. "I seriously have no idea what you're talking about."

"You expect me to believe Sofia planned this whole thing on her own?" I was already on thin ice with Damien, could barely tolerate him at work, but now I felt more betrayed than I ever had. "There's no way she could've come up with that plan on her own. It's so simple that it's brilliant, and no offense to her, but she's nowhere near brilliant."

His eyes shifted back and forth as he looked into mine, his brain trying to catch up with my thoughts. "All I know is that Maddox is dead. That's it. I came the second I heard, and I had no part in the whole thing. So, Sofia killed him?"

I couldn't control my temper, so I walked off. "Fine, be an asshole."

Damien walked after me. "How many times do I have to tell you? I'm just as shocked as you are. Why would I lie?"

I snapped back around. "Because you're a coward. Because you're worthless."

The confusion slowly drained from his face, and then a red tint started to flush into his cheeks. His anger heated up the air surrounding him. "You know what? Believe me. Don't believe me. Your opinion means nothing to me, so I don't give a shit." He shoved me hard in the chest before he turned around and left.

I almost pulled out my gun and shot him in the back, but that would be a cowardly thing to do, and I wouldn't sink to that level.

After everything was said and done, I scrubbed my hands until they were nearly raw so I could get every piece of Maddox off me. I'd burned his body, and I didn't want a trace of his corpse to stay with me.

I returned home and walked into my bedroom on the top floor.

Sofia was there.

After all the commotion of the afternoon, I'd forgotten about her. All I cared about was disposing of Maddox's body and getting that office cleaned as if a murder hadn't just taken place. It was the first time since I'd met her that she wasn't the biggest priority in my life.

She wasn't on the list at all.

I'd hoped to come home to have a drink in solitude. I wasn't in the mood for conversation. I wasn't even in the mood to listen to her talk. I stopped and stared at her, seeing her in just a dark blue dress, now that her black leather jacket was gone. "Where's Andrew?"

"I left him with Ash." Her arms were crossed over her chest, and her guard was up a bit.

"Ash?"

"He's great with him." She offered an explanation to a question I never asked. "I thought he would be the best protector if something happened to me and you. My mother would be a good nurturer, but I needed someone stronger than that."

I couldn't believe my brother was the caretaker of my son. He wasn't a fan of children or responsibility. But I knew he would take care of Andrew until Sofia could return home. "What you did was stupid and reckless."

"Doesn't matter if it was. He's gone."

My eyes narrowed. "It does matter. You have no idea what you risked."

"I risked my own life, which I was willing to do to save you. I couldn't let you live like that any longer. I couldn't sleep…I couldn't eat. I had to do something."

All I did was stare because I didn't know what else to do. I was angry with her for not doing something sooner, and I was also grateful she'd gotten me out of the situation. It had only been a matter of time until Maddox turned me into his fuckboy. She'd spared me from all of that, but I couldn't bring myself to thank her. "It was really dangerous…and you got really lucky."

"I didn't get lucky. I aimed the damn gun and pulled the trigger. That's not luck, that's guts."

I dismissed her last statement by walking to the bar and pouring myself a drink. I tilted my head back and let the liquid wash down my throat before I turned back to her. "You want one?"

"I'm breastfeeding."

I was never around Andrew, so I didn't know shit like that. I took another drink. "Then I guess you should leave." There was nothing for us to say. Maddox was gone, and that was the final thing keeping us together. We accomplished what we'd set out to do. Now it was time to move on.

She stepped toward me as her arms dropped to her sides. "What?"

I turned so I could face her directly. "There's nothing left to say, so you can leave."

She threw up her arms. "And that's it?"

I forced myself to say the words that I wanted to keep bottled inside. "Thank you." I was grateful she'd saved me, but I was resentful she didn't do this sooner. I was resentful that she'd saved me when I should've saved myself.

She came closer to me until we were within arm's reach. "I don't understand. It's like you're mad at me. You should be happy. Andrew and I can move back to Florence, and we can have what we've always wanted. We can get remarried…be happy. You're acting like everything is going to go back to the way it was."

I automatically took a step back without even thinking about it. "It is going to go back to the way it was. Why would it change?"

The color in her cheeks slowly faded away, and her lips loosened because her features slowly tightened with pain. "I don't understand…"

"None of those things are going to happen, Sofia. We aren't getting remarried. You aren't moving back here. We're over." I wanted her to get out of my house and give me space. She may have saved me, but I didn't owe her anything. I'd already given her everything possible. If anything, she was just paying me back.

The confusion in her expression only deepened. "Where is this coming from? Last time we were together, we were in love. That was barely a month ago. What happened?"

If I could breathe fire, I would. "What happened?" I asked coldly. "I'll tell you what the fuck happened." I moved into her, closing the distance because I felt so much rage. "You. Left. Me." As I stepped into her, she stepped back. I held up two fingers. "Twice. You fucking left me twice. I'm sick of bending over backward for you. I'm sick of putting up with your shit. When Maddox took you, I did everything I could to get you back. Every hour, every minute, every second, I was doing something to find you. I never gave up on you. But you gave up on me so fucking easily."

Her eyes gave away her emotion, the hurt and the unspent tears.

"You left me here alone and took my son with you. You abandoned me when I never abandoned you. You have no idea how much I've sacrificed for you since the day I met you. I'm tired of it. I'm over it."

The tears formed in her eyes at such a speed, she couldn't blink fast enough to keep them away. "I had to protect our son. If I weren't pregnant, I would've stayed. You have no idea how hard it was for me to leave."

"Couldn't have been that hard because you walked out and never came back." I had no pity in my heart, no reservations about speaking my mind. "I busted my ass to earn your love throughout our entire marriage. No, I worked my ass off since the first day you were mine. I loved you so fucking much, and you never gave a damn about me."

"That's not true…"

"Yes, it's fucking true. You showed your true colors when you left me. Marriage is forever, till death do us part. You walked away from us, you made me sign those divorce papers, and you moved on without looking back. I'm done with all of it."

The tears fell down her face, and her cries became sobs. "I don't understand. You loved me just weeks ago…and now you're a different person. I can understand you being upset with me, I can understand you needing space, but we're a family. We have a child together."

"I'm not going to stay with you because of Andrew. I can be a father and not a husband at the same time."

She sobbed a little harder when I tore her down.

"I don't want to be with you, Sofia." I stood my ground and stared at her tear-soaked face and felt nothing. She wasn't worth my time or my energy. She'd put me through so much, and she didn't deserve to have so much power over me. I was tired of being a pussy-whipped bitch. "Now, get out."

18

SOFIA

I stayed at the Tuscan Rose because I had nowhere else to go. I didn't even have any clothes because I hadn't packed anything. I assumed I would be staying with Hades, and there were a couple shirts lost somewhere in the closet or in one of the drawers. I also assumed we'd be spending time together…to appreciate what we'd regained.

But he dumped me instead.

He was a different person from the last time we were together. The warm and affectionate man I knew had transformed into a bitter and heartless man who wanted nothing to do with me. It was as if he didn't care if I lived or died.

What happened?

I spent time at the hotel, crying into tissues and ordering room service so I wouldn't have to go outside. I waited by the phone and hoped Hades would call with an apology and explanation, but he never did.

I'd looked forward to this moment for so long, and now that it had arrived, it was the worst moment of my life. It was worse than when Maddox raped me. I'd never been so destroyed ever before. Hades ripped me to pieces until there was nothing left.

When he'd kicked me out of his home, I'd wanted to argue with him, but I was so distressed by his coldness I couldn't think straight. I also wanted him to calm down and see if that would change anything. Maybe if we talked again, he would have a different attitude.

When I finally had enough courage, I returned to his home. Helena was nice enough to walk me to the third floor even though he had said he didn't want any guests. I knocked on his bedroom door and hoped I would see the man that I knew…not the monster that crawled out of his broken heart.

He opened the door a moment later, in his sweatpants with no shirt. When he realized it was me, he turned just as cold as the other day. He didn't want to see me. He didn't look at me like I was beautiful. He looked at me like I was nothing but a nuisance.

It hurt so much.

He opened the door wider and walked away so I could come inside. He helped himself to a glass of scotch and took a seat. "What do you want?"

After I'd shed my tears, I was more prepared for this conversation. Last time, he caught me completely off guard. "Don't talk to me like that."

"Like what?" He took a drink without taking his eyes off me. "This is how I talk to everybody."

"Well, that shit's not gonna fly with me."

He leaned back and rested his glass on his thigh. "Say what you want to say."

I couldn't believe this was the same man I'd married. "What happened? You're a totally different person."

"I've always been this way. Ask Damien. Ask Ash. I was only different with you because of our relationship. But now that that relationship is over, there's no reason for me to be that way." He took another drink.

"It's like you changed overnight."

He shrugged. "I guess I just snapped out of it…"

"Snapped out of what?"

He locked his gaze with mine. "Love."

As if he'd had a gun aimed at my heart, he pulled the trigger and shot me. "You don't mean that."

"I do." He set his glass on the table. "We've been divorced for a long time. That's just how it happens."

"But you loved me last month."

He shrugged in response. "We can talk about it all day, but that's not gonna change anything. We share a son together, and that's the only thing we should be talking about. I can go visit once a month and stay at the hotel. That's probably the most practical."

I couldn't believe we were having this conversation. "I only moved to Rome because of Maddox. Now that he's gone, I should come home. I've lived in Florence all my life. I'm not gonna stop now."

"Fine. Then I'll pick him up every couple weeks, and he can stay here."

We went from being madly in love to being a divorced couple with a kid. He was treating me like I'd cheated on him, like he hated me. "So, we just move him back and forth? We never spend any time together as a family?"

"We aren't a family. We stopped being a family when you divorced me."

I kept my tears back this time, but it was hard. "You know why I did it. And in the end, I fought for you."

"Six months later…"

"Hades, I was pregnant. You expected me to take on Maddox when I was pregnant?"

It was the first time he didn't have a rebuttal.

"I'm sorry that I hurt you. I really am. The last thing I wanted to do was leave you. But once I was able to actually do something about it, I did. You can't be mad at me forever. And you can't be this unreasonable."

"Unreasonable?"

I didn't want to provoke his rage, but I didn't want to roll over and let him trample me. "It was a complicated situation for everyone. But my decision didn't mean I stopped loving you. I love you more now than the day I married you."

"You didn't love me the day we got married. We both know that happened a long time afterward."

"It doesn't matter. In this moment of time, I love you."

"Well, I don't love you."

I felt like I'd been slugged in the stomach again. The tears were hot behind my eyes, but I still didn't let them fall. "I don't believe that. Say it as many times as you want, but I still won't believe you."

Hades rose to his feet. "Believe whatever you want. I really don't care." He walked around me and headed to the door. "I'm not sure why you came here tonight, but you can leave."

I kept my back to him so I could have a moment to compose my features. He continued to stab me everywhere, continued to make me bleed. I was dying over and over again, losing all my strength. I turned back around and walked toward him. When I was by the door, I faced him once more. "This is how I know you don't mean it."

He opened the door and let his hand rest on the handle.

"If you stopped loving me, you would be indifferent to me. But your anger and coldness tell me that I hurt you, tell me that you're in pain. The only way you could feel that way is if you felt something."

His eyes narrowed on my face.

"I know you still love me…even if you really believe you don't."

When I returned to Rome, I went to Ash's place straightaway.

He lived in a large apartment close to the Colosseum. It was a three-story building, and he had the top floor to himself. He didn't own a big mansion like his brother, but I suspected it wasn't because he couldn't afford it. I rang the doorbell when I was on his doorstep.

Ash opened the door a moment later, and judging by all the stains on his shirt, he'd had a long day taking care of Andrew. His eyes roamed over me quickly and interpreted my body language before he made his conclusion. "You look tired…mad… and a little sad."

"Because I am all those things." I walked past him and stepped inside. In the center of the living room was a large blanket, and Andrew lay on top with plastic keys in his grasp. He shook them gently and listened to the rattle inside. I'd thought all I needed was to see my son and everything would feel better.

But it didn't work.

I sat on the blanket beside him and placed my hand on his tummy. "How's my baby?" I picked him up then cradled him in my arms. He focused his eyes on my face before a smile followed. He recognized me…I could see it.

Ash joined us and sat across from me. "He ruined my favorite shirt."

"How?"

"I was trying to give him a bottle, and he kicked it. Boob juice everywhere."

"Lesson learned. Don't wear your favorite clothes while you're taking care of a baby."

"Well, I would be naked, but that would be weird."

"Very weird. Don't do that." I grabbed a pillow from beside me and placed it on my lap so I could put Andrew on top of it.

"So, what's happening? Are you moving back to Florence? Shacking up with my brother? I'm surprised he hasn't called and yelled at me yet."

Hades was too busy being angry at me. "We're moving back to Florence, but I'm not moving in with Hades."

He cocked an eyebrow.

"I don't know what happened, but he's not the same person. Even with Maddox dead, he's angry at me…said I shouldn't have left him. Says he doesn't want to be with me, that he doesn't love me anymore." There was no amount of comfort Andrew could give me to chase away the terrible feeling.

Ash turned skeptical. "What? What the hell are you talking about?"

I shrugged. "I really don't know what happened. He just woke up one day and didn't feel the same way."

"That doesn't make any sense. I just saw him a couple weeks ago, and he felt the same way. Said he would never move on from you."

It didn't make any sense. "I don't know what happened…"

Ash considered it for a long time before he suggested an explanation. "I wonder if Maddox did something to him…like turned him against you. Brainwashed him."

"Not possible. Hades is too strong to be manipulated like that."

"Well, he's been manipulated in some way. How could he feel so drastically different?"

I didn't have an explanation for that. "You should've seen him. I've never seen him be so cold, so cruel. I felt like I was talking to a different person."

"What are you gonna do?"

I looked down at my baby and shrugged. "I don't think there's anything I can do. He's in this mood, and nothing will get him out of it."

"You want me to talk to him?"

"Actually, yes. If you don't mind."

He nodded. "I'll get to the bottom of it. We're definitely missing a piece of the puzzle."

19

HADES

Damien sat across from me at the bar, hatred brewing in his eyes. "So, what do you want to do?"

Maddox was gone, and now I was in charge. I was going to take over the world, take over everything. "Business as usual."

"We kill all his men?"

"No. We inherit them."

"And what about us?"

I looked at him coldly. "What about us?"

"Are we gonna keep working together?"

I shrugged. "That's up to you. This business is mine. I was doing all the work when Maddox was around, so I'm not gonna leave."

He cocked his head to the side. "That only happened because Maddox hijacked the whole thing. Don't make it sound like I don't do anything. I bust my ass, asshole. We went into this together, and you can't kick me out…no matter how much you hate me."

"I'm not kicking you out. But I want to buy you out."

He shook his head. "No."

"I'd pay you fairly."

"It's not about the money."

"Then what is it about?"

He grabbed his drink and pulled it closer to him. "You know exactly what it's about."

Power. Prestige. Reputation. Those were the reasons I didn't want to walk away either.

"So, we'll keep doing things as usual."

Unfortunately.

Now that the conversation was over, Damien left his cash on the table and slid out of the booth without another word.

I watched him go with a mixture of hatred and resentment in my heart. After everything we'd been through, he'd betrayed me again. He was a weasel who couldn't be trusted. Since my gaze was focused on him, I didn't notice the beautiful woman who took the seat beside me. She had two glasses of scotch…one was for me.

"You drink fast. Just want to make sure you have a refill." She leaned close to me, pushing her brown hair over one shoulder. Her perfume wafted into my nose, smelling like peonies on a summer day.

My arm moved over the back of the booth, and I leaned close to her. "That was thoughtful, sweetheart." I grabbed the glass and took a deep drink. "It's got a nice kick to it." I continued a quiet conversation with her while the music played overhead.

Twenty minutes later, Ash fell into the seat across from me.

I was so distracted by the woman whispering dirty things into my ear that I almost didn't notice him. "What are you doing here, man?"

"I've been trying to get ahold of you for like two hours."

I'd silenced my phone because I didn't want to be bothered. "Then how did you find me?"

"Damien."

"Of course. Fucking snitch."

Ash turned to my date. "Scram. Let the men talk."

I kept my arm around her shoulders. "You're fine, sweetheart."

My brother gave me a heated stare. "What the fuck are you doing?"

"Getting laid. What are you doing?"

"What about Sofia?"

She pulled her hand from my thigh. "Who's Sofia?"

Before I could say anything, Ash blurted out the answer. "His wife."

"Whoa, I'm not married…" I pulled her closer so she wouldn't slip away.

She gave me a disgusted expression. "Pig." She pushed off me and left the table.

Since my brother chased off my tail, I shot him a pissed-off look. "What the fuck are you doing?"

"I want to ask you the same thing. Sofia kills Maddox and saves you, but then you dump her?"

"I didn't dump her. We haven't been together in months."

"You slept with her a month ago."

I hadn't expected my brother to corner me late at night in a bar. "That doesn't mean anything. I didn't want to sleep with her in the first place. I'm ready to move on with my life. It's been a long time coming, and I feel free."

"What about the conversation we had on your terrace?" my brother asked. "You said you could never move on."

"Well, I found a way. And if you don't mind, stay out of my business."

Ash stared at me in annoyance. "I wouldn't have to be in your business if you weren't being a jackass. I know this isn't what you want, so I don't understand why you're doing it."

"It is what I want. That relationship was bullshit from the start. It's always been a one-way street, me busting my ass for her. I'm over that shit. I want to be single again. I want to fuck whomever I want and then kick them out the next day. No more heart on my sleeve, no more relentless sacrifice. I'm glad I'm not married anymore, and I don't want to be married again."

Ash stared at me in disbelief, like he couldn't believe a single word that came out of my mouth. "Did Maddox do something to you?"

I immediately thought of the date Maddox made me attend, but it had been so uncomfortable that I didn't want to share that night with anybody. Nothing happened…but it was still creepy. "No. What kind of question is that?"

"It's like you're brainwashed or something."

"I'm not brainwashed. I just don't love her anymore. People fall out of love every day."

"Not in a month," he argued. "And not you. You've been infatuated with this woman since you met her. How can that just end? How can you be so committed to her throughout your divorce and then one day just stop? Do you really want to go home with that girl who only wants your wallet? Or would you want to go home with a real woman who killed your greatest enemy and gave birth to your son?"

When he described her that way, he made her sound like a saint. She was no saint. "Let's not forget that she left me. Twice."

"She was trying to protect your kid. And when was the other time?"

"When we first started seeing each other. I asked her to marry me. She said no."

"The explanation for that is pretty simple…because you'd just started to see each other. That was way too soon, and you know it. You're just making excuses, and I don't understand why."

I knew exactly why I felt the way I did. The gypsy cleansed my heart and made me feel nothing. It was freeing…not caring about anything. But I would never tell him what I did. It didn't matter anyway. I didn't love Sofia anymore, and that was the bottom line. "I just don't love her anymore. It's that simple."

"And what about Andrew?"

"What about him? I'll still be a father. Divorced couples do it all the time. I'm not reinventing the wheel here."

Ash didn't have any arguments left, but he was still surprised by my confession. "I could understand all of that if it hadn't happened overnight. But one day, you were lovesick over Sofia, and now that you can have everything you've ever wanted, you don't want her anymore."

I shrugged. "That's the way life is sometimes."

"No, it's not. Not for no reason."

I did have a reason…but that reason didn't matter anymore. "I appreciate you looking out for me and Sofia, but it will be fine. We'll work it out for Andrew."

"It won't be fine. She's heartbroken. She's in love with you, Hades. She risked her neck to save the man she loves, only to find out he doesn't give a damn about her."

I shook my head. "It's not that I don't give a damn about her. I just don't feel the way I used to. How many times do I have to say it?"

He stared at the surface of the table for a while and ran his fingers through his hair. "You loved her once. I think you could love her again if you wanted to. You wouldn't even have to try."

It was my turn to stare at the table. "But I don't want to try."

20

SOFIA

It took a few weeks for us to move to Florence. I put the house on the market and left it up to the real estate agent to sell before fall. Thankfully, my inheritance was sizable enough that we had been able to hold on to our old place close to the hotel. It'd been vacant for a while now, and my mom didn't have the heart to sell it.

I hadn't spoken to Hades since our last painful conversation because I dreaded talking to him now. He was a heartless asshole, and I could only take rejection so many times. Before I officially made the move, I stopped by Ash's place to say goodbye.

"Where's the little stud?" He didn't seem to care about me at all, just his nephew, whom he'd grown so fond of.

"He's not a stud…at least not yet. I'd like to keep it that way for a long time."

"If he's anything like me and Hades, he'll start young. I think I lost my virginity…"

"Anyway…did you talk to Hades?" Ash had never called me, so I assumed he only had bad news.

He crossed his arms over his chest and sighed. "He said

everything that you had already told me. It doesn't make any sense…I don't get any of it. But his story didn't change. He's just a different person. No idea why."

Ash had been my last hope to get something out of Hades. Damien would probably have been more helpful, but since they weren't friends anymore, he was useless. Now I felt even more devastated because I didn't know what else to do besides give up.

Ash gave me a soft expression. "I'm sorry…"

"Yeah…me too." If Hades was this cold to me, that meant he'd probably already moved on with his life. He had different women at his place, and my old wedding ring sat in the nightstand where it'd been forgotten. I didn't want to let him go, but I didn't know what choice I had. It wasn't like I could change his mind. "I guess that's it…" Tears burned behind my eyes, but I didn't let them rise to the surface. I'd lost the love of my life, and now he acted like he hated me. Just woke up one day, and everything was different.

"I don't think you'll ever understand his decision. And you probably won't change his mind. But maybe you could do something else."

"Like what?"

He crossed his arms over his chest. "I don't recommend this. Personally, I wouldn't do it because I have way too much pride. But if you still love him and want to keep fighting for him…"

"I do."

"Then you can make him fall in love with you again."

That seemed impossible right now. "I don't even know how I would do that."

"What did you do the first time?"

I shrugged. "I don't know. In the beginning, we were just hooking up…"

"Then try that again. Be the person in his bed…so no one can replace you."

I used to feel sexy when I was with him, but now I didn't feel sexy at all. My body was different after having a baby, so I wasn't the size zero I used to be. It wasn't the same as it was years ago. I doubted I was the kind of fantasy he had. "I don't think he'll want me."

"Trust me, he will."

"Why? I'm twenty pounds heavier than I used to be, and my boobs are different."

"A guy doesn't care about a woman looking perfect. He cares about a woman fucking perfect. Something tells me you have that down." He winked at me. "If you really love him, I would at least try. Because if you don't try…you'll probably never get him back."

My mother watched Andrew while I was at work at the hotel. She was a free babysitter, and she looked forward to spending time with her grandson every single day. I didn't have to worry about him because I knew he was in safe hands.

It was nice to be back at the Tuscan Rose. There were other vacant offices, so I could have worked somewhere else and avoided the crime scene, but I actually felt safe while working in the place where Maddox died.

Where I shot him.

It made me feel like the victor, the solution to my own problem. I wished Hades were more thankful for the sacrifice I'd made, but he seemed ambivalent about it. Brainwashed was the best description to explain his behavior. But whatever the cause, it didn't change the illness.

I thought about Hades often and tried to think of an excuse to see him, but my only reasonable move was to talk about the son we shared. But having the baby with us made it difficult for us to be ourselves. We couldn't scream at each other because it'd make Andrew cry.

I called Damien as I sat at my desk.

He answered after a couple rings. "It's been a long time…"

Damien and I had fallen out of touch when I'd moved to Rome. Now that he and Hades weren't close anymore, he drifted to the outskirts of my thoughts. I'd always thought the two of them would make up, but it'd been so long that seemed impossible now. "I know. Life just got hectic… You know how it is."

"Life is shitty, if that's what you mean."

Ain't that the truth. "How are things with you?"

He had a soft heart under that hard body because he continued to talk to me even though he really had no reason to. "Hades is trying to push me out of the business, and he thinks I'm a liar… and I haven't caught any good tail lately. So, things have been better."

"Why would he want to get rid of you?"

He sighed into the phone. "Because he's an arrogant bastard who thinks he doesn't need anyone anymore." The venom in his voice was unmistakable. Even if Hades apologized, Damien probably wouldn't give a shit. That bridge had been burned.

"Why does he think you're a liar?"

"He assumes I collaborated with you to kill Maddox when I promised I wouldn't get involved."

My heart sank when I realized I'd caused a greater rift between the two men. "It was me and Ash…"

"Yeah, I figured that out a couple hours later. But he's so stubborn, he can't think straight."

"Did you tell him that?"

His voice came out like ice. "No."

"Well, you should."

"Well, I don't want to. His opinion of me means nothing. I don't give a damn if he thinks I'm a liar and a cheat. I know I fucked up in the past, but I've always been a good friend to him. It's not my fault he can't see that."

Now I wondered if Hades had really lost his mind. Maybe being stuck with Maddox for so long messed with his head. It changed him, traumatized him until he couldn't handle it anymore. He responded the only way he knew how…by snapping to cope. "Yeah, he's definitely lost touch."

"When's the wedding?"

The question made me feel dead inside. Getting my husband back would be nearly impossible, not to mention marrying him again. I wasn't even sure I'd be able to seduce him anymore. "Hades is being…kind of an asshole."

"What's new?"

"He says he doesn't want to get back together."

This time, he took a long pause and stopped issuing smartass comments. "Why would he say that?"

"He's angry with me for leaving. Says he doesn't love me anymore." It broke my heart to say those things out loud.

"Not possible."

I smiled, but my tears also began.

"I've never seen a person love anyone the way he loves you."

I'd taken Hades for granted for so long. He was so loyal and committed to me, showed me love was real. I was afraid of having a marriage like my mother's, but he gave me so much more. Now that it was gone, I didn't know how to go on. "I know…but that's how he feels."

He was quiet again. "I noticed he was different when we last spoke. Didn't realize he was that different…"

"Something snapped inside his head. When he left me in Rome, he said he didn't want to see me again. That it was too hard. Maybe that decision made him realize life would be easier without me."

"Maybe for someone else…but not him." The line turned silent as Damien thought to himself. "What are you going to do?"

"I'm so hurt that I don't want to bother with him. But I love him so much that I can't just walk away. I want my husband back. I want my family back. So, I'm going to try to change his mind."

"Good luck with that. Maddox may be gone, but there's a new villain in town."

I didn't follow his logic. "Who?"

He sighed into the phone. "Hades…god of the underworld."

21

HADES

I PRODUCED THE HIGHEST YIELD OF CRYSTAL OF MY CAREER. I handed it off to our distributors then told my cooks to get back to work. With Maddox out of the picture and my power unrivaled, I intended to eliminate all other competition and kill anyone that got in my way.

Life was good.

I wasn't as relieved as I'd thought I would be that Maddox was gone. I hated to admit it, but I'd learned a lot from him. I understood how to delegate to my men, how to terrify my enemies, and how to get shit done with precision. His demise was great news because he couldn't control me anymore, but in terms of great businessmen, he really had been one of the best.

Now I was the best.

I'd acquired all of his men and tripled my force. Now I sat in my office with my feet on the desk, an invisible crown on my head. Getting rid of Damien was the last thing on my list, and I considered how to kill him.

But I knew I couldn't do it. Maddox could've…but not me.

My phone started to ring on the desk, and I glanced at the screen.

It was Sofia.

That name used to send vibrations into my heart, make my stomach tighten with both excitement and unease. But now, I felt nothing…except a sprinkle of annoyance. I'd made it clear I didn't want her anymore. I hope she took that seriously. My days of being a pussy-whipped little bitch were over.

She could find some other asshole to torture.

But she was the mother of my son, and of course, I would always care about her. Even if I didn't love her anymore, I would help her in whatever way I could. I took the call. "Yes?"

"Don't talk to me that way unless you want to get slapped." Her tone of voice was so different, I almost didn't recognize it. She wasn't the clingy, whiny woman she was the last time I saw her. Now, she was stern and hard, reminding me of the woman I'd originally met years ago.

"You don't know where I am, so how will you accomplish that?"

In a dead serious tone, she said, "I'll hunt you down."

I was quiet because I was surprised by her response.

"I've had Andrew for two weeks. I think it's time you took him for a while. There're some things I have to take care of, and it'd be nice to have a break."

I was curious about these plans she had, but I didn't ask. I'd had Helena make up a room for Andrew down the hall from me because I knew I would be watching him on my own at some point. Having a kid interrupted my bachelor life, but he was so special to me that I didn't mind. "That's fine."

"You want me to drop him off later? I'm going out anyway."

I didn't ask what she was up to. "Yeah. Any time after six."

She didn't even say goodbye before she hung up.

I listened to the line go dead, and I raised an eyebrow. "Did she just hang up on me?"

I'd just gotten out of the shower when there was a knock on the door. I left my towel on the bathroom counter and pulled on a pair of sweatpants before I opened it.

Sofia stood there holding a car seat with Andrew inside. He was so small that it was easy for her to carry him with one arm. On her shoulder was a blue baby bag with his favorite toys and blankets. "I packed enough bottles of milk to last you three days." There was no desire in her eyes when she looked at me shirtless. There was no affection either, like she was taking our separation well. "I got his favorite stuffed animals and other stuff he might need." She was dressed in a tight black dress with little straps over her shoulders. Her tits were bigger than they used to be, and they were proudly displayed in the sweetheart top. Her body wasn't thin and hard like it once was, but she had a lot of extra curves to make up for it. With silky, shiny hair and painted lips, she looked like a hot piece of ass.

It didn't look like she'd had a baby at all.

I thought I would want to stare only at my son, but I couldn't take my eyes off her. Where was she going dressed like that? Did she have a date? Was it too soon for that? "Thanks." I took the car seat from her and carried him into my bedroom. I placed him on the top of the bed so he could have a look around. It was the first time he'd been in my bedroom since he was born.

She set the bag beside him before she leaned down and kissed him. "I'm gonna miss you so much, baby. But I'll be back in a couple of days." She cupped his cheeks and rubbed his nose with hers. "I love you, sweetheart. Have fun with Daddy." When she bent over like that, the curve in her back was more noticeable, her ass stuck out, and her tits were practically falling out of the front of her dress. She stood up straight. "I gotta go. I'm already late."

Late for what?

She ran her fingers through her hair and walked past me. "Call me if you need anything. Even if it's in the middle of the night, I'm happy to help." Immune to my muscular attractiveness, she headed to the door.

My eyes glanced down to her ass. "I know how to take care of my son."

She turned around at the door. With one hand on her hip, she gave me a stare ripe with attitude. "But you don't know how to talk to a woman."

I took Andrew to the bank with me during the day. He sat in the car seat in one of the chairs facing my desk. As long as he had a toy or a bottle, he was usually fine. His cries were at a minimum. The only time he got upset was when I left the room. He hated being alone, so as long as I was nearby, he felt comfortable.

I would look up from my laptop from time to time just to stare at him. He was only six weeks old, but he'd grown so much in such a short amount of time. His face was more defined and less chubby, and his hair was starting to come in. I could see his distinct similarities to me, but I could also see so much of Sofia in his expression. He was a perfect combination of the two of us.

Damien stormed into my office. "That fucking prick Thomas is being a little bitch. He just gave us his money, and he wants to pull it out already. The guy expects results overnight, but he doesn't have a fucking clue—"

"Watch your mouth."

Damien straightened in front of my desk and gave me a quizzical expression.

I nodded to Andrew on the chair. "Don't want him to be a potty mouth like his father."

Damien glanced over his shoulder and stilled when he noticed my son. He hadn't seen him before since we had no personal relationship at all. He stared for a while before he leaned down and looked at him. "Hey, little guy. Your daddy must be somebody else because you are way too cute."

I let the insult slide.

Damien squeezed Andrew's foot before he turned back to me. "Sofia did a good job."

I raised an eyebrow. "I fucked her, didn't I?"

"Whoa, watch the language."

I rolled my eyes.

"She was the one who had to carry him for nine months. She literally made him and then pushed him out of a tiny hole. I think she gets all the credit."

No argument there.

"Are you gonna bring him to work often?"

I nodded. "I can leave him with Helena, but then I'll never see him."

"True." He set the papers on my desk. "You want to talk to Thomas?"

The last time we spoke, I'd tried to buy Damien out of the company, but he wouldn't go. It was a little awkward, but Andrew's presence seemed to smooth it over. It was hard to hate each other when there was a baby in the room. "Yeah, I'll handle it."

"Can you still do the meetings with Andrew?"

"Yes. He'll be fine."

Damien clearly didn't have anything else to say, but he continued to linger at my desk.

I turned back to him and stared. "Yes?"

He slid his hands into his pockets. "You and Sofia are done for good?"

He must've spoken to Sofia if he knew that. "Yes. Not that it's any of your business."

"She's not gonna be on the market for long…"

My eyes narrowed. "Don't stick your nose in my business."

"I'm not." He stepped away from my desk. "Just wanted to give you a heads-up before I go after her."

Andrew liked the changing colors and shapes of the TV, so I held him in my arms as we sat on the couch. He rested against my chest while he held his favorite plastic keys. A blanket was over both of us.

There was a cartoon on and I was bored out of my mind, but I was also grateful I got to spend time with him. I had no experience with children, and I hadn't thought I would be a father so soon, but it was a lot easier than I'd thought it would be. All you had to do was pay attention to them…and love them.

My phone was on the table beside me, and it rang with Sofia's name on the screen. It'd been three days, so she probably wanted him back.

I kept thinking about the last thing Damien said to me, that he wanted to go after my ex-wife. Of course, that annoyed me because friends didn't do that to each other. But then I remembered we weren't friends…and Sofia didn't owe me anything.

Damien obviously heard about our falling out from Sofia

herself, so it made me wonder if they'd already started to see each other. When she dropped off Andrew, she was dressed like she was about to hit the town. If she was fooling around with Damien, it was just a rebound.

But it made me uncomfortable anyway.

I wasn't jealous… I just didn't like it.

Or did me not liking it mean I was jealous?

I didn't want to be with Sofia, so I didn't know how that could be true.

I took her call. "Yeah?"

It was obvious in the background that she was driving. "What did we talk about?"

"It's not personal, I just—"

She hung up.

I heard the line go dead then stared at the phone incredulously.

She called again.

When I answered, she spoke immediately. "Let's try this again."

I was annoyed with her pissy attitude, but I didn't antagonize her. "Hello, Sofia."

"Ahh…much better."

My eyebrows furrowed at her condescension, but I was also intrigued she didn't let me push her around.

"I'm in the neighborhood, so I wanted to see if I could pick up Andrew. If you want another day with him or whatever, that's fine. But I thought I'd ask."

"Yeah, you can come get him."

"Great. I'll be there in ten minutes."

"He and I—"

She hung up.

I set the phone down hard and noticed that Andrew had turned to stare at me. He held my gaze for a while before he reached for my phone.

"Yes, that was your mother. I hope you'll be a better conversationalist than she is."

This time, Sofia let herself inside my bedroom. Like last time, she was oblivious to my rock-hard chest and my chiseled abs. She used to melt into a puddle at the sight of my tanned skin, but now she seemed completely indifferent to it.

All she cared about was Andrew.

She walked over to him in the car seat on the bed because I'd already packed him up to go. "Oh my god, did you get cuter in three days?" She picked him up then brought him into her chest. Just as she had been a few days ago, she was dressed in a tight dress with heels, her hair a curtain of silk. Her eyes were smoky, and her lips were red as a ripe apple. She cradled him against her breast and gently bounced him from side to side. "I missed you so much, baby. I missed hearing you cry in the middle of the night. I even missed changing your diapers." She kissed his forehead and ignored me because all she cared about was him.

When she was done getting reacquainted with him, she put him back in the car seat. "I was so afraid you were gonna forget me." She grabbed the bag and put it over her shoulder.

"He definitely didn't forget you." I put my hands in my pockets as I watched my ex-wife dote on our son. "When you called a while ago, he recognized your voice."

"You did?" She turned back to Andrew and gently tickled his stomach. "You didn't forget your momma, huh?" She leaned down and smothered him in more kisses. When she was satisfied with his affection, she stood up to leave. "Was he good?"

"I took him to work every day, and he was great."

Her eyes lit up in flames. "You did what?"

"The bank." She should have assumed I wouldn't take him to the factory or anywhere else dangerous.

"Oh, thank god."

"Give me more credit than that."

Her look turned cold. "I'll give you credit when you deserve it."

My eyes narrowed. "You've been hostile lately."

"You get what you give." She grabbed Andrew and made her way to the door.

As much as I hated myself for doing it, I glanced down to her ass.

"Let me know when you want him again." She opened the door.

I came up behind her. "I can carry that for you." She had two flights of stairs to manage with the car seat along with the baby, which was a burden.

"I don't need you to carry anything for me." With her head held high, she strutted in her heels like she was walking on air.

I watched her ass shake from side to side. Her behavior was so different from how it was the last time we spoke that it was disconcerting. I found myself confused…even a little annoyed. "Sofia." I walked after her before she reached the landing.

She turned back around. "Yes?" She cocked her head slightly and gave me a spiteful look. "Annoying, isn't it?"

I ignored the way she got back at me for answering the phone like that all the time. "Are you fucking Damien?"

She stepped back slightly like I'd pushed her in the chest,

seeming truly surprised by the question. That either meant she was surprised Damien said anything to me, or nothing was going on at all. "I can't believe you just asked me that."

I stepped closer to her. "And I can't believe you haven't answered the question."

She put one hand on her hip and looked at me with nothing but disgust. "You made it clear you don't want to be with me. So how dare you stick your nose in my personal life. You told me you didn't love me anymore. You watched me break down in sobs. Who I let inside me is none of your fucking business." She grabbed the rail and started to descend the stairs without looking back.

I stayed on the landing and watched her go, pissed at myself for caring in the first place. I wasn't sure what bothered me about the situation. Was it the idea of Sofia with somebody else? Or was it the fact that my former best friend was screwing my ex-wife?

When she was at the bottom of the stairs, she stopped and looked up at me. "And just so you know, Ash was the one who helped me. Not Damien."

22

SOFIA

I called Damien. "Did you tell Hades we were sleeping together?" I couldn't imagine why Damien would do that, but I also couldn't understand how Hades had jumped to such a ridiculous conclusion. There was no way I would sleep with someone so soon, let alone his former best friend and business partner.

"No, but I did say something."

I started to yell into the phone in my office. "Why the hell would you say that? I'm trying to get him back, not piss him off. What did you say to him?"

"I told him I might ask you out."

I gripped my skull with one hand. "And why would you say that?"

"Just wanted to piss him off."

"Well, thanks for throwing me under the bus…"

"Before you get all mad at me, think about what happened. When he thought you and I had something going on, he got mad, right?"

I got up to shut my office door because I was being so loud. "What does that matter?"

"It means he cares, Sofia."

"Just because he cares doesn't mean he wants to get back together."

"No. But it does mean he thinks you're sleeping with somebody else, so if he doesn't sleep with you, somebody else will. Now, you're a hot commodity. He knows what will happen if he's not in the picture anymore. Maybe it will only make him jealous, but maybe that's all you need to get his attention."

When I thought about the question Hades had asked me and the ruthless way he said it, it did seem like he was upset about the idea of Damien and me being together. He'd turned red in the face and even followed me all the way to the stairs. That wasn't how I wanted to get him back, but I would take anything at this point.

"What did you say when he asked you?"

"I didn't say anything."

"Good. Neither confirm nor deny as long as you can."

"I'd feel like such a whore for sleeping with my ex-husband's best friend."

"We aren't friends. We're enemies. And that makes it so much worse…which works in your favor."

Maybe this would destroy what little chance I had with Hades. Or maybe it would give me a chance at all. "Now what?"

"We'll see what happens."

"What if he says something to you?"

"I'll string him along without answering his question directly."

"And what should I do?"

"Look hot. That's all."

A few days later, Hades made a surprise visit at the Tuscan Rose.

I was sitting at my desk when he stopped by unannounced. Now that I was back at work, I assumed he would leave the care of the hotel to me, but then I remembered half the hotel still belonged to him after our divorce.

He stepped inside wearing a dark blue suit and tie. There was a nice shadow along his jawline, just the way I liked. His hair was styled, and he had a watch on his wrist, but it wasn't the one I gave him.

He was such a sexy man, and I hated to think about the women who were enjoying him now that he wasn't mine. The thought was so painful, it made me want to hurl everything I'd had for lunch. It made me so weak, I wasn't sure I could stand in these heels.

He straightened his tie with his palm as he approached my desk, that same hostile expression in his eyes. He was behaving the same way as he had when I'd rejected his marriage proposal years ago. He treated me like he hated me, hated me more than Maddox.

I held his gaze and felt my fingertips go numb. I had to keep up the pretense of indifference because that was the only thing he responded to. That was the only thing that interested him. "Is there anything I can help you with?"

"There's a meeting with the board today. I've been handling all those while you've been gone. Do you want me to continue to do so?"

"No. This is my hotel. I can handle it."

His mood visibly soured. "Our hotel. Half of it is still mine, and I made some changes around here."

I knew what kind of changes he was referring to. He was drunk on power and used the hotel as a perfect base for his criminal activities. Without me in the picture, he tarnished the pure reputation of the hotel and turned it into a mafia paradise. "I can still handle it. I know you have other responsibilities."

He continued to watch me with that cold stare. The love in his eyes had been extinguished a long time ago, and now he stared at me like I was a burden more than an asset. I'd been replaced by the beautiful women who threw themselves at him wherever he went. Even if he was still married, they wouldn't care.

I rose to my feet and shut my laptop. "Anything else?"

"No."

I waited for him to leave and kept up my own form of coldness. He only seemed to pay attention to me when I was heartless and cruel. If I wore my heart on my sleeve and told him I loved him, it would just push him away. It was difficult to lie instead of just telling the truth…but I wanted him to be my husband again. "Then why are you still here?"

He broke eye contact with me. "Not sure."

Maybe Damien was right. Maybe the stupid thing he said to piss off Hades was actually beneficial to both of us. "Well, I have things to do. So, if you'd excuse me…"

He pulled his hands out of his pockets and adjusted his watch. "Ash is the one who helped you?"

I nodded. "You owe Damien an apology."

"I wouldn't have accused him in the first place if he'd had a clean record."

"That's a terrible excuse. Innocent people will commit crimes, and criminals will abide by the law. You should never make assumptions."

His eyes narrowed slightly.

"Be a man and admit you were wrong."

"Don't be a coward and not answer my question."

I stilled at the accusation. "What question?"

"Are you screwing Damien?" His brown eyes were so hot, they started to steam. They were like a hot cup of coffee on a winter day. He was definitely angered by the idea, but it wasn't obvious why.

My heart started to beat so fast. "If it has nothing to do with raising our son or running our hotel, then it's none of your business, and I don't have to answer your question. I've never asked you what you do with your evenings, so how dare you ask what I do."

Instead of letting it go and being rational, he continued to push it. "This isn't some random guy. This is Damien. I run two businesses with him, so I have the right to know if he's fucking my ex-wife."

"Why don't you just ask him, then? Because he's obligated to answer you. I'm not."

His anger rose. "He won't answer me."

"Then let it go."

He took a deep breath and slowly let the air escape through his flared nostrils. "Just fucking answer me."

"No. What does it matter if it's him or somebody else? What if I told you I was hooking up with a guy I met at a bar last week? I'm a single woman. I can do whatever I want."

His shoulders squared and his body visibly tightened as he absorbed my answer. He wasn't getting what he wanted, and it only infuriated him. "Are you hooking up with some guy?"

It was the first time I felt hope for us. He was so cold and cruel to me that I assumed he didn't give a damn about me. But now he was struggling with the idea of me screwing his former friend, and also the idea of me screwing anyone. There was only one explanation for that.

He still cared.

Despite my delight, I had to keep up my ferocity. "Get the fuck out of my office, Hades."

I was home with Andrew when Damien called me.

"You got plans tonight?"

"Depends. Are you asking me out?"

He chuckled quietly. "No. You're pretty but not my type."

"Then what's your type?"

"I don't know…I'm not picky. I guess I still see you as a sister."

It was a sweet thing to say, and it made me more frustrated with Hades that he wouldn't let the past go. He'd lost a good friend when that person should've been in his life forever. "You're not my type either."

"What? Sexy, tall, rich… That's not your type?"

I rolled my eyes even though he couldn't see me. "You said I'm not your type either, so what does it matter?"

"Just want to make sure you're not blind or anything…"

I definitely wasn't blind. When Hades walked into my office the other day, I saw him well—all of him. "So, why did you call?"

"I overheard Hades talking with some clients. He's going out tonight. I thought you could show up, looking all conspicuously sexy in a tight little dress. And skip the panties. Let a bunch of guys hit on you to piss him off."

"I don't like to play games."

"You're gonna have to play the game if you want to win. Are you gonna go for it or what?"

I'd already taken off all my makeup; I was tired from working all day and taking care of Andrew when I got home. But if I didn't intercept Hades, some other woman would snatch him. It was a disturbing thought, and it made up my mind quickly.

"You really only have to sleep with him once. Because the second it happens, it's gonna make everything complicated. That's good for you…bad for him."

I knew I would never love anyone but Hades, so I had to do everything I possibly could to get him back. I wanted the life I'd lost, wanted the family I'd never got the chance to enjoy. "Which bar is it?"

23

HADES

I SAT IN THE BOOTH WITH RHETT AND TONY, TWO BIG CLIENTS I'D acquired over the last two months. They dealt with oil in the Middle East and sold most of their product to the States. Despite the world moving toward renewable and sustainable energy, there was still huge revenue from oil.

And my clients needed to launder it.

That was where I came in. I could make problems disappear.

After a few rounds of chitchat, a couple brunette girls joined us at the table. The guys were about forty years older than me, so their days of picking up women would soon be over. They were rich, but cash wouldn't cover the wrinkles.

The blonde who'd approached me kept drinking out of my glass even though she had her own red wine. "How do you drink that?" She stuck out her tongue and made a face, acting like a child. She was a little young for my taste, probably in her early twenties. For me, it felt like thirty-five was fast approaching.

When the girls got bored of Rhett and Tony, they excused themselves and moved on to something else. Maybe they had been interested in me, but the blonde beat them to it.

Rhett looked across the bar to find new tail. "Those girls weren't that hot anyway."

Yes, they were.

Tony agreed with him. "What about that brunette over there?"

"Where?" Rhett asked, looking at the front of the room where the barstools were and the bartender stood making drinks.

"She's wearing the backless dress," Tony explained. "Brown, curled hair and stripper heels."

When Rhett spotted her, he whistled. "Damn."

"But there's only one of her," Tony argued.

Rhett shook his hand. "Then may the best man win." Just as he was about to get out of his seat, he stilled and sat back down. "Shit. Some other guy's already there."

"A few guys have been there," Tony said. "She has like six glasses sitting in front of her, and most of them are full."

Initially, I hadn't cared about the hot woman across the bar. All women were hot. Blondes, brunettes, redheads, whatever. It took a lot to impress me, so they all seemed the same to me. But I'd never heard of a woman getting that many drinks, so I turned to get a glance.

Fuck me.

It was Sofia.

I could recognize that long dark hair anywhere. I'd fisted the strands so many times that I'd completely memorized the texture of her hair, the way it slid through my fingertips when I held her close to me. Even if she just got a trim at the salon, I noticed it. I noticed the way her hair framed her face and trailed to her shoulders.

The rest of her features were even more distinguishable, like her tanned skin, her chiseled back, the sky-high heels that made her ass look dangerously perky. She had her lips painted red the way I liked, and the smoky effect around her eyes was another thing I enjoyed. She certainly didn't look like she'd just had a baby. That dress was tight and flattering, and her sexy chest was distracting to any straight man with eyes.

Did she know I was there?

Was this just a coincidence?

It had to be, because there was no way she could've figured out my whereabouts. I never told Ash or Damien, so unless she was following me, there was just no way. I stared at her with a mixture of shock and annoyance.

Seeing the handsome man talking to her just annoyed me more.

Then she laughed, throwing her head back and gripping her stomach because whatever the fuck that guy said was so hilarious. Her hand rested on his wrist on the surface of the bar, seeming innocent but also purposeful. All the guys before him had struck out based on the untouched Long Island iced tea, vodka cranberry, glasses of red wine, and a screwdriver.

The drink she was actually consuming…was a scotch.

That pissed me off more.

"Damn." Rhett genuinely looked devastated he never got his chance with Sofia, even though he knew nothing about her, hadn't ever even listened to her voice.

Damien's words came into my head. *She won't be on the market for long…*

I grabbed my glass and took a deep drink, feeling unbridled rage coming from nowhere. I was up the stairs and tucked into the back of the bar, so she probably had no idea I was there. She really was out on the town, picking up handsome strangers to erase my memory.

I didn't give a shit.

At least, I didn't want to give a shit…

Forty-five minutes later, she'd been hit on by three other guys and had so many drinks that, if she drank them all, she would be in the hospital for alcohol poisoning. To make it worse, the guys hitting on her weren't ugly weirdos. They were handsome men who could have anyone they wanted…but they thought she was worth their time.

The blonde was grabbing my thigh under the table, doing her best to get my attention. She pouted her lips and whined like a child. "Why are you in such a bad mood?"

"I'm not," I said defensively.

"Well, you haven't paid attention to me all night."

"Then why are you still sitting here?" I snapped.

Rhett and Tony had drifted off when they'd paired off with other women they found that night. I would've gone home and taken the blonde with me, but I chose to stick around and watch Sofia drain every wallet in that place. There was no reason for me to stay, no reason for me to care, but I couldn't bring myself to go.

Sofia would eventually walk out of there…and she wouldn't be alone.

The blonde eventually threw in the towel and smacked me on the arm. "Forget it." She grabbed her clutch then stormed off.

I didn't bother to watch her go. My eyes were on the woman who used to be my wife, the woman I'd once loved and lost. She'd left me at my darkest hour, and the betrayal had never gone away. I gave up on us because it seemed like we had no chance. I didn't feel the way I used to.

But I fucking hated this.

It was getting late, so I knew this night would conclude soon. She and the guy stopped ordering drinks and just continued to talk. She never dismissed him, and it didn't seem like she was going to. Maybe this was the guy she liked. Maybe this was the guy she wanted to take home.

The guy she wanted to fuck.

I downed the rest of my scotch to get rid of the bile.

I couldn't explain what I felt. I was pissed she was there. I was pissed she was flirting with guy after guy. I was pissed she hadn't shooed this one away. That anger was rising in ferocity, and now I wondered if she was hooking up with Damien on the side while sampling what else the city had to offer.

I was out of my seat before I realized what was happening. My feet carried me forward without my thinking twice about it. I had no plan for when I arrived at my destination. I had no idea what the fuck I was doing, but that didn't stop me from doing it.

My heart beat faster as I came close. One hand tightened into a fist because I wanted to break that guy's nose even though he'd done nothing wrong. I wanted to grab her by the wrist and yank her out of there even though she could do whatever she wanted.

I could hear her voice as I came closer, hear her laugh at something he said. The guy had a deep voice and chiseled arms, looking like a man pretty enough to be with her. They seemed like a good match, her beauty and his muscles.

What the fuck was I doing?

Before I could second-guess my decision, it was too late.

Sofia turned and looked at me, and after the initial surprise on her face, her features slackened into an expression of confusion. "Hades? What are you doing here?" She glanced at her date like she was immediately uncomfortable by my unexpected visit. Her eyes glanced back and forth like this was the most intense moment of her life.

I couldn't bottle my rage for a second longer. It was illogical and irrational, fucking stupid. But whatever, it was happening. "Leave." I stared at the guy sitting beside her and promised him a painful death if he didn't excuse himself.

The guy glanced at Sofia for explanation.

"Don't look at her. Look at me." I stepped into his line of sight so he couldn't see Sofia. "Leave."

"Hades." Sofia smacked her hand into my back. "What the hell are you doing? I like him. He's not bothering me."

I opened my jacket and pulled out a small knife. "You don't speak our language? Or do you just speak stupid?"

The guy raised his hands in the air then hopped off the stool. He was gone in a couple seconds, making the right choice.

I slipped the knife back into my jacket and turned around to look at Sofia. I had no idea how I was going to excuse that tantrum. This conversation would not end well. I'd probably get slapped, maybe kicked in the groin. Sofia had never done that before, but I'd never deserved it before.

She looked pissed. Her eyes were wide with danger, and her hands were up with skepticism. "What the hell was that? Who do you think you are? I'm talking to a cute guy, and you think—"

"Shut up."

Her mouth hung open because she couldn't believe my audacity. She grabbed her clutch off the table then slid off the stool to get to her feet. With impressive speed, she pulled her hand back and slapped me hard across the face.

I knew it was coming, so I didn't bother blocking it.

"You have a lot of nerve, asshole." She turned around and stormed off.

I watched her sexy body move in those impressive heels as my hand went to my cheek to feel the heat that flushed my skin.

People automatically moved out of her way, and she still turned heads everywhere she went, despite her violent outburst.

It took me a few seconds to compose myself before I went after her. I had no justification for my behavior, no excuse that would vindicate me, but I went after her anyway. I caught up with her once we made it outside and onto the sidewalk. It was almost midnight, so it was pitch black. Her heels echoed against the concrete as she continued her speed to the car.

"Sofia." I walked behind her.

Without turning around, she flipped me the bird and kept going.

This time, I jogged to her and grabbed her by the wrist. "Sofia."

She spun out of the grasp like a pro and slapped me across the face again. "Fuck off, Hades."

This time, she hit me so hard I turned with the hit.

"You said you didn't want me. You said you didn't love me. So you had no right to do what you did. You can't have it both ways. You can't break my heart and then block me from moving on. I never really thought you were an asshole until now." She turned to leave.

I grabbed her by the wrist again. "Let me talk."

She squirmed out of my touch again and tried to hit me.

Now I was ready for it, so I squeezed her hard and restrained her.

Her eyes burst with hatred when she realized how easily she was overpowered. "I don't care what you have to say. I killed Maddox so I could be with you, and you acted like such an ass. I gave you a son, I risked my life for you. If you don't want me, fine. But don't stop me from being with other people."

I stared at her beautiful green eyes and loved how pretty she was when she was mad. Her eyes lit up like emerald fire, and her mouth was so sexy when it was pursed like that. Her entire body was tight with adrenaline, and her palm against my cheek was a turn-on too. "I don't know why I did that…"

"Then you shouldn't have done it." She pushed against my chest so she could be free. "You can play your games with your bimbos, but I'm better than that. I deserve more respect than that as the mother of your child. Don't pull that stunt again." After one final look of viciousness, she turned around to leave.

I couldn't think straight anymore. I couldn't reason with my emotions. I couldn't understand what I wanted. Now my thoughts were dead in my head, and instinct kicked in. I rushed her, and this time when I grabbed her, I pulled her hard against me and kissed her.

Kissed her good.

My hand moved into the hair I'd been admiring all night, and my lips burned when they were reunited with hers. My arm pulled her lower back close to me so I could feel every curve of her frame. My breath left my mouth and entered her lungs, and my heart started to beat once again.

Instead of slapping me again, she kissed me back. Her arms circled my neck as she pulled my face down to hers. One moment she hated me, and the next, she desired me as much as I desired her. It was instant chemistry, instant fire. Passion ignited both of us, and now I couldn't stop touching her, couldn't stop kissing her.

I didn't want that guy to have her because I wanted her all to myself.

Since it was late on a weeknight, the sidewalk was empty of pedestrians. It was just the two of us, combined lips and tangled limbs in a patch of illumination beneath the streetlight. I could've gone home with someone else, and it would've been much simpler if I had, but I was wrapped around the person I wanted to be free of instead.

My mind was long gone in the gutter, and I backed her up into the alleyway shrouded in shadow. It wasn't romantic, especially with the dumpster and the pile of wooden crates that sat beside it, but it gave enough privacy that no one would ever see us.

I cornered her against the wall and continued to kiss her, my hands on her hips. I could feel the changes in her body, the way her hips were slightly wider after passing my son. I could feel the curves of her thighs and stomach, feel the changes she embraced as she stepped into motherhood. Even if I were a bachelor who'd met her for the first time that evening, I would find her body to be incredibly sexy. I actually preferred the curves over the sharp angles that she used to have.

Instead of coming to the realization that I had just acted like an asshole a minute ago and pushing me off, she slid her hands under my t-shirt and up my hard body until her fingertips pressed into my chest. She sucked my bottom lip before her tongue moved into my mouth, accompanied by her warm and sexy breath. She went from zero to sixty in a single instant, wanting me despite the shitty way I treated her.

I'd stopped loving her, but this innate passion was permanent. Once our mouths were together and our tongues danced erotically, it felt so right. She was the epitome of good sex, the heat and intensity people searched for their whole lives and never found.

She slowed down her kisses as if she was about to stop. Then she pulled away and looked at me, her lips slightly opened and her eyes on mine.

I didn't want her to end this. I didn't want her to come to her senses and march off again.

Her eyes flicked down to my lips for a moment before she looked at me again. Her hands moved down my tight stomach before her fingers began to loosen my belt. In a sexy whisper that only I could hear, she said, "Fuck me."

I liked dirty talk, but that was the sexiest thing I'd ever heard. I was living a fantasy I didn't know I had. I was about to screw this beautiful woman in a dark alleyway, and despite dirt and danger, I didn't give a damn.

She undid my belt and popped my button open. She pushed my jeans and boxers over my hips so my cock could be free. Her eyes studied her movements before they flicked back to mine, her green eyes filled with undeniable desire.

Jesus.

I was paralyzed by the intensity, drowned by the flood of arousal. I couldn't even move because my body couldn't process what was happening. I was about to have the best sex of my life, and I knew it.

My hands finally started to work again, and I pulled up her dress so her toned thighs were visible in the darkness. My fingers yanked her black panties over her hips and down her legs. They fell to her ankles, and she quickly kicked them away, where they would remain in the alleyway long after we were gone.

Fucking hot.

She grabbed the front of my shirt and tugged on the fabric so she could pull my lips to hers. It was her signature move that had always made me weak. Her leg hiked over my hip, and she grabbed my ass and pulled me as close as possible. She was blocked from view by the dumpster, and my large mass hid the rest of her if someone made the mistake of walking by.

Our lips were entangled in a heated embrace as I gripped the back of her knee and kept her leg over my hip. I smothered her into the wall and ground my hard length against her aching clit.

Quiet moans echoed in the alleyway, and I was so focused that someone could have robbed me and I wouldn't have even noticed. Wouldn't have even cared. I pulled on the left strap of her dress so it could slide down a bit. The fallen fabric eventually exposed one gorgeous tit, plump with milk she used to nourish my son. My palm gripped it tightly, and I squeezed as I continued to grind against her and kiss her at the same time.

This was the last place I thought I would end up tonight, but I was glad I hadn't ended up in bed with that blonde. Our kisses wouldn't have been this hot, our touches wouldn't have been so scorching, and our bodies wouldn't writhe like this. Only one woman could make me pant like a dog, could make me plead like a beggar.

I grabbed the base of my dick and pushed my tip inside.

Wet.

Tight.

Perfect.

I closed my eyes for a moment and moaned against her face because pussy never felt so good. I hadn't been with her since she'd had Andrew, and I was surprised she was exactly the same as she was before. Her body bounced back with incredible resilience, and the body part that could give life could also give incredible pleasure.

When she had every inch of me, she stilled and breathed deeply. Her hand was underneath my shirt and against my back, her nails clawing at my skin. Her fingertips stopped moving because she wanted to pause and enjoy the incredible feeling between her legs. She acted like it was the first time in a long time. She gave the sexiest sigh, so quiet that only I could hear it. It was stupid not to wear a condom with her when I had no idea where she'd been, but I refused to wear anything with her. She was different from the others. She was special to me.

When she pulled on my lower back, I knew she was anxious for me to move. She yanked on me so I could slide deep inside her before I pulled out again. She determined the pace, slow and steady, with even strokes that made for a sexy cadence.

I wanted to kiss her but couldn't. All I could do was hold her close and look into those excited eyes. I was breathing too hard to kiss her at the same time. I was feeling too much to do two things at once. I picked up her knee a little higher and pushed her into the wall so I could take her at a deeper angle.

So fucking good.

A group of drunk guys passed on the sidewalk, yelling and laughing as they got kicked out of the bar, but it didn't shatter our moment. We were oblivious to the world around us, just a man and a woman doing what they were meant to do.

She rested her face against mine and breathed with me. "Hades…"

I closed my eyes and moaned because my dick became just a bit harder.

Her hands slid down to my ass, and she dug her fingernails deep into the muscle. She started to change the speed, making it deeper and faster. As she breathed harder and her body tightened, her eyelids started to flutter open and closed. A beautiful red tint flushed deep into her cheeks, the warning she always gave before an explosion. I'd fucked her enough times to know exactly what that look foretold.

Made my dick want to combust.

When the pleasure imploded between her legs, her head tilted back against the wall and she opened her mouth wide to release a gasp the echoed down the alleyway. Her nails became relentless and clawed at my skin like daggers. She forced her mouth to shut to stifle her orgasmic screams. She started to moan between closed lips, her eyes watery from the high.

My eyes were locked on to her face because I was mesmerized by the show. Watching her come was the sexiest thing I'd ever seen. Feeling her body tighten around my throbbing dick made me feel like the biggest man in the world. This wasn't like old times when we were home and I could last forever. It was an off night because it'd been so long since I'd had pussy like this, had a woman like this. I felt all my muscles in my body tighten as my body prepared to fill her with my seed. I breathed harder and harder and pushed her deeper into the wall as I prepared to finish.

She relaxed when she was finished and wrapped her arm around my neck to pull me close. "Come inside me."

I couldn't stifle the moan that escaped my throat. It was deep and loud, like a bear roaring in the woods. I turned into an animal that only understood carnal desires. My hips rocked faster and faster, and I reached my trigger point in seconds.

I pushed myself entirely inside her as I released.

My face went into her neck to cover my deep moan. "Fuck…" I just came inside my ex-wife in a dark alleyway like this was a dream or a fantasy I'd made up in my imagination. It was not where I expected to be at any point in time, but my cock was like a magnet and her pussy was steel. They found their way back to each other regardless of the distance, the resentment or the fights.

I knew I would regret this, but in that moment, I felt too good to question my decision. I enjoyed every second of the high and decided to deal with the consequences later.

It was a quiet drive home.

She left her car parked near the bar, and I gave her a lift back to the place where she used to live with her mother. I drove with one hand on the wheel while the other was set against the window. We didn't talk about what had just happened…even though my dick was still wet.

She was the one with no panties, so she would seep onto her dress or the leather seats.

Just picturing that turned me on again.

Minutes later, I pulled through the gate outside her property and got out of the car. I wasn't obligated to take her home or walk her to the door, but it was almost two in the morning, and I wanted to make sure she got through the door safe and sound.

She ran her fingers through her hair to tidy up the mess while her clutch was tucked under her arm. She moved to the front door then turned to look at me. Heartbeats passed as she stared, her thoughts a mystery.

I expected an annoying conversation about our relationship, an interrogation about what I wanted. My feelings hadn't changed; I'd just had a slipup. If she asked me, I would tell her that, but I'd rather she didn't.

She sighed before she spoke, like she was going to give a long-winded speech. "Thanks for the ride." She turned around and walked inside without saying goodbye. She didn't even turn around to look at me before she shut the door.

I continued to linger in front of the door, surprised by the way she'd dismissed me. She didn't ask for anything, and she didn't expect anything. She seemed to have used me even more than I'd used her. It took me a few seconds to process her indifference before I finally walked away.

24

SOFIA

As hard as it was for me, I didn't contact Hades.

I knew I should seem indifferent toward him, because the less I cared, the more it bothered him. Watching me get free drinks all night shattered his resolve, and he ended up exactly where I wanted him.

So I had to keep going.

That was exactly the way I'd behaved before he asked me to marry him…the first time. So, if I ever didn't know what to do, I referred to the past for guidance. The old me would use him unapologetically. I wouldn't care about leaving my panties next to a dumpster, and I would shut the door in his face once his services were completed.

I just hoped it worked.

It was hard to behave this way when it contradicted my feelings. I didn't want to play games; I didn't want to act like he meant nothing to me. Being with him only reminded me how much I loved him, how much I wished I could go home with him and be his wife again.

I missed it so much.

But this was working, and I had to see it through. I couldn't wonder about the other women he must be seeing. I couldn't think about where he was every night. I had to keep my eyes on the prize and not get distracted by the obstacles in my way.

It was almost two weeks before he called me.

I was home in my room with Andrew when he called. Andrew was on a blanket on the floor while I sat in a chair and watched him lie on his stomach and examine his toys. I thought being a mother would be hard, but it was a lot of quiet time. Maybe that would change when he became a toddler.

I stared at the phone for a while before I answered. I acted like a completely different person with him because my behavior didn't reflect my true self at all. "You want to take Andrew for a couple of days?" I was proactive and made the subject the one thing we had in common. It showed I wasn't interested in talking about our night in the alleyway—even though it was all I thought about.

He was quiet for a while, as if he were taken aback by my comment. "Yeah, I think I should."

I hid my disappointment. "You want to pick him up? Or would you rather me drop him off? I'm on my way out anyway." I didn't have plans. I never had plans. I spent all my time with Andrew because the idea of dating was disheartening. I already knew the man I wanted to spend my life with. No other guy could compare.

"If you're leaving, may as well drop him off." His deep voice lacked any emotion. He was the strong and silent type, but ever since we'd gone our separate ways permanently, he was even more of an enigma.

"Alright. I'll be there in fifteen minutes."

I had to quickly throw on my makeup and fix my hair because I'd been in my pajamas before he called. I threw on a deep navy blue dress and pumps before I got Andrew in the car and drove to Hades's place. My attire would suggest I had specific plans for the evening. Maybe that would make him jealous again. Maybe that would make him drop his pants again.

I arrived at his place then carried Andrew and the bag to the third floor. I did all of it barefoot because it would be way too hard in heels. When I made it to the top landing, I slipped on my heels again and knocked on his bedroom door.

He opened the door and showed off his hard chest and chiseled abs. His skin was always slightly tanned even though he wasn't outside shirtless often. He was just gifted with beautiful Italian skin. He was as powerful as a statue and as beautiful as a piece of art.

I thought about our night in the alley and felt my skin flush.

His eyes quickly glanced over me, taking in my tight dress with the same thought.

I helped myself inside and carried Andrew to the bed. "I just fed him, so he doesn't need dinner. He had a cold a couple days ago, but it cleared up. If you hear him sneeze, don't worry about it." I opened his bag and pulled out a few extra toys. "The dinosaur is his favorite toy right now. It's the best way to get him to stop crying." I glanced at Hades to see if he was listening.

He stood beside me with his hands in his pockets, so strong that it was distracting. His eyes were focused on my face, and he gave me the usual look of intensity that he was known for. His face was impossible to read. His mood was even more mysterious.

"I'll be back in a couple days." I leaned down and kissed Andrew on the head and the tummy. I rose to my full height and squeezed his little feet. "I love you, baby." Leaving my baby was always hard, but since I was giving him to Hades, it didn't hurt as much as it would if I gave him to a sitter or my mother.

I looked at Hades again and swallowed my feelings. I wanted to move into his chest and wrap my arms around his neck so I could hold him. I just wanted to feel my husband love me. I wanted to feel like we were a family.

But I continued my ruse. "Call me if you need anything." I stepped around him and headed to the door.

His voice made me stop. "Sofia."

My heart started to race when I heard him say my name. It immediately made me weak, made my ovaries come to life. I wanted to love this man. I wanted to make so many babies with him. I wanted this place to be my home again. But when I turned around, I didn't let any of those thoughts creep into my expression. "Yes?" I was cold, indifferent, even a little bitchy.

His eyes narrowed slightly, and he looked so sexy when he was focused. His already hard features hardened even more, making his jawline razor-sharp. He must've shaved that morning because there was no shadow on his face. "Where are you off to?"

I was thrilled he cared, but I acted pissed instead. "You've gotta be kidding me."

"I can't ask you about your life?" He stepped toward me, his bare feet tapping against the hard wood.

"If I asked you, would you answer?" One hand moved to my hip, and I flexed my full attitude.

He stopped in front of me, his hands in his pockets.

"That's what I thought." I grabbed the handle and opened the door. "Our alleyway fuck was a mistake, and I don't want to talk about it. Let's just forget it happened."

His eyes shifted back and forth slightly as he regarded me.

"I'm seeing someone, and that's not the kind of person I want to be." I turned away and shut the door behind me. Once he couldn't see me, my heart started to race, and I felt sick because of the lie I'd just told. Playing games like this wasn't my forte. I wasn't even sure if I was convincing. I walked down the hallway and headed to the stairs, the blood slowly draining from my face.

The bedroom door opened, and his footsteps sounded behind me. "Sofia."

I stopped walking and took a deep breath. I wanted this nightmare to end. I wanted Hades to come back to me so I could just be myself, tell him I loved him whenever I felt like it, never worrying about what he was doing when I wasn't around.

When I didn't face him, his footsteps grew louder behind me. I felt like prey that could sense a predator's attack. Before I turned around, I turned into the stone-cold bitch I'd been a few seconds ago.

He stopped in front of me, anger in his eyes that wasn't there a minute ago. "What do you mean, you're seeing someone?"

"What do you think it means?" I snapped. "It means I met a guy I like. I wouldn't say we're serious, but eventually it might go there, so I can't fool around like that again. It was stupid for a lot of reasons, but I don't want it to sabotage this relationship's potential."

His eyes narrowed farther like he didn't like that response. "You don't think that's too soon?"

"Please tell me you're joking."

His voice was ice-cold when he spoke. "Do I ever joke?"

"You made love to me, then told me you didn't love me anymore a few weeks later. You don't think that's too soon?" I hissed. "You made it clear this isn't going to happen again, so I'm not going to wait around for the slim chance you might change your mind. I'm still in my twenties, so I have time to find someone else. I'm too young to waste my time crying over a man who doesn't want me." I headed to the stairs.

He grabbed me by the arm. "I'm not done talking to you."

I shoved him in the chest. "Grab me again and see what happens."

His nostrils flared with rage, and he pressed his lips tightly together to contain his frustration. "Whatever guy you bring around will be around my son. That makes it my business."

"My mother watches him when I stay over. So they've never met. If I want to marry the guy, then I'll introduce them. So, calm down." If that was really his only concern, he would let me go. I headed to the stairs again.

This time, he didn't grab me, but he quickly maneuvered his body in my way. His hard chest blocked my entrance to the stairs. "Who is he?"

"What?"

"I asked who he is."

"What does it matter? You probably don't even know him anyway. He owns a winery in Tuscany and has a shipping business. He makes an honest living, so I doubt you have any idea who he is." I was making this up on the spot, and I was surprised I could keep going.

Hades didn't like that answer. "So, you pick up guys at bars and then meet this guy?"

"How's that any different from what you do?"

He turned silent because he had no rebuttal.

I tried to move around him.

His arm slid around my waist, and he positioned me in front of him again.

This touch was different from the others. This time, it was

gentle rather than aggressive, and he wanted to get me close versus stopping me from leaving. His arm formed a leash around my waist, and he kept me close to his body so we were practically one person.

My heart was beating so fast, I was afraid he could hear it. The sizzling energy was between us again, possession, jealousy… It all radiated from him. I tried to control my breathing, but it was chaotic. I didn't want to go home and sleep alone. When I left Andrew here, it made me cry because I wished I were with them both. There was nowhere else in the world I'd rather be than right here. I wanted him to ask me to stay. I wanted him to snap out of this weird trance and be the man I remembered.

He looked into my eyes as he spoke. "Stay."

My heart was about to burst out of my chest. "What?"

"Stay with us."

I couldn't feel my legs or my fingertips anymore.

"Andrew deserves to have both of us in the same room together. We're still a family."

I wondered if this was a ploy so I wouldn't see my fake boyfriend. Or maybe it really was a heartfelt request. But either way, there was nowhere else in the world I would rather be. And it made me so happy that he wanted me to stay. "I already have plans…"

"What's more important? Some guy or your baby?"

I still wasn't sure if he was just using this as an excuse to keep me away from the imaginary guy, but he gave me a good excuse to get out of it so it wouldn't seem like I'd caved. "Let me call him…"

We had dinner together just the way we used to. Helena's home cooking was exactly the same…warm and delicious. I had only been in his bedroom one other time since our split, and I hadn't really had the opportunity to examine the details of the room.

Now I noticed the bed was different, the frame made out of a different kind of wood, and the sheets had been changed. His watch no longer sat on the nightstand, and a few other things were out of place. The room didn't feel as warm as it used to. It was sterile and dry.

The entire time we were together, I was nervous and tense. I kept hoping something would happen, and I had to remind myself to behave like he didn't matter to me. That required me to look at Andrew instead of him, to make conversation about subjects I didn't care about like the weather, politics, and other nonsense.

We sat together on the couch with the TV on. There was a cartoon show on the screen, and Andrew liked to look at the colors and characters. He lay against Hades's chest so he could see the TV easily. He was in a blue onesie, his eyes wide open with interest.

Hades never looked sexier than he did right now. Lying back with our baby on his chest, his arms wrapped around Andrew's legs so he wouldn't move. He was a protector, a father, but he didn't have a dad bod at all.

I wanted to cry because I wished this was my life.

I wished we were married again and watching TV on the couch was something we did every night.

I slipped off my pumps and pulled my legs closer to my body as I stared at the two of them.

Hades didn't make a move to sleep with me; he didn't ask me any more questions about the guy I was supposedly seeing. Now that he'd gotten me to stay, he didn't chase me anymore. I wasn't sure what would happen next, if he would ask me to leave once Andrew was asleep.

But I could just go to my "boyfriend's" house then...

Thirty minutes later, Andrew couldn't keep his eyes open. He was so fascinated by the show that he wanted to keep fighting his fatigue, but he was just a little baby so the fight didn't last long. His eyes finally closed and stayed closed.

I stared at him for a long time, so happy he was in my life. He was an unplanned surprise, but when he got here, he just fit. He brought me more joy than anything else ever had. "He's so cute..."

Hades looked down so he could see our son's face. "He always tries to stay up late like his dad, but he never wins."

I wanted to pull out my phone and take a picture of the two of them, but I thought that would ruin the moment.

Hades placed his hand over Andrew's stomach and held him in place while his other arm moved over the back of the couch. He turned his gaze on me and stared at me for a while. He didn't have a stern expression anymore. Now, it was slightly soft, his lips relaxed and his eyes warm.

I felt like I was back in time.

"I should put him to bed." He rose to his feet and carried our son with one arm.

"Does he sleep with you?" I slipped on my heels and followed him.

"No. He has a crib in the other room."

I always had Andrew sleep with me, so I was surprised he didn't scream when he was left alone.

We entered the room next door, which was painted gray and blue. There was a crib in the middle of the room, along with a changing table and other supplies. Whales were painted on the wall.

Hades gently set him in the crib where his stuffed animals were tucked in each corner. Hades quickly swaddled Andrew, keeping him safe in a cocoon. Hades straightened and gripped the rail as he looked down at our son.

"This room is so nice." I hadn't expected Hades to do something so thoughtful. I assumed he would just have Andrew stay with him during his short visits. If I were living here, we would've designed this room together. It wasn't what I would have done myself, but I wouldn't change anything in any way.

Hades turned toward me while he continued to grip the crib. "All Helena."

I nodded. "I figured." I came to the edge of the crib and looked at Andrew, who was the most handsome baby in the world. "I regret a lot of things…"

Hades turned his head toward me.

"But I don't regret anything that led me to him." My heart immediately slowed with peace as I looked at the little boy without a care in the world. "Even if we marry other people and have other children, I still wouldn't change anything. He's the single most important thing in my life. I wasn't ready to have children, but when Andrew arrived…I was ready."

Hades's hands loosened on the rails, and he rested his elbows on the surface instead. His thoughts were a mystery as we stood together in the dark room, only Andrew's night-light for illumination. Hades's warm expression reminded me of the man he used to be, the man who wasn't afraid to wear his heart on his sleeve. He'd disappeared overnight…but there were still pieces that remained behind. "You're a great mother."

I couldn't stop the smile from spreading across my lips. "Thank you. You're a good father."

He continued to stare at me, his gaze growing more intense by the second. He pivoted his body toward me slightly so our faces directly faced each other. He towered over me, his chest stronger than the Great Wall.

I could feel the tingle in my fingertips, feel the vibrations of my pulse under my skin. My breathing changed because I knew what would happen before it happened. That magic was still here…that inexplicable attraction that constantly brought us close together. I could feel that special quality the night we met, and the sensation only grew as the years passed. A divorce and a series of mistakes couldn't diminish what we felt for each other. I thought I'd have to try harder to demand his attention, but once the conditions were right, it just happened.

All on its own.

When he moved closer to me, I knew what was next. His large palm moved to the small of my back, and he gripped the fabric of my dress before he pulled me close to him. He lowered his face to mine for a few heartbeats as we gazed at each other. His hands slowly glided up my back until he reached my neck. Then his fingers gripped the warm skin, his thumb brushing over the pulse in my neck.

I wanted to reach for him, but I continued to restrain myself. I had to pretend to be resistant, like he was the one convincing me this should happen. But I knew it should happen…like I knew we should be together.

He brushed the hair out of my face before he leaned down to kiss me. This time, it wasn't a heated embrace beside a dumpster outside a bar. This time, it was in our home, right next to the baby we made together. The world around us was silent, and there were no distractions to keep us apart. It was so quiet I could hear our lips move together and break apart.

When I felt that electric current down my spine, my hands moved to the crooks of his arms, and I gripped his biceps to feel those strong and sexy muscles. My fingers could feel the network of veins just underneath the skin. And he was warm, so warm that it reminded me of when he heated the sheets all night long.

I kissed him back heatedly. I moaned quietly even though it was far too soon for that. But this was what I wanted, a slow and tender kiss between two people who loved each other. The screw in the alleyway was fun, but this was what I really wanted.

I wanted to make love.

And it seemed like he wanted to make love to me.

We continued to kiss beside the crib, our eager mouths making louder noises as our speed quickened. We became braver by touching each other under our clothes, slightly yanking on the fabric if we wanted it to come loose.

Hades eventually took the lead and picked me up. His arm scooped under my ass and held me to his chest as he carried me out the door and gently closed it behind him. Then he carried me down the hallway, back into the bedroom that used to be mine. He laid me down on the bed before he grabbed the baby monitor on the nightstand and turned it on.

Instead of breaking the moment, it made me want him more. No matter what he was doing, he still put our son first. Now that I was a mother, that was the sexiest quality in a man.

He was wearing very few clothes, so all he had to do was push off his sweatpants and boxers, and he was ready to go. Tall, strong, and proud of his physique, he stood over me and gave me a fearless expression.

He grabbed my legs and pulled me to the edge of the bed so he could slide his hands up my thighs and pull my panties free. Just like in the alleyway a few weeks ago, he pushed up my dress and left it on.

I'd rather take it off, but I was too eager.

He stood at the edge of the bed and positioned me so he could take me in that position. His hands pushed my thighs open, then he gripped my hips for anchorage. With his eyes on me, he guided himself inside me and sank until he claimed me completely.

I closed my eyes and moaned.

He leaned over me so he could fist the back of my hair and take me gently. Sometimes he kissed me and sometimes he just stared at me, but it was the way he used to be. He was loving, gentle, affectionate.

He was the man I loved.

25

HADES

I HAD ONLY BEEN ASLEEP FOR AN HOUR WHEN I WOKE UP AGAIN.

An arm over my stomach shattered my dreams. I was used to sleeping alone, having the whole bed to myself, so a touch was jarring.

I opened my eyes and looked at Sofia beside me. I felt like I'd gone back in time to when she was beside me always. Her brown hair was stretched across the pillow, and her lips were still red from her lipstick. Her eye makeup was smudged, but of course, she still looked like a million bucks.

I was transfixed as I stared at her.

But then I was annoyed.

What the hell was I doing?

Why did this keep happening?

She wasn't even coming on to me. I was instigating all of it, so I couldn't even blame her. Every time I thought she would end up in another man's bed, I did whatever I could to stop that from happening. I had no idea why.

I grabbed her shoulder and gently shook her so she'd wake up. "Sofia."

She blinked her eyes a couple times before she was awake enough to understand I was talking. "Hmm…"

"You should go home."

She propped herself up on one elbow and looked at me. She blinked a couple more times before she became focused enough to understand what I'd just suggested. Then she looked pissed. "I'm not going anywhere. I'm staying right here because I'm not some stranger you'll never see again. I'm different from all of them, and you know it." She got comfortable under the sheets again. "I'm sleeping here, and I'm going to fuck you in the morning before I go."

When I woke up the next morning, she made good on her word.

I tried to get out of bed, but she grabbed me by the arm and pushed me down. She straddled my hips then sank down onto my hard dick and didn't give me a choice in the matter. She took me like I was already hers.

Once I was inside her, I was defeated. My dick was in the best pussy I'd ever had, and my eyes had never seen a sexier lady. She had a little belly from her pregnancy, but I liked it. Her stretch marks were badass, and her hips made her easier to grab on to.

And her tits…damn.

I lay back on the pillow and watched her bounce up and down on my dick like a professional. She kept her promise and fucked me good, fucked me so good that I forgot our circumstances altogether.

She brought herself to a climax in just a few minutes, and I followed behind her as soon as she was done.

With her, I couldn't last long anymore.

The second she was done with me, she got off me and grabbed

her clothes from the ground. She pulled on her old underwear and pulled the tight dress over her head and down her body. After quickly fixing her hair in the mirror, she pulled on her heels and walked off.

She didn't say goodbye.

I may not feel the same way anymore, but everything else was the same.

I got addicted to her quickly…just as I did years ago. I was hypnotized by her beauty and totally mesmerized by her. My dick fell in love with her pussy instantly, and now he didn't want anything else.

In just a short amount of time, I was right back to where I was.

Not that I wanted to be.

What was it about this woman that made me so damn infatuated?

I used to be a man, but she turned me into a little bitch.

I left my office and walked down the hallway until I pushed in his door. I was in a bad mood, so I didn't care if he was with clients or doing something important.

Damien was on the phone, and he kept talking as he raised an eyebrow.

I snatched the phone out of his grasp and slammed it down onto the receiver.

Damien raised both arms in protest. "What the hell are you doing?"

"Stay the fuck away from Sofia."

He slowly lowered his arms. "Hades…"

"I mean it. Go near her, and I'll fucking kill you."

"Why the hell do you care anyway? You don't want her, right? She's free to do whatever she wants, as am I."

The idea of the two of them together made me angrier than I'd ever been in my life. The idea of him between her legs and her calling out his name made me want to pick up his desk and slam it on his head. Her sweaty body, her sexy curves naked on his bed while she rocked with him, made me so sick. "Did you fuck her?"

Damien got to his feet. "How is that any of your business?"

"Answer. The. Fucking. Question."

He slid his hands into the pockets of his slacks and gave me a bored look.

"Motherfucker, do you want to die?"

"You know I don't kiss and tell."

I grabbed the phone on his desk and slammed it down like a gorilla, and then I shoved everything onto the floor. His laptop snapped in half, and his coffee destroyed all his papers.

Damien glanced down at the pile of his things. "You owe me a new computer."

"Answer me, or you'll be broken too."

He stared at me for a long time without answering.

This was eating away at me. Damien had an ownership stake in a winery and also had stock in a shipping company. If he was the one Sofia was seeing, my head would explode. If it was him, she would lie about it. I couldn't handle that kind of truth.

"Instead of focusing on me, why don't you just get your wife back?"

My nostrils flared at his lack of response.

"Alright, I'll answer you." He raised his hands slightly so I would calm down. "But regardless of my answer, you should get her back. You're losing your fucking mind. I've never seen you lose your shit like this before. If it's not me, it's going to be someone else."

"Just answer me."

"No."

"No, you won't answer me, or is no your answer?"

He answered calmly. "No. I haven't slept with her."

Fucking hallelujah. My hands went to my forehead, and I slowly dragged them down my face in relief.

"But you clearly want to. So why don't you go do that instead of wasting your time with these women you don't care about?"

I still resented her for what she did to me, but these feelings were pouring in again. It happened so quickly, I couldn't believe it. I was so jealous, I turned into a psychopath. What the hell was wrong with me? "I'll handle the meeting with John tonight."

He raised an eyebrow. "So…you're just gonna pretend this little tantrum didn't happen?"

I glared at him.

"And you better buy me a new computer. I'm not kidding around about that."

"If you care about your shit, don't go sniffing around my wife."

He grinned.

"What?"

His smile only grew. "Ex-wife."

Most of my meetings took place in bars because rich and

powerful men liked to show off just how rich and powerful they were. Their wives already knew what they were worth and were entitled to it, so they wanted to impress somebody new.

John was dull and stupid. He handed his money over for other people to manage, but he did it blindly, which was incredibly dumb. Good news for him, I was actually an honorable man when it came to business. But he hadn't realized I was one of the few.

When we stopped talking and he became distracted by an admirer, I excused myself to the bar and got another drink.

I kept thinking about what Damien said.

Ex-wife.

I'd called Sofia my wife when she hadn't been my wife in eight months.

Was that an honest mistake? Or was it an indication of my real feelings?

One thing was for sure—I was so fucking happy she hadn't fucked Damien.

I probably would've killed him.

A brunette came my way and placed a drink in front of me. "Hi, I'm Veronica." She was young and perky, with a high-pitched voice and a bubbly personality. She was the talkative type. You could tell just by looking at her.

"Hey."

She pushed the drink toward me, a vodka cranberry. "I thought I'd buy you a drink before someone else does."

I'd stopped being flattered by advances because they'd stopped meaning anything. They were just another person, another stranger. I knew there were women I'd slept with whom I wouldn't recognize if I came face-to-face with them again. I wasn't ashamed of my decisions, but now I found them pointless.

The best sex of my life had happened with one person.

I started to feel like shit, to feel ashamed of what I'd done.

Veronica began to talk about herself, her hobbies, like reading and rock-climbing.

I faced her head on, but I didn't really pay attention to anything she said. I kept thinking about the way I'd screamed at Damien. I kept thinking about the way Sofia had told me off when I'd tried to kick her out of my bed. I thought of the way she'd fucked me the next morning.

My imagination must've run wild because Sofia appeared right before me.

In a tight purple dress, she placed herself in front of Veronica so she blocked her from view. She looked up at me with confidence, not anger or jealousy.

It took me a second to realize my eyes weren't playing tricks on me.

Sofia grabbed the front of my shirt and pulled my lips to hers to kiss me.

As if I was under a spell, I didn't resist at all. I kissed her back and closed my eyes like we were alone.

When she pulled away, she spoke so only I could hear her. "Do you want to go home with one of these dumb girls? Or go home with the only woman you actually want?" She stared at me possessively with those beautiful eyes, her hand still gripping the front of my t-shirt.

I didn't want to cave. I didn't want to lose. "We just slept together. I'm sorry if I misled you."

Her confidence didn't wane. "I think you only misled yourself. At least that's how Damien made it sound when he told me you ransacked his office today…" She looked at me with victory in her eyes, like she knew she'd beaten me. "Do you usually call me your wife by accident?"

That fucking rat.

She smiled slightly before her fingers relaxed on my shirt. "Let's go home."

Veronica didn't take her loss with grace. "Bitch, I was here first. Move."

Sofia ignored her. "Come on."

I wanted to fight my way out of this, but I knew there was no escape. She had me by the throat, and she knew it. We both knew I didn't want to go home with anyone else. She knew I felt all those old emotions every time we were together. She knew she was the only woman I wanted to fuck.

Veronica didn't give up. "Bitch, don't make me ask again." She grabbed Sofia by the wrist.

My reflexes were quicker than a striking cobra. I grabbed her hand before she could make contact. "Don't touch my wife."

All Sofia did was give me a smile, but that smile said everything.

It was the middle of the night.

I'd ended up exactly where I didn't want to be, but I wasn't surprised by it either. Fighting got me nowhere, and it sucked to lose over and over again. I went outside on the terrace and sat at the table. The end of summer was here, but it was still hot and humid like fall was nowhere in sight. In just my sweatpants, I sat there and looked at the lights from the city. A slight breeze moved through my short hair, and I rubbed the scruff on my jaw and realized I hadn't shaved in days.

Sofia was right… I hadn't wanted to go home with that girl.

Any girl.

But I didn't want to be here either. I sat there for a long time and reflected on how much my life had changed. My biggest adversary was gone, and I was a man running the streets once again. But everything was different because everyone in the shadows knew I was the one who'd overthrown Maddox.

The terrace doors opened behind me, and Sofia joined me in the darkness. "Can't sleep?"

No. I just didn't want to sleep.

She moved to the seat across from me, wearing one of my oversized shirts. Since there was a slight breeze, her nipples hardened through the thin fabric of my t-shirt. When she sat down, her long legs stretched out before her, beautiful and tanned from the long summer. There was no baby monitor because Andrew was with his grandmother.

Her hands rested together on the table as she looked at me. Her hair was a mess, like a hurricane had passed directly through it

I was that hurricane.

Her brown strands were scattered across her shoulders, and her eyes had a sleepy look. Her skin was such a beautiful color because she was well rested and satisfied. With no makeup and nothing fancy to wear, she was still the most provocative thing in the world to look at. It was obvious she didn't grasp just how truly stunning she was.

She gave me the opportunity to respond, but when that clearly wasn't going to happen, she broke the silence with her feminine voice. "It's ironic. I haven't slept so well in a long time."

Just a few months ago, I would've said I hated her. There was so much rage and resentment in my heart that I didn't think I could feel anything positive for her. But now, my heart softened when she said those romantic words.

"And the second you leave the bed...I just know."

It was exactly the way it used to be when we were married. She knew the instant I was gone. That was why I could never sneak out in the middle of the night. That was why I woke her up every time I came home, no matter how quiet I was.

Her eyes reflected the lights from the buildings behind me, giving them a special glow. I hated the way I felt about this woman, and no matter what I did, feelings always came rushing back. It didn't matter what she did to hurt me…I always bounced back to her.

"You're angry." She could read my silence like my mood was words on a page. She kept her voice steady so she wouldn't provoke me.

My eyes narrowed on her face.

"Why?"

"Because no matter what I do, I always end up here." I always ended up on my knees for this one woman, so infatuated that I couldn't see straight. My heart grew to three times its size, and I felt emotions I thought were impossible to feel.

"I know you want to end up here, Hades."

My eyelids twitched in anger. "Trust me, I don't. Since the day we met, I worked my ass off to be with a woman like you. I was honest, loyal, the most committed guy there ever was. And you treated me like shit."

She didn't overtly react. She seemed to digest the harsh insult I'd just thrown at her, but she did it with grace. "When we first met, you rushed me into something I wasn't ready for. We'd only been hooking up for a few months when you asked me to be your wife. Then when we did get married, I wasn't ready for that either. My experience with marriage had always been negative, borderline depressing…"

"You said all that already."

Her eyes flashed with annoyance. "But I haven't told you that you've completely changed my opinion about marriage. You made me believe in it, made me want to be your wife until death took me. You made me fall in love when I didn't think that was possible. You made me trust a man when I didn't think that was an option either. You opened my eyes to a whole new world I could never see. Now I want that life back more than anything in the world. I loved being married to you…and I would do anything to be married again." She paused to take a breath, to gather her emotions. "I admit that I didn't appreciate you as much as I should've. I admit I wasn't the wife you deserve. I understand that I hurt you and now you don't trust me…" Her eyes started to cloud with tears. "But I would spend the rest of my life trying to earn that trust back. I would be the wife I should've been before. I would bust my ass, work every day to make you happy. Hades, give me another chance."

That speech should've meant nothing to me, but it tugged on my heart and made me bleed.

"I haven't been seeing anybody."

My chest stopped rising mid-breath.

"It wasn't a coincidence that we were at the same bar. And all those men buying me drinks…they never had a chance. Damien and I never had any type of flirtatious relationship. I made all that up because I thought it was the only way to get your attention. Begging you to take me back wasn't getting me anywhere. I've never given up on you… I'll never give up on you."

She'd played me like a fool. "You lied to me."

She took a deep breath. "Yeah…I did. And I don't regret it."

I was relieved she hadn't been screwing all those random guys for the last few months. She'd only been with me.

"Please give me another chance…"

My eyes diverted to the scenery around us, the dark buildings with little spots of light. Seconds passed before I looked at her again. I didn't know what to say. I wanted to tell her it was never going to happen, that she had no chance, but I knew I would end up in bed with her over and over again. I was in this relationship even if I didn't want to be. "You aren't moving back in here, and we aren't getting remarried."

Her face relaxed when she understood what I said. "That's fine."

I'd gone to the gypsy so I could be free of this woman forever, but there was no spell strong enough to erase my feelings for her. I'd wiped them away once, but they grew back overnight.

"Thank you." Her eyes started to gloss over with moisture.

"No one else…just the two of us." I didn't owe her my fidelity, but I didn't want to be with anyone else anyway. And I definitely didn't want her to be with anyone else either. I was slightly annoyed with myself for caving, but there was also this huge weight that lifted off my chest.

She left her chair and came toward me until she lowered herself into my lap. She used to sit like this all the time, keeping me company while I suffered one of my moods. She rested her forehead against mine and laid her palm against my chest.

My hand moved into her hair, and I held her close. My heart had already softened for this woman. This was exactly where I wanted to be…because it was the only place I ever felt happy.

26

SOFIA

I LOOKED AT MYSELF IN THE MIRROR AND APPROVED OF THE DRESS I'd thrown on. It was blush pink, with little straps and a short length. I wore white heels on my feet, looking like a spring rose in the heat of summer. I curled my hair and pinned it over one shoulder. My lips were painted the same color as my dress, and I went a little crazy with the mascara.

"What do you think?"

Andrew sat in his car seat and just stared.

"Good enough for me." I pulled out my phone and called Hades.

He took the call on the first ring, just the way he used to. It was nice to revisit old times. "Sofia." He no longer spoke with attitude and coldness. His voice wasn't blanketed with affection, but it was a major improvement.

"Are you free tonight?"

He paused before he answered. "Depends. What do you have in mind?"

"I thought Andrew and I could come over for dinner." I basically invited myself over, but since I lived with my mom, it was a little awkward to invite him here. Besides, I viewed that place as my home. I wanted to move in as soon as possible.

"Alright."

I could tell he was still on guard, letting me in but only a little bit. "We'll be there in fifteen minutes." I glanced at the baby bag on the bed. It was full of bottles and diapers and a change of clothes, but it also had some of my things inside…because I hoped to spend the night.

He hung up.

I grabbed Andrew, and we headed downstairs.

My mom met me by the front door and looked me up and down like a guy checking me out. "Wow, look at you. I hope you're putting that dress to good use. And not on the street corner."

I rolled my eyes. "We're having dinner with Hades."

"Ooh…" She put one hand on her hip. "Operation: Get your husband back."

"Pretty much."

"Well, I hope I don't see you two until tomorrow morning." She started to walk away. "In my experience, if you want to get a guy to stay, give him a good blow job."

I quickly turned around and gave her an incredulous look. "Mom?"

"What?" she asked innocently. "I want all of us to live together again as soon as possible. I would give him a blow job…but I don't think he'd like it."

We sat together at the table inside and enjoyed the dinner Helena prepared for us. Andrew was too young to sit in a highchair, so I held him with one arm and breastfed him while I took a few bites of my food. One strap was pulled over my shoulder so my breast was free. It wasn't the most elegant look for dinner, but since Hades was the father, it was no big deal.

Hades stared at me as I fed Andrew, his eyes focused on my exposed tit. He continued to eat without watching what he was doing, so transfixed on our son having dinner. He'd been giving me heated looks all night.

Must like the dress.

When my nipple really started to ache, I switched Andrew to the other breast and left both my tits exposed.

Hades picked up his fork and tried to place the food in his mouth, but he was so focused on us that he accidentally stabbed his piece of chicken into his face. He flinched at the contact and quickly placed the food where it belonged.

I smiled because it was the first time I'd seen Hades be uncoordinated. "He does this pretty much all day, and then I also have to pump." My tits were so much larger than they used to be, and they were swollen and achy all the time.

"It's hot…"

"Yeah?"

He nodded. "Watching you feed our son with your tits hanging out like that…it's the sexiest thing I've ever seen. Must be an evolutionary thing."

"Yeah, must be." I held Andrew close to my chest and continued to eat my dinner. "How was your day?"

He shrugged. "Fine."

"That's all you're gonna give me?"

"My job is not that interesting."

"You're a drug dealer. There are movies and TV shows about it."

He shook his head slightly. "They never get it right."

I didn't want to tell Hades what to do, but I hoped he would leave the business on his own. I hoped he would understand we couldn't take any more risks now that we had a son. But our relationship was too raw right now, so I wouldn't dare say anything. "And the bank?"

"That job really is boring."

"I hope you and Damien are getting along better now."

Now that his plate was clean because he'd eaten everything, Hades leaned back in his chair and stared at the two of us. "I had to buy him a new computer."

"Why?"

"Because I broke everything in his office when I lost my shit."

I cupped Andrew's head with my other hand and kept him close. "That was nice of you."

"I just wanted him to shut the fuck up."

"Now that you know Damien was never really interested in me and Maddox is gone, maybe the two of you can bury the hatchet and move on…"

His eyes held a dead expression, like there was no possibility that could ever happen.

I didn't want to provoke his anger when I was trying to repair the rift between us, so I let the conversation die. "My mother misses you. She wants us to get back together so she can live with us again."

He took a drink of his wine then licked his lips. "She's still a package deal, huh?"

"No…but it would be nice if she could watch Andrew while I'm at work."

All he gave was a slight nod.

"On the way out, she basically called me a hooker because of this dress."

His eyes looked me over. "I like that dress. A lot."

"I guess she has good taste. She also told me the best way to get a man is to give him a blow job."

His expression didn't change, but his eyes narrowed slightly. "She's a lot smarter than I realized…"

Hades lay beside me in bed, with Andrew sleeping on his chest. Our baby was so small in comparison to Hades's large physique. Together, they breathed at the same rate, like Andrew was copying his father.

I was in Hades's t-shirt beside him, my hand resting around his bicep. The three of us were cuddled close together, snuggling like a family. I almost wanted to cry because this was exactly what I wanted.

I pressed a kiss to his shoulder and rested my face in the crook of his neck. "I love you." He told me he didn't love me anymore, and I'd believed him at the time, but now I wondered if that had ever been true.

Could a love like ours just stop?

He didn't say anything back. The silence stretched on for a long time, never-ending. He eventually turned his lips to my forehead and pressed a kiss there. That was the only reaction he gave me.

I tried not to be wounded by his rejection, but that was difficult. I missed being loved by this man so much. But I told myself to be patient, that it would happen eventually. I remained still and kept my breathing even so he wouldn't sense the hurt in my quiet sigh.

After Hades put Andrew to bed in the other room, he stepped back inside and approached the bed.

I never asked if I could sleep over, but I wasn't leaving unless he explicitly told me to. If I had it my way, I would just live there forever. I wouldn't even go back to get my clothes. I grabbed the baby monitor off the nightstand and flicked it on.

Silence.

He stopped in front of me and grabbed the top of his sweatpants.

I stared at his perfect physique and felt my heart race as I waited for him to reveal more.

He dug his thumbs into his waistband and then pushed his bottoms off until he was naked. He was already hard, like he already had something in mind. "I want that blow job."

This was the Hades I missed, the authoritative, bossy man who wasn't afraid to tell me what he wanted because he wasn't afraid to want me in the first place. He'd spent so much time acting like I meant nothing to him, probably wanting to believe his own lie. But he'd now stopped doing that and wore his desires on his sleeve.

It was already a major improvement.

I would gladly suck his dick every night if he would be my husband again.

I pulled his t-shirt over my head so I was just in my pink thong. I wasn't as confident as I used to be because the stretch marks over my stomach and thighs were so noticeable on my body, but all those doubts disappeared when he looked at me like that. He could spend his evening with anyone else, but he was there with me.

Just me.

I slid off the bed and fell to my knees in front of him on the rug.

I positioned myself before him and grabbed both of his hips. He was hard as a statue, so tall and straight, he seemed to be made out of marble instead of flesh.

I began by pressing a gentle kiss to his balls.

He took a deep breath at the initial touch, as if that was exactly the spot he wanted me to kiss first. His hand moved to my shoulder, and he squeezed me gently before his fingers moved into my hair and wrapped it around his hand to fist it. "You want to be my wife again?"

"Yes…"

His hand moved to the bottom of my chin, and he gently pushed down so my mouth would open wide. Then he grabbed the base of his dick and prepared to push it inside my throat. "Then prove it."

27

HADES

Sofia and I fell into a routine where she would come over several nights a week and we'd spend the evening in my bedroom, having dinner and spending time with Andrew. When he fell asleep, we'd put him in his crib in the other room and then have our own fun in bed.

Now that I'd agreed to give her another chance and knew how sorry she was, I started to trust her again. I wanted to be mad at her forever, but I simply couldn't. I could read people well, and I knew her act of contrition was true. She came to Florence to kill Maddox, and after that was done, I'd rejected her love, but she didn't give up on me.

She knew I'd been out with other women, but she still didn't give up on me.

She lied to me. She manipulated me.

But it was all to get me back.

That was the reason I had faith in us again. It would've been easy for her to find a new husband and move on. I'd said a lot of cruel things to her that were unforgivable, but she still put up with me.

She wasn't loyal before, but she was now.

But every day, she told me she loved me…and I couldn't say it back.

She never asked me about it. Never showed a look of rejection every time I ignored her confession. She let me hold my silence and never asked me to break it.

Andrew cried a couple times during the night, so Sofia was in and out of the room to feed him and rock him. He wasn't usually a fussy baby, but that night, he wanted attention. I had to work in the morning, so I let her take care of it.

When my alarm went off the next morning, I showered and got ready for work while Sofia continued to sleep. Instead of going back to work full time right away, she chose to spend most of her time with Andrew, so she usually slept in, then left while I was gone.

I had a meeting at the bank, so I put on a suit and tie then opened my drawer where my collection of watches laid. I usually grabbed a different one every day, and the one Sofia gave me was off to the side in a whole different pile. I stared at it and considered slipping it on my wrist, but something stayed my hand.

I grabbed a different one instead.

I slipped on my shoes and prepared to walk out the door.

Sofia woke up and stared at me for a few seconds before she got out of bed. "I'm glad I get to say goodbye before you go." She looked sexy as hell in my black t-shirt with nothing underneath, not even panties. A more beautiful woman hadn't been anywhere near me since she left. They were trolls compared to her. And when I thought about them, I was filled with disgust and guilt. I felt like I'd cheated on my wife after the fact, even though she wasn't my wife at the time. I still felt dirty…like I'd done something wrong.

The guilt overwhelmed me so much that I avoided her gaze.

She probably picked up on my mood swing but didn't comment on it. "I'm taking Andrew in for a checkup at one if you want to join us. But if you're busy, I can handle it."

I headed to the door. "I have an important meeting I can't get out of."

"Then don't worry about it." She followed me then rose on her tiptoes to kiss me goodbye. She cupped my cheeks and gave me a full kiss, showing the depth of her love in that simple embrace.

She could make me feel so much…with so little.

She pulled away then squeezed both of my biceps through my jacket. "Have a good day… I love you." The insecurity in her eyes told me she didn't expect me to say it back. She didn't want to make it awkward either, so she turned away so we wouldn't have to face the tension.

I stayed rooted to the spot instead of walking out. "Sofia."

She turned back to me.

I slid my hands into my pockets. "I'm sorry."

"Don't apologize," she whispered. "Whether you say it back or not, I want to say it anyway."

"Not for that."

She raised an eyebrow.

"I'm sorry I…stopped being totally faithful to you." My gaze dropped because I was too much of a coward to meet her look. "I don't feel good about what I did. I'm sorry that I hurt you." I'd celebrated my freedom at the time, but I didn't get much pleasure out of it. I'd stopped loving her and I'd tried to jump back into my bachelor life, but once these feelings started again, I realized that wasn't me. Whether I loved her or not, she meant the world to me. I was glad I'd never actually had sex with any other women.

Her eyes filled with emotion before she walked back to me. Her hand rested on my bicep before she looked up at me. "We've both done things that we regret. We are supposed to be together, so let's forget the past. We're a family now. That's all that matters."

Ash was in town, so I met him after work for a drink.

"So…you and the missus are Mr. And Mrs. again?" He swirled his scotch on the rocks then took a drink. The bar was quiet that evening because it was in the middle of the week.

"Where did you hear that?"

"Sofia talks to Damien, who talks to me… We love to gossip."

I noticed Sofia had a closer relationship with Damien and my own brother than I did. She was just easy to love. "We're working on it…"

"Good. Sofia has too nice of an ass to get away."

I grabbed the top of my glass and slid it toward him. "Just because you're my brother doesn't mean I won't shatter this into pieces then shove the shards up your ass."

His response was completely inappropriate; he grinned like an idiot. "I missed you."

I cocked an eyebrow.

"You know, this huffy-puffy wolf guy. I love pissing you off. It's so much fun."

I took a drink and ignored what he said.

"So, when do they move in again?"

"We're just taking things slow right now."

"But have you seen how cute your kid is?"

"Yes," I said sarcastically. "I made him."

"Wouldn't you want to see him every day?"

I didn't reply because the answer was obvious.

"Wouldn't you want to see your woman every day?"

I'd started to miss her on the nights she was gone. There was a distinct hole in my bed where she was supposed to be. It had happened so quickly, I could hardly believe it.

"I think they should move back in, and you should get remarried. What's the point in waiting? You know it's going to happen anyway. But I guess that means you have to walk away from everything…and I'm sure you don't want to do that."

I was about to pull my glass closer and take a drink, but I flinched at what he'd said. "What's that supposed to mean?"

Ash pushed up the sleeves of his shirt. "I just assumed you would retire."

"Why the fuck would I do that?"

He gave me a look like I was stupid. "Uh…maybe because terrible things happen to your wife because of it? Because now you have a son whom people could target? Because you're probably going to have more kids? I thought that was obvious."

The thought hadn't crossed my mind. I'd been taking things slow with Sofia and not thinking too far into the future. But I knew she would be my wife again, and I knew we would have another son. After everything that had happened with Maddox, it would be foolish to think something like that could never happen again.

Ash continued to drink as he stared at me. "Maybe you should talk to Sofia about it."

I didn't want to talk about it. I didn't want to think about sacrificing my life's work for a simple reason. To someone else, it was just crime and money, but to me, it was so much more. It was my life's work…my blood.

"You want my advice?"

"No. But you'll give it to me anyway."

"Your job has brought you the worst agony you've ever known. Yes, there's good stuff like money, power, and enemies' bloodshed, but for the most part, it's fucking stressful. Sofia and Andrew have only brought you joy. I think the answer is pretty obvious."

Summer had ended, and now it was late September. Toward the end of the month was when things started to change. Leaves turned from green to red, and the humidity slowly turned into fog. Fall had arrived, bringing crisp days with sunshine.

Sofia and I had spent our time having dinners in my bedroom while spending time with Andrew. We never went out to dinner because it was too hard to bring a baby, and a lot of times Sofia didn't want to leave him home. She quickly turned into one of those mothers who was obsessed with their son.

Not that I minded.

She continued to tell me she loved me…even when I didn't say it back.

It happened when I left for work, when we were in bed together, and it was the last thing she said before she went to sleep. It was the first time in our relationship when there were no expectations for me. She was the one doing all the work, the one fighting for me.

It was nice.

Without any pressure or expectation, I relaxed and stopped worrying about getting hurt again. I lived in the moment, watching my son grow so quickly and Sofia's happiness blossom. Being committed wasn't hard because I was never really fulfilled by my promiscuous lifestyle.

I was much happier now.

We sat on the couch together and watched TV. I had Andrew lying on my chest with his face close to my neck. He was in a onesie, and he held his favorite stuffed animal as he drifted off to sleep. His fingers eventually went slack, and he dropped the doll onto the couch.

Sofia sat beside me. "Looks like he's out."

"He had a long day." My hand rested on his back so he wouldn't slip away. I got used to our evenings when we cuddled like this. Like most fathers, I looked forward to it. It was something just he and I did, and I already dreaded when he would be too old to do this anymore. One day, he would grow into a man, be independent and strong, and he wouldn't need me anymore.

Such a depressing thought.

Sofia hooked her arm through mine and rested close to me. She'd been working out with a trainer to get her body back in shape. Now she was a lot tighter and fitter, and while she looked great, I actually liked her body before.

At least I could enjoy it again when she was pregnant a second time.

She gently rubbed her fingers up and down my arm and stared at my face instead of the TV. She usually only had eyes for Andrew, but I was the center of her focus tonight. "You're such a good father…"

"I am?"

"Absolutely." She smiled slightly. "You're so good with him…and he loves you so much. I'd like to have a girl, but I like raising a son to be like his father." She leaned down and pressed a kiss to my shoulder.

I missed being loved by her this way. When we were married, she was all over me all the time. She didn't have to tell me how she felt because she wore it on her sleeve. The woman was infatuated with me…the way I'd always been with her. It was nice to have that back. At the end of the day, her opinion was the only one that mattered. "I've decided to walk away from the business."

It took her a long time to process my announcement. Her smile slowly faded away, and the brightness in her eyes dulled into a look of confusion. We had been having a warm moment, but now everything turned serious. "What do you mean by that?"

"I'm leaving the business to Damien."

"Why?"

"You and Andrew." I continued to watch the reaction dance across her face as she went from being surprised to being touched. "I can't risk anything happening to either one of you. Not again."

She was still shocked. She tucked her hair behind her ear and stared at Andrew for a few seconds before she looked at me again. "I…don't know what to say. I guess I'm just surprised that you made that decision. I know how important your work is to you."

It used to be the most important thing in the world. But now it seemed like a reckless choice, a risk too great when I had something so valuable at home. Now that my heart had been fixed, I didn't need the job anymore. Everything I needed was here. "I love you." I looked into her gaze and watched the shock quickly turn into joy. "So don't be surprised."

I entered the factory and moved down to the basement floor, where all the equipment was set up. Clouds of steam rose to the ceiling and were carried outside through the pipes. There were two cooks making the crystal, while other men boxed the product and prepared to ship it.

Damien was there, watching everyone to make sure their jobs were done right. He may have screwed up with me, but he was a good boss. He instilled fear into the men, along with a healthy dosage of inspiration. He watched the containers being placed on the pallet so they could be taken to the surface in the industrial elevator.

I came up behind him. "You got a minute?"

Damien looked at me over his shoulder, his arms crossed over his chest. "I've got shit to do. I never have a minute."

My eyes narrowed in annoyance. "It's important."

He rolled his eyes. "Everything in this business is important." He walked off to the office on the other side of the room. It had been overtaken by Maddox at one point, but now it was ours again. He walked inside first and stood in front of the desk.

I followed him, and it was hard not to imagine Maddox sitting there with his feet on the desk. He'd been gone for months, but his ghost continued to haunt me. I didn't have nightmares, but he was on my mind often.

Damien leaned against the desk with his arms across his chest. In a black t-shirt and jeans, he was fit and strong, and with that attitude, he could be quite the adversary. "This isn't a date, so we don't have all night."

"Fine. I'll just get to the point."

Damien stared at me, his eyes guarded but also full of interest.

"The business is yours. I'm bowing out."

He cocked one eyebrow before he straightened. "Huh?"

I knew he wouldn't be happy about this, so it would be a long conversation. "I'm not doing this anymore. It's time for me to move on."

With Damien's temperament, he would probably throw a fit and lash out. We'd been doing this together for years, and doing it on his own would mean he'd have to do all the work himself. Having a partner you could rely on was crucial to success. "If you're gonna have a wife and kid, I guess that's smart."

Now it was my turn to be surprised.

"Your family deserves to be safe. Sofia deserves the quiet life she always wanted."

I could hardly believe what he was saying.

"Hades, you know I don't need you. I can do all this shit on my own in my sleep. But the reason we were partners was because we were friends. But that isn't true anymore, so there's not much point."

His harsh response made me feel a little dead inside.

"What about the bank? I can handle that too if you want to leave."

"No. The bank is fine. If I don't work, I'll lose my mind."

Damien dropped his arms to his sides and stared at me for a long time. His expression was vivid, but his thoughts were concealed. There was a slight shift in his eyes as he took in my appearance.

"That was easier than I thought it would be."

"You overestimate your value." His tone was sarcastic but also slightly playful.

Damien and I didn't interact at the bank often, so our time together would be diminished significantly. We'd set out to start this business when we left university, believing we would be friends forever. But now we were going our separate ways… permanently. "Good luck." I headed to the door.

"So, that's it?"

I stopped before I reached the door and slowly turned around.

"We've known each other for over ten years, and you're walking away just like that?" Hurt was in his eyes...along with other things.

I stared at him. "What do you want me to say?"

After a full minute of silence, he shook his head slightly. "Nothing. A friendship like ours doesn't deserve more than nothing. It deserves to be forgotten." He took a step closer to me, his eyes filled with disappointment. "You don't give a shit about me, and you never did."

"Let's not forget how this happened..."

"Asshole, I didn't try to get your wife raped. Don't put that shit on me. Sofia doesn't, so you shouldn't either."

"She has a bigger heart than I do."

"No. You don't have a heart at all."

My eyes narrowed.

"Just forget it." He threw his arms up. "We'll only speak to each other at work when we have to, and we'll spend the rest of the time pretending the other one doesn't exist. You'll have more kids that I'll never meet, and all the shit going on my life will be a mystery to you. We'll turn into strangers, and after enough years pass by, maybe we'll forget we were ever friends in the first place." He walked past me and shoved me aside with his arm on his way to the door. "Have a good fucking life."

28

SOFIA

Hades told me he loved me, that he was leaving the business that had caused so much suffering for both of us. It was a relief that he'd made the decision on his own because I never could've asked. After everything he had done for me, I would stick by his side no matter what. But he'd made the right choice for our family.

And I didn't even have to ask.

Now, I wouldn't have to worry about someone coming after me to get back at him. And I wouldn't have to worry about someone hurting my baby boy. The best way to disappear from danger was to disappear altogether.

While things had definitely changed, he hadn't asked me to move in yet.

Things were going so well that I didn't want to risk our happiness by asking for too much. I wanted to be in my old bed with Hades beside me every night. I wanted to feel safe, knowing he was there to protect me and our son. I wanted to feel the weight of my diamond ring on my left hand every night as I slept.

But I had to keep being patient.

I got Andrew ready before I called Hades.

He answered right away, but he was clearly in a bad mood. "Yeah?"

He hadn't spoken to me that way in a long time, so I let it slide. "Everything okay?"

"Just a shitty day."

"I was going to see if we could come over, but I'll give you your space." It was another reason why I missed being married, because I couldn't comfort him when he walked through the door. I couldn't be a part of his bad days as well as his good days if I had a different address. I had to give him space…even if I didn't want to. "I'll talk to you later."

He didn't respond. He lingered on the phone but didn't have anything to say.

"Bye."

"Baby, I want you to come over. Both of you."

It'd been so long since he'd last called me baby that it brought tears to my eyes. It was such an affectionate endearment, a warm blanket that wrapped around me so tightly. I preferred it over my real name, at least from his lips. I was glad he couldn't see me so he wouldn't have to see how red and puffy my face instantly became. "Good…because being with you is the only place I want to be." The tears escaped in my voice and made it obvious I was crying.

He paused again. "Bring some extra stuff to leave here this time."

It was hard to remember what my life was like before Andrew because he was so wonderful. But there was one thing I missed about my previous life, and that was having Hades whenever I wanted.

When I walked through the door, he was shirtless and beautiful, with the scruff around his jaw that I liked. The fire in the fireplace was roaring, so he looked like a sexy man on the cover of a romance book. I wanted to push his sweatpants over his narrow hips and take him then and there.

But I had a baby now.

I set the car seat on the bed then kissed him on the lips. "Hey."

He slid his hand into my hair then kissed me again, as if that first embrace wasn't good enough. He kissed me harder and devoured my lips, leaving me breathless before he pulled away. "That's how I expect you to greet me."

My hands moved up his chest, and I rested my forehead against his chin. "I'd love to."

He kissed my forehead before he turned his attention on Andrew. He picked him up out of the car seat and held him with a single arm. "Hey, boy." He kissed him on the forehead then came back to me.

There was nothing sexier than watching him hold our son like that.

After we talked about Andrew for a little bit, we moved to the couch and sat down. Hades played with Andrew for a while until he got tired. Then he just held him. He seemed to be in a much better mood than he had been on the phone earlier.

"Tell me about your shitty day."

His body tensed again. "Damien and I butted heads a bit…"

"You always butt heads. Was he upset when you told him you were leaving?"

He continued to watch Andrew. "He seemed to be fine with it. But then he confronted me about our friendship…and shit hit the fan. We ended on bad terms."

It'd been so long since they'd stopped being friends that I'd given up on them a long time ago. "Hades, this is your last chance to bury the hatchet. I think it's time you forgive and forget."

He ignored me like he hadn't heard what I said.

"You love him. He loves you. You know that."

Still, no response.

"Something is going to happen one day, and it'll be too late. I don't want you to live with that kind of guilt."

He turned to me, his eyes cold. "I've made my decision. Leave it alone."

I'd tried to talk him out of it many times, but nothing ever stuck. It was time to move on. "Alright."

He lay in bed beside me, on his back with his powerful chest directed at the ceiling. There was a gleam of sweat on his skin from the workout he'd just performed making love to me. Now, his chest rose and fell quickly as he recovered from his exertion.

I moved on top of him and kissed his chest everywhere, feeling his hard pecs against my soft lips before I felt the valleys between his abs over his stomach. My kisses continued because I couldn't get enough of this man. I could have him every minute of the day, and it still wouldn't be enough.

He moved his fingers through my hair as he watched me. "I thought I was doing a good job, but I guess not. You're never satisfied."

I looked up and met his gaze. "I'm not unsatisfied. I'm addicted."

His eyes darkened like he enjoyed that response. "Move in with me."

The request was so sudden, I didn't react right away. "Yeah?"

"This is your home."

I'd wondered if and when he would ask me to marry him again, but I should be grateful he was offering me this. As long as I got to live with him and see him every day, I was okay with never getting married again—even though I wanted it more than anything. "I want nothing more…"

"And bring your mother."

"You don't have to do that."

"She told you to give me that awesome blow job. So, I like her a little more."

I smiled at his playfulness, loving the fact that he was himself again. "You know, you can have one of those every day."

"I know…but I get distracted by that perfect pussy of yours."

"Perfect?" I rubbed my palm across his chest. "I had a baby… I doubt it's perfect anymore."

"It's even better now." He stared at me with a loving gaze. "Knowing you gave me a son is the biggest turn-on ever." He continued to run his fingers through my hair.

When I'd thought about the women who'd replaced me during our estrangement, it made me so sick. His admission that there had been others made it worse. But now that I had him back and he loved me, I had to force myself to let those thoughts go. None of them mattered…only I did. "You seem to love me, no matter what."

His eyes grew intense before a slight smile moved across his lips. "You have no idea how true that is…"

29

HADES

Sofia moved back in to the house.

My closet was full of her clothes again. The top drawer of the dresser was full of her delicate panties and bras. On the bathroom counter were all her hair supplies, makeup, and her favorite perfume.

It felt the way it used to.

Her mother came as part of the deal and returned to her old bedroom downstairs. I could negotiate her removal, but since it was important to Sofia, I let it be. Besides, we always had a trusted babysitter on call.

Now when we had dinner together, we had true privacy. Sofia didn't have to breastfeed during her meals so her food wouldn't grow cold. And when we hit the sheets, we never had to be interrupted by a crying baby.

It was like a second honeymoon.

She sat across from me now on the terrace, wearing a long-sleeved sweater with her curled hair pinned back. She slowly ate her food and looked up at me from time to time, letting the silence linger because she didn't feel the need to fill it with unnecessary conversation. She understood I was the strong and silent type and let me be.

She understood me better than anyone.

I set my fork down even though my food was only half eaten. "I want to ask you to marry me, but there's something I have to tell you first."

My statement was so unexpected that she jerked noticeably when she heard what I'd said. Her fork fell and clattered against the plate, making a loud tapping noise. Then she took a deep breath and rubbed her hand across her chest, disconcerted by the abrupt change in tone. "Okay…" She took another deep breath. "But there's nothing you can say that would stop me from wanting to marry you, so there's really no point in saying it at all."

I appreciated her enthusiasm and commitment, but she'd made the wrong conclusion. I had no wrongs to confess, no secrets to expose. I just wanted her to know the truth about us, to understand the intensity we had experienced over these last few years. "You're not going to believe what I'm about to tell you. I didn't believe it myself until it became more blatantly obvious that it had to be true. But please trust me."

She rested her elbows on the table and blinked a few times as she prepared.

"When I was twenty-one, I visited a gypsy in Marrakech who read me my fortune. I assumed it was silly and just a way to take my money. Her prophecy stated I would only love one woman, and she would never love me back."

Sofia's eyes narrowed.

"I thought it was bullshit. But then I met you eight years later. I felt things I'd never felt for anyone else, and then I stupidly asked you to marry me without thinking about what I was doing. You said no…and that's when I got scared."

Instead of objecting to everything I said, she continued to listen.

"When I found out you needed a husband, I realized the prophecy was true. The gypsy told me I would marry you. She told me we would have two sons. And she told me we were soul mates."

Her eyes softened.

"That was why I married you…because I was supposed to. I was in love with you, and I couldn't control it. I tried to move on, tried to forget you, but it was impossible. This curse was placed upon me because I killed my father. It was a punishment. So, we were living together as husband and wife, and I hoped you would somehow love me on your own…but you never did."

She stayed quiet.

"I knew you would love me if you could. We're soul mates, so in any other circumstances, it would be organic. So I went back to the gypsy and tried to break the curse. She told me my only chance was to make amends with my brother…or she could make me stop loving you altogether. I chose the first one."

She released a gasp. "That was why you wanted me to meet your brother. That was why you were trying so hard to earn his forgiveness…"

I nodded. "And I loved you so much that I never wanted to stop, even if it would be easier to do so. The plan worked, and in a short amount of time, you felt the same way. You gave me that watch, and I knew I'd finally succeeded. I finally had what I wanted…and I was so fucking happy."

Her eyes started to well up with tears.

"Then everything went to shit. Maddox ruined everything, and I lost you. It didn't matter if I broke the curse, we were never going to be together. I couldn't move on after our divorce, and I was so depressed I considered taking my own life."

She closed her eyes, and two streams of tears fell down her face.

"But then you called me, and that changed my mind. I was still living with the torment, so I did the only thing I could… I went back to the gypsy and asked her to make me stop loving you. Instantly, I felt different. I stopped caring. I stopped feeling. And then you killed Maddox…"

She wiped away her tears and sniffled. "It makes sense now…"

"You fixed everything, but I didn't feel the same way anymore. I didn't want you anymore. But in time, you made me fall in love with you again. It wasn't even that hard…because I'm supposed to love you."

She reached across the table and grabbed my hand. "It's because we're soul mates…"

I looked at her with surprise. "You believe me."

She nodded. "I don't believe you. I just know it's true. Now that I know everything you did to keep us together, to fight for me no matter how much pain it caused you…there are no words. I'm just so relieved that you're here with me now, that you never gave up on me."

Now I felt my own tears start in my throat. "It feels so good to tell you this. I wanted to say something before, but I thought you would assume I was crazy. I thought it would make it worse."

She shook her head and squeezed my hand. "No…only made it better."

All the weight was lifted from my chest, and I finally found peace. I'd worked my ass off for this woman, and she was finally mine. No one could ever take her away from me now, take away the love we had for each other. We were soul mates…we both knew it.

"The gypsy told you we would have two sons?"

I nodded. "Why?"

She reached into her pocket and pulled out a pregnancy test. "It looks like he'll be here soon."

EPILOGUE

SOFIA

The sun had just set on the square of the bazaar, so the flames from the bonfires started to burn brightly. There was music coming from everywhere, followed by the sounds of clinking pots, camels moving around the area, and the occasional altercation.

My husband took me by the hand and guided me through the chaos.

My husband.

I could call him that again…and I would never take it for granted.

"You still know the way?"

He glanced down at me with a handsome smile on his face. "Baby, I know everything."

I laughed then gave him a playful tickle on the side.

He didn't react the way I would because his body was hard, with just muscle and skin.

He guided me around the fire dancers and cobras then took me down a separate alleyway that was much quieter than the rest of the bazaar. There was a pottery stand and a lone purple tent.

He pointed. "That's it."

When Hades had told me the story of the gypsy and the fortune she'd read, I believed it immediately. Throughout our entire relationship, I'd always felt like there was a swirling fog clouding my thoughts and restraining my true feelings. If that had never been there, I suspected I would've fallen in love with him on our first night in that hotel room.

But something had stopped me the entire time.

I distinctly remembered the day my heart started to ache with so much love that I thought it would burst. I went from simply respecting him to loving him a lifetime's worth overnight. It sprang on me so quickly that my body couldn't acclimate fast enough.

So, once I was in love…I was deeply in love.

I couldn't imagine my life with anyone else. I couldn't imagine taking another man as my husband. I was loyal and committed, even when I had no reason to be.

Because I always knew, deep down inside, that this man was my soul mate.

He stopped in front of the tent. "Are you sure you want to do this?"

"Yes." I rose on my tiptoes and kissed him on the lips.

His arm nestled deeper into the curve of my back, and he placed his other hand on my small belly, where our second son was slowly growing inside me.

I pulled away first then strutted fearlessly into the tent. "I'm not scared of anything."

He followed me inside.

A woman in a purple shawl sat there, covered in jewelry on her earlobes, on her neck, and her wrists. She was playing with a deck of cards, oblivious to the two of us. "I suspect this is the last time I will see you, Hades." She grabbed all the cards and returned them to a neat stack then she lifted her chin to meet our gazes.

Hades stayed behind me. "I hope so."

The gypsy turned to me. "How can I help you, Sofia?"

Did Hades tell her my name? "I want to know my fortune." I took the seat across from her.

"Are you sure about that?" She glanced at my husband. "Because it can ruin lives…"

I shook my head. "I know we're going to have a happy ending."

She grabbed the cards again and only took the top half of the deck. She did some shuffling before she laid out the cards in front of me.

Hades stood behind my chair and placed his hands on the wooden frame.

After studying the cards for a while, she picked out two from the arrangement and pushed them toward me. "Are you sure?"

I nodded. "Yes."

"Your boys will grow to be men. The women they marry will be daughters to you, not in blood, but in water. Your lifetime will be short, not in duration, but in speed. Happiness and bliss pass much more quickly than sorrow and despair, which you will have very little of. You will outlive your husband in old age, but by only two days…because you will die of a broken heart."

Tears welled in my eyes because that was exactly what I wanted for the rest of my life, to live a long and happy life with the man I loved, and not to live long without him. I felt Hades place a hand on my shoulder and grip me gently.

The gypsy gathered the cards and returned them to the stack. "Are you satisfied with your fortune?"

My hand rested on his, and I looked up to see him staring down at me. "Yes."

ALSO BY PENELOPE SKY

Hades retired from the business.

Now it's just me.

Look at me now...bitter...angry...depressed. I resent my former friend so much, even hate the guy, but I've never been the same since he refused to forgive me.

I meet a woman. She's like all the others...beautiful, interesting, good at the fun stuff, but I don't feel anything.

One woman will love you for you, not your money or your power, but you'll lose her. And once she's gone...she's gone.

That gypsy wasn't right about me too, right?

I've got trouble on my doorstep when the new Skull King shows up. He wants a cut of my business.

Like he's getting anything. This is all I have left.

Once again I become swallowed by the underworld.

Will I survive it?

Order Now

Printed in Great Britain
by Amazon